RALPH COMPTON

HE WAS A NOBODY.
A NOTHING.
UNTIL HE BECAME…

D0034903

THE MAN FROM NOWHERE

A RALPH COMPTON NOVEL BY JOSEPH A. WEST

SIGNET

SIGNET

$5.99 U.S.
$7.50 CAN.

ISBN: 978-0-451-22741-6

50599

EAN

Dogfight

Oates kicked out at the female coyote and the hard sole of his right foot took her full on the snout. The canine yipped in pain and backed off, snarling. The dog coyote, hearing his mate's cry of hurt, was startled and he too bounded back a few steps.

The first round to Oates. But, wiser now, the coyotes attacked again.

This time both of them jumped on Oates, and he collapsed under their weight. He smelled the feral stench of the animals and felt their fangs rip into his back and thighs.

Desperately, Oates tried to sit up, striking out with his right arm. He hit the dog a couple of times, but his punches were weak and ineffective. Blood sprayed around him and dripped like rubies from the muzzles of the coyotes.

Then the flat statement of a rifle shot racketed through the hollow quiet of the evening. The dog coyote shrieked and fell away, landing on its back, its legs twitching.

Another shot. The female dropped without a sound, her deadweight suddenly heavy on Oates.

He felt the coyote being lifted from him and a bearded face with good-humored hazel eyes swam into his view. "You all right, pardner?" a man's voice asked. Oates tried to answer, but darkness took him and he knew no more.

Ralph Compton

The Man from Nowhere

A Ralph Compton Novel
by Joseph A. West

A SIGNET BOOK

SIGNET
Published by New American Library, a division of
Penguin Group (USA) Inc., 375 Hudson Street,
New York, New York 10014, USA
Penguin Group (Canada), 90 Eglinton Avenue East, Suite 700, Toronto,
Ontario M4P 2Y3, Canada (a division of Pearson Penguin Canada Inc.)
Penguin Books Ltd., 80 Strand, London WC2R 0RL, England
Penguin Ireland, 25 St. Stephen's Green, Dublin 2,
Ireland (a division of Penguin Books Ltd.)
Penguin Group (Australia), 250 Camberwell Road, Camberwell, Victoria 3124,
Australia (a division of Pearson Australia Group Pty. Ltd.)
Penguin Books India Pvt. Ltd., 11 Community Centre, Panchsheel Park,
New Delhi - 110 017, India
Penguin Group (NZ), 67 Apollo Drive, Rosedale, North Shore 0632,
New Zealand (a division of Pearson New Zealand Ltd.)
Penguin Books (South Africa) (Pty.) Ltd., 24 Sturdee Avenue,
Rosebank, Johannesburg 2196, South Africa

Penguin Books Ltd., Registered Offices:
80 Strand, London WC2R 0RL, England

First published by Signet, an imprint of New American Library,
a division of Penguin Group (USA) Inc.

First Printing, July 2009
10 9 8 7 6 5 4 3 2 1

THE IMMORTAL COWBOY

This is respectfully dedicated to the "American Cowboy." His was the saga sparked by the turmoil that followed the Civil War, and the passing of more than a century has by no means diminished the flame.

True, the old days and the old ways are but treasured memories, and the old trails have grown dim with the ravages of time, but the spirit of the cowboy lives on.

In my travels—to Texas, Oklahoma, Kansas, Nebraska, Colorado, Wyoming, New Mexico, and Arizona—I always find something that reminds me of the Old West. While I am walking these plains and mountains for the first time, there is this feeling that a part of me is eternal, that I have known these old trails before. I believe it is the undying spirit of the frontier calling, allowing me, through the mind's eye, to step back into time. What is the appeal of the Old West of the American frontier?

It has been epitomized by some as the dark and bloody period in American history. Its heroes—Crockett, Bowie, Hickok, Earp—have been reviled and criticized. Yet the Old West lives on, larger than life.

It has become a symbol of freedom, when there was always another mountain to climb and another river to cross; when a dispute between two men was settled not with expensive lawyers, but with fists, knives, or guns. Barbaric? Maybe. But some things never change. When the cowboy rode into the pages of American history, he left behind a legacy that lives within the hearts of us all.

—*Ralph Compton*

Chapter 1

At ten o'clock sharp on a fine spring evening, the Honorable Company of Concerned Citizens, City of Alma, New Mexico Territory, hanged the Hart brothers: Billy, Bobby and young Jimmy.

Next morning, at dawn, they came for Eddie Oates, the town drunk.

Let it be noted that at first the four Concerned Citizens present tried to wake the sleeping Oates almost gently. But when the little man continued to snore and slobber in his sleep, the boots went in.

Even after he woke, red-eyed and puking, kicks slammed into Oates' ribs, none driven harder and by more rage than those of Cornelius Baxter, Alma's only banker and richest citizen.

To even the most casual observer, the reason for Baxter's anger would not have been hard to find.

His expensive patent leather ankle boots, hand sewn by Rigby and Sons of New York, Boston and Denver, were splashed with the green bile that had erupted from Oates' mouth.

God alone knows how it would have ended had not John L. Battles, proprietor of the Silver Nugget saloon, stuck out a pudgy hand and pushed Baxter away.

"Let it be," he said. "We didn't come here to kill the man."

It took the banker a while.

The others present saw the boiling fury in Baxter bubble away gradually, then settle to a low simmer. He lifted pale blue eyes to Battles, for the saloon keeper was a tall man, and said, quiet and even, "John, don't ever lay a hand on me again or I'll kill you."

After twenty years on the frontier, Battles was not a man to take a step back from anyone. He said, "Anytime you want to heel yourself, Baxter, we can have at it."

Baxter's face was crimson, the mouth under his mustache a thin, hard line, white and pinched at the corners.

Tall, stringy Jeddah Piper, the town undertaker, saw the danger and decided to act. "Here, this won't do," he said. "The Apaches have us under the gun and we're all on edge. Gentlemen, let's not start fighting among ourselves."

The fourth citizen present, Clem Hamilton, who owned a dry goods store, tossed in his two cents' worth. "Jed's right," he said. "Are we going to fight over a drunken nothing like Eddie Oates when we got Mescaleros all around us?"

Piper saw hesitation in the faces of Baxter and Battles and said quickly, "Get him to his feet. We'll take him outside, where he can join the rest of them."

"Wait," Baxter said. He began to wipe his shoes on Oates' shirt and pants. "The little son of a bitch can't smell any worse."

John L. Battles laughed, and with that, the bad blood that had lain between him and the banker was forgotten.

Chapter 2

Eddie Oates blinked like an owl against the morning light.

His sides hurt from the kicking he'd taken and there was the taste of blood in his mouth. He needed a drink but doubted there was one to be had.

When the Concerned Citizens had found him, he'd been asleep in the alley where he had fallen into unconsciousness shortly after the hanging of the Hart brothers. Now, suspended between Baxter and Battles like a crucifixion victim, his bare toes dragging behind him in the dirt, he was manhandled into the street and tossed in the zinc horse trough outside the Silver Nugget.

Oates sank, then rose, sputtering, gasping like a just-landed trout. Somebody rammed his head under the surface again. He was down there, swallowing water for what seemed a long time, then was suddenly released. He floundered, kicking, into a sitting position and heard laughter.

As he watched the bodies sway and heard the hemp creak, Oates had a sudden moment of clarity. He'd been puzzled before, but now he knew why he was being hanged. He was not a fighting man either.

"Get over there, you."

A hand pushed Oates in the small of the back, and he crashed heavily into the gallows. Around him men laughed as he bounced off the pine boards and staggered, but a helping hand reached out from somewhere and steadied him.

"What are they going to do with us, Mr. Oates?"

Oates blinked at the owner of the hand, then slowly recognized the frightened, freckled face of young Sam Tatum. He remembered that he liked Sam. He was the only person in Alma, or any other town, who had ever called him Mister.

"I don't know, Sammy." Oates' voice sounded like the hinges of a rusty gate. "I don't know anything."

"Will we get hung, Mr. Oates?"

Oates turned away. He didn't want to think or look at Sam anymore. God, he needed a drink.

His mind screamed as the whiskey hunger raked him, giving him no peace.

He wanted to cry out, "Hang me, you bastards. Get it over with, but let me have a drink first," but he could not form the words. Besides, who would listen?

Later, the citizens of Alma who'd crowded around the gallows that morning would recall that Eddie Oates had been in truth a pathetic sight.

"Standing there, dripping water, rubbing his mouth all the time. Poor thing."

"Like a little drowned rat, wasn't he?"

"He smelled bad too. How does a man get to smell like that?"

"Well, who cares? He's probably dead by this time anyhow."

But that was then; this was now.

Cornelius Baxter stepped among the crowd and threw up his hands, demanding silence. Deciding that his portly five foot seven was less than impressive at ground level, the banker stepped up onto the gallows platform and stood in front of the purple-faced bodies.

Again he raised his arms and slowly the hubbub died away to a ragged silence.

"Fellow citizens of the fair city of Alma," Baxter began. Up went a cheer, which the banker acknowledged with a smile and a slight inclination of his head. Then he continued. "As you are all aware, I am talking to you at the time of our greatest peril."

Baxter waved a hand, encompassing the whole town. "As you can see, we have alert sentinels posted at each end of our city, and stalwart riflemen on our roofs. I have tasked them with one duty—keep keen watch for Victorio and his bloodthirsty fiends."

The banker stopped, as though expecting another cheer. But there was none. People looked uneasily over their shoulders and then at one another, the very name Victorio enough to cause a ripple of fear to go through the crowd.

"The trails in and out of town were cut by the Apaches days ago," Baxter said. He paused and then added ominously, "There will be no more supply wagons for some time to come, and already our food supplies are running perilously low."

Against a background of worried murmurs, the banker said, "But who better to tell us where we stand than our very own Will Jackson."

All eyes turned to a small, round-bellied man who, even at this early hour, was wearing a spotless white apron. Jackson owned the only general store in town and was a founding member of the citizens' committee.

Without any preamble, the little man began to tick points off on his fingers. "Flour, one week's supply; bacon, five days'; salt pork, ditto; coffee, one week; sugar, ditto." He paused, thinking, then continued. "Cheese, eggs, butter, red meat and beans . . . as long as they last, which won't be long. Ditto salt, pepper and other spices. I've already run out of canned milk, canned meat, peaches and most other canned goods.

"Now, as to prices, I'm afraid that from today I'll have to increase—"

"Yes, yes, Will, we understand," Baxter interrupted quickly. He addressed the crowd again. "Given the Apache menace and our shortages of food, last night the Honorable Company of Concerned Citizens, myself presiding, decided that we can no longer tolerate parasites within our community. In short, there will be no more useless mouths in Alma."

Baxter indicated the hanged men. "This was a start, but there are others." He took a slip of paper from the pocket of his frock coat, then said, "Pike, Sanderson, you others, bring them forward." Then, to the expectant crowd he said, "The loafers, shirkers and slackers who would take the very bread from our children's mouths."

To yells of approval, three women and Sam Tatum were pushed beside Oates.

"There they are," Baxter said. "All wear the Mark of Cain and flaunt that vile brand as bold as brass. Look into their faces, citizens. I assure you, you will find not the slightest trace of remorse for the wasted, sinful, lustful lives they have led."

One of the women, a hard-faced blonde Oates knew as Stella, spat in Baxter's direction. "You should know, Horny Corny!" she snapped. "You've been working your spurs on this here sinner for months."

Laughter rose from the men in the crowd, but the few women present looked as if someone were holding a dead fish under their noses. For his part, Baxter shuffled his feet and looked sheepish, like a small boy caught with his hand in the candy jar.

A mean-eyed man with a belted Colt around his waist stepped closer. "You shut your trap, Stella," he growled.

The woman was defiant, her hands on her hips. "An' if I don't, Pike?"

"Then I'll shut it for you."

"Miss Stella, better do as he says," Sam Tatum said. The boy was trembling. "I don't think Mr. Pike is a very nice person."

The man nodded. "You got that right, kid."

Her eyes blazing, Stella opened her mouth to speak again, but a voice from the crowd stopped her. A huge silver miner wearing a plug hat and plaid shirt yelled, "Hey, Baxter, you aiming to hang these folks?"

The people crowded around the gallows fell silent, waiting for Baxter's answer.

Oates looked on with dead eyes, beyond caring. He wanted, craved, hungered for whiskey—raw, red whiskey beading in the bottle. Lots of it. He had no other thoughts. No fears. No hopes. No interest.

Baxter was speaking again. "In reply to the gentleman's question, the low persons who have been brought before us here will not be hung." He paused for effect, then said, "Let all present bear witness to the decisions of the Honorable Company of Concerned Citizens of Alma. For the more respectable element here gathered who may not know these people, each of the accused will be brought before you as his or her name is read."

Baxter consulted his paper.

"Edward Oates, laborer—"

"Drunk, you mean!" a man yelled.

The banker waited until the laughter had stilled, then continued. "Edward Oates, laborer, vagrant and dance hall lounger. Sentence: banishment."

Oates was pushed back to the gallows platform. Then Sam and the women were dragged out one by one.

"Samuel Tatum, orphan and simple boy—banishment.

"Stella Spinner, known as High Timber, fancy woman—banishment.

"Lorraine Sullivan, fancy woman—banishment.

"Nellie Carney, known as Cottontail, fancy woman—banishment."

Baxter stepped to the edge of the gallows platform. Behind him the bodies of the three Hart brothers stirred in a rising wind. To the northeast, above the cone-shaped peak of Round Mountain, dark clouds were gathering, threatening rain.

"Sentence to be carried out immediately," he said.

Chapter 3

"Mr. Baxter, if you will, just a moment."

The banker hesitated on the steps, then recognized the man who had just spoken. "Oh, it's you, Reverend Claghorn," he said with a noticeable lack of enthusiasm.

"If I could just say a word?"

Baxter hesitated, then nodded. "All right, say what you have to say."

Claghorn was a thin, bent man with a gray beard that fell in sparse strands to the waistband of his pants. He mounted the steps and spread his arms to the crowd.

"My dear friends, the poor souls you see before you, a drunk, three scarlet women and a simple boy, will soon be gone from our midst. They have neither reaped nor sown, and thus we who have done so can no longer give them bread."

"You tell 'em, preacher," a man yelled. He turned to

the others around him. "We're gonna miss them scarlet women though—eh, boys?"

"Then why don't you take them home an' feed 'em, Lou?" a miner asked loudly.

"Because my old lady won't let me," Lou answered, a response that brought ribald laughter from men and disapproving looks from the women present.

"Please, please, good people," Claghorn called out, "before we cast them out, even as Adam and Eve were cast from the Garden of Eden, let us bow our heads in prayer and ask that these unfortunates may travel their lonely road in peace."

Perhaps fearing that his invitation might be turned down, Claghorn immediately clutched his Bible to his chest and stared up at the threatening sky.

"Oh Lord, protect your five wayward children from the perils of the trail, outlaws, savage Apaches and wild animals. And may they not starve but find grub in the wilderness, even as you fed manna to the Israelites as they wandered in the desert.

"And Lord, most of all, we ask that the nigger cavalry from Fort Bayard will arrive soon and free our fair city from the Apache yoke."

There was a scattering of "Amens" and, emboldened, Claghorn began to sing in a weak, quavering tenor.

There is a land that is fairer than day,
And by faith we can see it afar;
For the Father waits over the way
To prepare us a dwelling place there.

In the sweet by and by,
We shall meet on that beautiful shore;
In the sweet by and by,
We shall meet on that beautiful shore.

Baxter cut the hymn short. "Yes, thank you, Reverend," he said, clapping his hands. "Now, you Company members, get them damned parasites out of our town."

Eddie Oates had watched all this with eyes of glass, a disinterested man attending a boring play. He made no protest when he was pushed away from the gallows with the others, as limp and unresisting as a rag doll.

The three women had stuffed what few possessions they could find into carpetbags and had obviously dressed hurriedly before they were bundled out of their tiny cribs in the Silver Nugget.

Lorraine Sullivan, a dark-haired woman, the wear and tear of eleven years of frontier prostitution showing on her, wore only her shift and a ragged plaid mackinaw.

Like Oates, Sam Tatum carried nothing.

As they were prodded at rifle point in the direction of the town limits, Stella Spinner lashed out with her bag at the bearded man who was pushing her roughly between the shoulder blades. Her face, free of paint, was pale and tired, but her mouth twisted in fury as she rounded on the people crowded close to her.

"You sons of bitches," she screamed, "you're killing us. You know we'll die out there."

"Shut up, Stella," the bearded man said. "Take your medicine quiet, like the rest."

"We have as much right to live as any of you, and maybe more," Stella yelled. "We won't last a day with the Apaches surrounding the town."

A respectable young matron dressed in rustling, rust-colored silk pushed forward. "We won't waste food on whores," she snapped, her mouth as hard and mean as the clasp of a steel purse. "Now . . . just . . . leave."

Stella's eyes flared. "Bitch!" She jumped on the woman and they tumbled to the ground in a flurry of white petticoats and popping buttons.

"Get her off me!" the woman cried as she tried to fight off Stella's raking nails.

A couple of grinning men dragged Stella to her feet and one, a miner, pushed her bag into her hands. "You go quiet now, girl," he said. "There ain't nothing left for you in Alma."

"John Turley," Lorraine yelled, "how do you expect us to go quiet? We could all be dead within hours."

"Yeah, you could," the miner named Turley said, grinning. "Maybe you should have thought about that afore you took up the whorin' business, Lorraine."

"Turley," Lorraine said, "the other girls always told me you were a dickless son of a bitch. Now I know it for sure."

As scornful laughter rained down on him, Turley's face turned ugly. "Lorraine, I hope fifty Apache bucks take turns on you afore they gut you like a sow." He motioned with the muzzle of his rifle. "Now git goin'."

The young matron had been helped to her feet, and the women around her, angry now, yelled, "Whores!" and threw rocks and clumps of horse dung. Lorraine and Stella were hit several times. A cut opened up on Lorraine's forehead, trickling blood, and dung matted on the hair of all three women.

After a while Cornelius Baxter put a stop to it.

"That's enough!" he yelled, pushing through the eager crowd. "Damn it to hell, how many of you does it take to get three whores out of town?"

"Hey, Baxter!"

The banker turned toward the soft but commanding sound of the voice, as did most of the others.

Dark, handsome, Warren Rivette, the Mississippi steamboat gambler, lounged on the porch of the Silver Nugget, a Henry rifle in the crook of his left arm. The word in town was that the Cajun was trying to outrun a losing streak, but he had prospered in Alma, thanks to silver miners and the free-spending cowboys from the surrounding ranches.

Since Rivette was rumored to be good with a gun, no one had ever questioned the honesty of his poker. Nobody had tested his speed with the Colt either.

"What can I do for you, Rivette?" Baxter asked, walking toward the saloon. He was wary of the Henry. The gambler was not a man to be trifled with.

Rivette smiled. "I want to talk to Eddie Oates, if that meets your convenience."

"I'm throwing him out of town," Baxter said, a note of challenge in his voice.

"So I've heard. But I'd still like to talk to him."

Rivette saw Baxter hesitate and said, "A few moments of your time. Surely you can spare the poor wretch that much?"

The banker made up his mind. "One of you men bring Oates over here."

None too gently, a rifle butt prodded Oates forward. Rivette looked down at him. The gambler's black eyes showed little emotion, the result of years spent with the cards, but there was a hint of something—pity, maybe.

"Eddie, do you understand what I'm saying to you?" Rivette asked.

Oates nodded, then shook his head. The gambler's words had been a blur of sound.

"Suffering this morning, aren't you?"

That much Oates understood. He rubbed his stubbly mouth. "I could use a drink." He studied Rivette's lean face. "You want me to play the fetch game?"

Then he remembered that the gambler had often spun him a silver dollar and had never ordered him to play the game. Funny, him recollecting that when he couldn't even think.

"Stay there."

Rivette turned and walked into the saloon. When he stepped outside again, he had a brimming glass of whiskey in his hand. He held it out to Oates. "Drink this."

"We're running out of whiskey too, Rivette," Baxter said sourly.

"I know. But we can spare this much."

Oates reached out and took the glass in trembling hands. Without spilling a drop, he lifted the glass to his mouth and drained it dry. The raw whiskey hit his stomach and exploded into fire. Every jangling nerve in Oates' body, every deprived, tormented brain cell welcomed the alcohol like a long-lost friend. It was both wife and child to him, his hope and his salvation. Before him the image of Rivette shimmered for an instant, then regained its solid form. The whiskey had worked its demon magic.

Eddie Oates had begun to feel whole again. But he knew it would not last. He held out the glass in a steadier hand. "More, Mr. Rivette?"

"No, Eddie, that's all you can have." The gambler's eyes searched Oates' face. "Now do you understand what I'm saying to you?"

"You said no whiskey."

"That's right, I said no whiskey."

Rivette took the rifle from under his arm and held it out to Oates. "This is a Henry .44. It holds sixteen rounds of ammunition and it's loaded. I want you to take it with you."

Oates looked puzzled and the gambler said, "Have you ever shot a rifle before?"

"No." Oates shook his head. "And if I'd ever owned a fancy rifle like that, I'd have sold it for whiskey."

Rivette looked over Oates' shoulder at the three whores standing dung spattered and forlorn in the middle of the street. "Stella Spinner will show you how to use it. She shot a corsets drummer over to Denver a few years back, so she's not bashful around guns."

His face mirroring his growing concern, Baxter said, "Here, Rivette, this won't do. When the Apaches hit us, you'll need that Henry."

"I won't send any man into harm's way without a weapon, Baxter." The gambler motioned toward the door of the saloon. "When the Apaches charge through there, I'll start shooting and I won't need a rifle for that." He smiled without a trace of humor. "I've always been better at close work."

Baxter thought about it, then let it go. He promised himself that one day he'd find out just how good the damned New Orleans half-breed was with a gun. But now wasn't the time.

He shrugged. "The rifle won't make a difference anyhow. Oates is already a dead man. You know it, I know it, and if he ever sobers up enough, he'll know it."

"Call it idle curiosity, Baxter, but why do you hate them so much?"

The banker waved an arm toward the whores. "Them?"

"Yes, them. And a harmless drunk and an orphan boy who can't read or write or put two words together that make sense."

Baxter smiled with all the warmth of a grinning cobra. "Everybody lives, Rivette. Not everybody deserves to."

The gambler, a tall, elegant man with still hands, nodded. "I guess it's only right that a man who owns a bank and a fine house, who dresses in broadcloth and has a wife with three chins, should be the one to decide who lives and who dies."

"Yes, Rivette, the strong decide. That's always been the way of it."

The eyes Baxter raised to the gambler were not those of the jovial banker he pretended to be. Gray and cold, they were the eyes of a predator, a lobo wolf.

"Rivette," he said, "a word of advice—don't push me too hard." He let that warning hang in the air for a few moments, then said, "I wasn't always a banker."

"I know," Rivette said. "I have a fair notion of what you were and still are."

Baxter nodded. "Then keep it in mind." He grabbed Oates by his skinny upper arm. "Let's go, Eddie. You've already been in Alma way too long."

"Wait." Rivette shoved the Henry into Oates' hands. "If you have to make a fight with Apaches, see you save the last five rounds." The gambler's eyes searched Oates' face. "Do you understand what I'm saying to you?"

Oates needed another drink. He could think of nothing else. He carried the rifle gingerly, like a maiden aunt holding a snake.

"Do you understand me?" Rivette said.

The little man nodded. "Five ... yes, five. Five rounds."

Baxter grinned. "When he sees his first Apache, he'll understand right quick."

"Good luck, Eddie," Rivette said.

Oates made no answer as Baxter pushed him toward the others.

Under a hammering rain, Oates, Sam Tatum and the three women left Alma and walked into a dark blue morning that offered them nothing.

Warren Rivette watched them go and smiled to himself. "You're holding a full house, Eddie," he said aloud. "Three queens and two knaves."

Chapter 4

Stella Spinner, who was the strongest of them, led the way across the high desert country.

At her suggestion, they headed east and followed the bend of Silver Creek. Around them rose the big-shouldered peaks of the Mogollon Mountains standing eleven thousand feet above the flat. Ahead lay a wide, buffalo grass valley studded with sagebrush and cedar. Thick forests of ponderosa pine, aspen and sycamore grew on the mountain slopes and the thin wind talked constantly, whispering secrets no one could understand.

The sky was heavy with rain and a few random drops scattered over Oates as he trudged after the others, trailing the Henry behind him.

He was in the grip of demons and around him the hissing land was full of snakes. The whiskey hunger lashed at him, giving him no rest. He neither saw nor heard and young Sam Tatum had to physically stop and redirect him when the women turned into the cottonwoods and alders along the creek bank.

"We've got to rest for a spell, Mr. Oates," Sam said. "Maybe we can find something to eat." The boy smiled and rubbed his hands. "Corn bread an' buttermilk. Now that would be good."

Oates looked at Sam with dull, uncomprehending eyes, his mouth slack. He said nothing.

"I'll take you into the trees, Mr. Oates. It's fixin' to rain again."

Stella was sitting with her back against a cottonwood, her elbows on her knees. A strand of yellow hair had fallen over her forehead. "Sam, take that rifle off'n him before he shoots himself," she said. "Bring it over here."

Oates let go of the Henry without protest, then found himself a place among the alders. He sat and drew his knees into his chest and shivered, looking around but seeing nothing.

"Stella, what are we going to do?" Nellie Carney asked. She had white-blond hair and huge, frightened blue eyes.

"First thing we're going to do is strip and wash off the stink of Alma."

"But it's raining," Nellie protested. "Lorraine, tell her."

"Honey, the creek is already wet," Lorraine said, "or haven't you noticed?"

Lorraine looked tired, beaten. At forty-three she'd been too old for the whore's profession. She knew she was too old by far for what lay ahead of her.

"Strip off . . . but there's men present," Nellie said. "I don't want to bathe in front of men."

Stella's laugh was harsh and unpleasant. "Nellie, neither of them two exactly qualify as men. I wouldn't worry about it."

A rainbow trout jumped in the creek, then another. Exclamation points of rain covered the water's surface and wind set the tree branches to rustling.

Rising to her feet, Stella began to strip. "You coming, Lorraine?"

The older woman nodded. Then she too rose. "What about Apaches?" she asked.

"What about them?"

"Suppose they come on us when we're nekkid?"

"Nekkid, clothed, what difference does it make? We're all dead, Lorraine. It's just a matter of when."

"Don't say that, Stella," Nellie cried. "We'll meet cowboys on the trail, or find a ranch. I know we will."

Stella's face took on the look of a scolding mother. "Nellie, all the cowboys have been pulled back to protect their range. We didn't see a drover in Alma since two weeks ago." She stood under the tree, naked and unselfconscious. "As for finding a ranch, we could go looking. But my advice is to get out of this country as fast as possible." The woman smiled. "Maybe it's not good advice, but it's all I got."

"Where will we go, Stella?"

"I'll tell you after I have a bath and wash the horse-shit out of my hair."

Lorraine had stripped and her pale skin was covered in goose bumps. She reached out a hand to Stella. "You ready?"

The younger woman nodded and took the proffered hand. "Let's go!"

Together they ran down the slope of the creek bank and jumped, shrieking with laughter, into water still cold from the spring snowmelt.

"Oh hell," Nellie said. She quickly took off her clothes and joined them.

Sam Tatum had watched all this in slack-jawed amazement. He grinned, reached into his ragged coat and pulled out a stack of paper and a few pencils. He rushed to the creek's edge and began to sketch furiously.

The three women ignored him, intent on their icy baths.

And so did Oates. He had no interest in Sam or in naked female flesh for that matter. At that moment he would have traded the most beautiful woman in the world for a jug of forty-rod whiskey.

Around Oates green-eyed serpents hissed and coiled in the splintered light, and beyond those a herd of scarlet buffalo moved through a mist of their own making, the smoke of ten thousand frosted muzzles.

Ol' Wild Bill was there, as ever was, pushing the herd astride a big roan horse. In Deadwood, whenever it was, maybe a hundred years ago, maybe yesterday, Bill had treated Oates to many a drink and never made him play the go-fetch game.

But Bill was dead and had lain cold in the grave this three year.

Oates shook and hugged his knees. He was locked in his own personal hell that had neither windows nor doors but only darkness streaked with fire. The darkness had eyes that watched him, ruby red, unblinking and soulless.

He shivered. He was in hell and could no longer sell his soul for a glass of amber whiskey, because he'd made that bargain with the devil years before.

But then came deliverance.

Bill was standing over him, the ivory handles of his revolvers plain to see, that wry grin on his mouth that used to set female hearts aflutter.

"For you, ol' hoss," Bill said. "Looks like you need it." He held out a beaded glass of bourbon, the fragrant, glowing ambassador of reason and human happiness.

"Thank you, Mr. Hickok," Oates said. He reached out a quivering hand . . . but clutched only the slate-colored mist of the rain.

A man needs to be alive to cry, but Oates had been dead from birth. He laid his forehead on his knees and trembled, aware of nothing but his own pain.

Sam Tatum was still sketching on the creek bank, one hand sheltering his paper from the rain, the other busy with his pencil. The boy was fifteen that spring. At least that was some people's guess, the few who cared enough to speculate, but he was tall and big in the arms and shoulders and looked years older.

Led by Stella, the three women kept diving into the water, clutching at its pebbly bottom, and Sam squealed in delight as he sketched.

Then the boy discovered the reason for such strange female behavior.

Stella, water dripping from the hair that had fallen over her face, held a wriggling trout in her hands. She quickly tossed it onto the bank. "Sam, make sure that damned fish stays there," she yelled. "It's supper."

Sam stuffed his papers into his coat and with his foot shoved the fish onto grassier ground. Stella threw another rainbow that landed at his feet. Lorraine also caught a fish, but Nellie had no luck.

Shivering, the three women left the creek and hurriedly dressed on the bank. Once she was clothed, Stella crooked a finger at Sam and said, "Come here, you."

Wary of the stern note in the woman's voice, the boy shuffled reluctantly close to her. "Yes, Miss Stella?"

"What was all that stuff you was writing when we were in the creek?"

"I wasn't writing, Miss Stella."

"You were doing something, you little pervert," Nellie said, frowning.

"Show us, Sam," Stella said. Her fisted hands were on her hips, a bad sign as the boy knew from his bitter experience in foster homes.

Quickly the boy took the papers from inside his coat and passed them to Stella. The woman shuffled through them, quickly at first, then more slowly, her face changing from irritation to wonder.

"What's he say?" Lorraine asked. She was looking closely at Stella.

"Come see this. You too, Nellie."

The women crowded round Stella and began to pass around the pages.

Nellie looked from the paper she was holding, to Sam, then back again. "It's like we're alive, right there on the page."

"Hell," Lorraine said, "is my ass really that big?"

"Yeah," Stella said, "and so are your tits."

"Your own ass ain't so small either, Stella," Lorraine said, irritated. She looked over to the embarrassed Sam. "Hey, boy, how come you're not a famous artist?"

Sam shrugged. "I just draw what I like."

Stella thought for a few moments, then seemed to make up her mind about something. She stepped to Sam and held up four fingers of her left hand. "How many fingers do you see, Sam? Count them."

The boy looked confused. "I don't know my ciphers, Miss Stella."

"All right then, get out your pencil and write your name."

Sam's cheeks reddened. "I don't know how. I don't know my letters either."

"He's simple in the head," Nellie said. Her interest in Sam's sketches was already fading.

"How can he be simple and draw pictures like that?" Lorraine asked. "His mind works different than other people's, that's all."

Stella nodded. "It's us, but better than us. He changed us and made us . . . beautiful."

"Uh-huh, big asses an' all."

"You shut up, Nellie," Lorraine snapped. "What do you know about anything?"

"You're such a whore, Lorraine."

"And you're an uppity little bitch, Nellie. And may I remind you that you're also a whore?"

"But I won't be when I'm your age. By then I'll have a fine house and a carriage and servants."

Stella laughed the strident, practiced bray of the saloon girl. "We're surrounded by Apaches, Nellie. If you're lucky, the house you'll own will be a Mescalero wickiup."

"We haven't seen any Apaches," Nellie protested, even as her face paled.

"That's true, but don't you think they already know we're here?"

In that, Stella was right.

Chapter 5

The Mescaleros came just as the light of the spring day was fading and the sun was a red pool shadowed by rain clouds.

Four men riding wiry mustangs rode up on the creek, then sat their ponies, watching Sam and the three women as they huddled around a small, smoking fire.

"Well, they've arrived," Stella said. "Hell, and just when the trout is almost cooked."

A tight, frightened gasp escaped between Nellie's lips. She was used to men, but the Apaches looked more like lean, hungry wolves. What appetites they might possess, she did not want to guess.

Stella rose to her feet and levered a round into the chamber of the Henry.

The Indians noticed and their black eyes glittered. For now at least, they would be wary of the rifle.

The Mescaleros slid off the backs of their ponies and approached the fire. All wore black headbands and were painted for war. Three carried Winchesters, the stocks decorated with brass and iron tacks, and the tall man who seemed to be their leader cradled a Sharps .50 in his arms.

"What do you want from us?" Stella asked. She motioned to the fire. "We have fish but too little to share."

The tall man said nothing. He walked to Oates, lifted his head by the hair and stared into his face. "What ails this one?" he asked.

"He's a drunk," Lorraine said. "*El es un borracho.*"

The Apache nodded. "In the white towns, does this sit with men?"

"No," Stella said, "he does not."

"It is just as well." The Apache let Oates' head fall. "Would there be any honor in killing such a one?"

"No," Stella said. "He's sick and will die soon."

The Apache raised his foot and contemptuously kicked Oates onto his side. The little man groaned, raised his knees to his chest and lay where he'd fallen.

The hard, obsidian eyes moved to Sam Tatum, measured the boy, dismissed him. A fighting man, the Apache could recognize that quality in others. He saw nothing in Tatum to alarm him.

But Sam read it wrong. The big Indian meant him harm.

The boy reached into his coat and pulled out the sketches he'd made. He proffered them to the Apache. "Pretty pictures," he said. "A gift." He waved to the women. "Pictures of them."

Scowling, the Mescalero pulled the papers from Sam's hand. He glanced at the drawing on top and bent his head to study it more closely. Then he looked across the fire to Lorraine, grinning.

He said something to his companions, and they crowded around him. Soon they were passing the sketches back and forth, laughing and slapping one another on the back.

Indians are notional, none more so than Apaches. Their meeting with the women could have ended badly but for Sam's clumsy attempt to make friends. The sketches of three naked women splashing in the creek amused and excited them. For now it was enough.

A young warrior with a terrible saber scar down one cheek laid his Winchester on the ground and bounced his cupped hands in front of his chest. He pointed to Lorraine and grinned. Another lifted his breechcloth and slapped his naked rump. Again Lorraine was the target.

"I told you, Lorraine," Stella said. "You've got a big ass."

The tall man motioned to the others, and the Apaches immediately swung onto their ponies. They rode away yipping and hollering, and waving Sam's sketches over their heads.

It was over, for now. The pictures of the naked women had satisfied them, something to show around the *ranchería* fires that night.

But it was the Henry that had tipped the balance, the rifle and the confidence of the cold-eyed woman who held it.

Stella leaned back against a cottonwood and brushed

a lock of hair off her forehead with an unsteady hand. "For a moment there, I thought we were all dead," she said.

Lorraine looked from the woman's pale face to the Henry. "Can you use that thing?"

"I don't know," Stella said. "I've never tried. Where I was raised, the price of this gun would have kept my folks in grub for a year."

Nellie was sitting on the ground, her face in her hands. She raised tear-stained eyes to the other woman. "It takes a man to shoot a rifle gun like that," she said.

"Well, we don't have one o' them handy," Lorraine said. "Now, let's eat the fish before it burns to a crisp."

Sam and the women shared the trout around their feeble fire. The trees were alive with wind and the rain was falling heavier, ticking from the branches.

Nellie looked over at Oates, who was still lying on his side, moaning softly. "What about him?" she asked.

"What about him?" Lorraine said.

"Shouldn't we feed him?"

Stella looked at the younger woman with the cool, bruised eyes of the professional whore. "Sure, Nellie, you can give him yours."

"I just said—," Nellie protested.

"You'd only be wasting food, honey," Lorraine said. She sounded as detached as Stella. "Unless he finds whiskey soon, he'll curl up and die."

"Why does a man get to be like him?" Nellie asked.

Lorraine shrugged. "Life, I guess."

"Or he just can't handle whiskey," Stella said absently.

"Nellie, Eddie Oates is a man who might once have looked at his life stretching away from him and saw nothing but ten thousand miles of empty road," Lorraine said. "Maybe that's why he stays drunk all the time."

Nellie shivered as drops of cold water fell from the trees and trickled down the back of her neck. Oates already forgotten, she said, "Stella, what are we going to do?" She hugged herself and tried to get closer to the fire. "I'm scared, Stella."

"We're all scared." Stella wiped her hands on the wet grass beside her. "There's a town east of here called Heartbreak. Maybe we can make it."

Lorraine smiled slightly. "Unless the Apaches get bored with the pictures and decide they want the real thing."

"They're men," Stella said. "Of course they'll want the real thing."

"How far away is Heartbreak?" Nellie asked.

Stella shook her head. "I don't know. Fifty miles, a hundred, I've no idea."

"Do we even know it's there?" Lorraine said.

"It's there," Stella answered. "I knew a girl who worked the line in Heartbreak. She said it was a fair-sized town, miners mostly, but there are some ranches around."

Nellie brightened. "Miners are high rollers. We can set up in business, the three of us, run our own house."

"Can I come, Miss Stella?" Sam asked.

"Sure you can. I think there's money to be made from you, Sam. I just have to figure a way how."

"What about Mr. Oates? Can he go to Heartbreak?" Tatum asked.

"If we can wake him." Stella searched around in her carpetbag. She found a flat tin, opened it, took out a thin cheroot and held it up for the others to see. "Anybody else?" When no one answered, she lit the little cigar with a brand from the fire.

Another search produced a nickel-plated Smith & Wesson .38 with ivory grips. Stella handed it to Lorraine. "Shove that in a pocket of your mackinaw," she said. "It's handy for up-close work."

"So, when do we take the Heartbreak Trail, Stella?" the older woman asked, dropping the revolver into her pocket.

"We'll sleep for a few hours, then hit the road while it's still dark."

Lorraine stared into the guttering fire for a few moments, then said, "Stella, it seems you've become our leader, so tell me: how do you rate our chances of reaching that Heartbreak place alive?"

Stella didn't hesitate. "Slim to none, Lorraine, and slim's already saddling up to leave town."

Chapter 6

Eddie Oates woke as the first light of morning bladed though the cottonwood branches. He lay still, listening to the small sounds of insects in the grass around him.

He tried to move—and groaned deep in his throat.

Immediately iron mallets pounded in his head and lightning flashed, searing streaks of white and scarlet, hellfire from the forge of a demented god.

Oates buried his face in the wet earth, deep into its musky fragrance, as soft and welcoming as the breasts of a beautiful woman.

His heartbeats thudded in his ears, the rapid, hammer-trip cadence of the alcoholic that threatened to rip his chest apart.

Dear God in heaven, he needed a drink.

It took a supreme effort of will and a battle against pain for Oates to rise up on all fours. Again he waited for the blinding agony in his head to subside. Then he struggled to his feet.

The world spun around him, trees, creek and sky cartwheeling past at dizzying speed. He bent over and retched, blood rushing into his face, which swelled like a red carnival balloon.

After a few minutes he straightened again, wiped his mouth with the back of his hand, blinked and peered around him. He was alone.

What was he doing here in this wilderness? Desperately Oates tried to remember. . . .

Alma . . . they threw him out . . . a useless mouth to feed . . . the saloon whores . . . Sammy Tatum. A rifle. Somebody had given him a rifle. He could sell it and buy whiskey. . . .

Where was the damned rifle?

Oates stumbled along the creek bank. Something fluttered from a cottonwood trunk; a white thing— paper—spiked on a broken branch.

He staggered to the tree and tore the sheet free. It took him several minutes to read the words and three times as long to understand what they implied.

We headed east on the
Heartbreak Trail.
Follow if you can.
You was asleep and
could not be waked.

Oates glanced around. The whores were gone. They'd taken his rifle and headed east—where the sun was touching the blue peaks of the Mogollons with golden light. He stumbled from the creek and started to walk.

He needed that rifle for whiskey money.

After an hour, Oates came on a game trail that ran parallel to the north bank of Gilita Creek. This was grassy country, heavily forested by wild oak, piñon and juniper, here and there stands of cactus and thistle. Once, a huge bull moose crossed his path, not yet displaying the antlers that would grow an inch a day by midsummer. The moose stood and watched Oates, intently, evaluating him as a potential danger. Seeing nothing to alarm him, he moved on and disappeared into the trees.

To the south soared the high peaks of the Gila Wilderness, their slopes heavily timbered by aspen and Douglas fir. Long before the Apaches came, this country had been the home of the Mogollon Indians, who had fished its creeks and hunted its canyons. Around AD 1300, the entire tribe had mysteriously vanished, leaving no scars on the land and only their ghosts to mark their passing.

Of this, Oates was unaware. He was conscious only of the whiskey hunger and the pain in his thin, undernourished body. He was unaccustomed to exercise and crossing this hard land was rapidly draining what little strength he had.

His bare feet were cut and bruised from the trail, and the heat of the climbing sun began to punish him.

A tall, undercut rock, wedged among a stand of juniper and a single, wind-racked pine, offered the promise of shade and a chance to rest. Oates stumbled into the blue shadow at the base of the rock and threw himself on the ground. He let a dreamless oblivion that wasn't sleep take him. . . .

Eddie Oates felt himself rising, leaving the earth. He kicked and struggled, afraid of soaring too high and falling. But then he was shaken like a rat and a man's laughing voice said, "Feisty little cuss, ain't he?"

Oates opened his eyes. A big, bearded man wearing a buckskin shirt had him by the back of the neck and continued to shake him hard.

Another voice said, "What's he got, Clem?"

"Nothing that I can tell, Pa." The bearded man wrinkled his nose. "Smells like the business end of a polecat, though."

"Bring him here."

Oates was dragged from the rock into the open. Two men sat mustangs, grinning at the sight of him. The older of the two had a mane of dirty, silver hair that hung over the shoulders of his buckskins and a beard of the same color fanned out across his chest. The other man was a carbon copy of his companion, except that his hair and beard were black. Both carried Winchesters across their saddle horns.

"Well, what ill wind blew you here, boy?" the older man asked.

Oates had trouble focusing his eyes. He opened his mouth to speak, but managed only a mangled croak.

The big man shook him again. "Answer my pa."

"He's tetched in the head, maybe." The older man grinned.

"Alma . . . I'm a couple of days out of Alma," Oates said.

"Where you headed, boy?"

Oates remembered the note. "Heartbreak. It's a town east of here."

"Heard o' it," Pa said. "Never been there, though."

The man's pale blue eyes grew shrewd. "Here, what's ailing you, boy? You sick?"

Oates shook his head. "I need a drink of whiskey, Mister. I need a drink real bad."

Pa turned to the man beside him. "Now, that's not a bad idea, is it, Reuben? Pass me the bottle."

The man called Reuben reached behind him and produced a bottle of bourbon from his saddlebags. Oates noticed that it was three-fourths full, glowing gold in the sunlight.

Pa drank, then wiped his bearded mouth with the back of his hand. He looked down at Oates and smiled.

Oates tried to match the man's smile and succeeded only in stretching his mouth in an insane grimace. "Mister, I appreciate this," he said.

"You got money, boy?" Pa asked.

Oates shook his head. "But I got me a fancy rifle gun."

Suddenly all three men were wary, looking around at the trees where the wind was playing. "Where is it?' Pa looked stern. "Don't you lie to me, boy."

Oates tried to think, an effort that was rewarded by

a cuff on the back of his head from Clem. "Where is the rifle?" Clem asked.

"It's . . . friends of mine have it. Three women, whores, and a simple boy."

"Where are they?" Pa asked.

"East on the trail. They're headed for Heartbreak."

Clem looked up at his father. "Pa, we haven't had us a woman since the Apache squaw we jumped in Burnt Corral Canyon."

Pa nodded. "It's been a spell right enough." He looked at Oates. "Whores, you say? Are they real purty?"

"Pretty enough," Oates said.

"And a simple boy?"

"Yeah. Just tell them I said for them to give you my rifle."

"Victorio might have 'em by this time, Pa," Reuben said. "Or ol' Nana."

"It's worth a look-see," Clem said. "Last I heard, Victorio's young bucks were playing hob west of here, raising all kinds of hell."

Pa leaned forward in the saddle. "Boy, if you're lying to me . . ."

"I ain't lying, Mister. Now, can I have a drink?"

"Naw, this is prime whiskey. It ain't for trash like you."

Oates couldn't believe what he just heard. "But . . . but you said . . ."

"I didn't say nothing about giving you whiskey."

Anger, the first he'd felt in years, flared in Oates. "You dirty, lying, son of a bitch!"

Pa's face hardened. "Clem, you gonna let trail trash speak to your old man like that?"

Oates heard Clem laugh. A fist as big as a ham crashed into his face. Then he doubled up when the man rammed a punch into his belly. Oates fell to the ground, retching, as Clem's boots went in hard.

Chapter 7

Eddie Oates woke to pain.

He lay unmoving, but opened his eyes, checking on the day.

The afternoon was far gone and the day was shading into a violet twilight. He turned his head, wincing as the movement brought new pain, a blinding agony that lanced into his brain. Above him the sky was the color of a duck egg and a single star stood a lonely picket to the north.

The salty, smoky taste of blood was in Oates' mouth and he twitched in painful shock as his fingertips touched his left eye. It seemed to be enormously swollen and, judging by his vision, almost closed shut.

Carefully, favoring his right side where his ribs ached, Oates struggled into a sitting position. Using his hands as crutches, he inched his way back to the rock and laid his back against the cool stone.

He was hurt bad, but it did not trouble him. Some men know they should never have been born, and suddenly Oates felt strangely content to be one of them. In all his life, no one had ever been happy at his coming or sad at his leaving. If he died here, he would not be missed.

The whiskey hunger had left him, and he found he was no longer mourning his lost friend. His boon companion, for so many years both wife and child to him, would not be coming back, and about that, there was nothing to be done.

He would stay there, right where he was, and pass away as the wind sang his requiem in the trees.

But Eddie Oates was not to be allowed the privilege of choosing the manner of his dying.

The coyotes were a hunting pair and the smell of blood was strong.

Wary, they kept their distance from Oates, studying him, calculating his strength and ability to fight. They were in no hurry. Coyotes will often battle a full-grown moose for eighteen hours before they bring it down or admit defeat and quit. This pair suspected they had found a much weaker and more vulnerable prey.

Oates looked around him for a weapon, a tree branch or rock. He found neither. The ground under the stony overhang was covered in sand that offered nothing.

Yelling at the top of his lungs, Oates bunched up a fistful of sand and threw it at the coyotes. The sand sifted apart in the wind and drifted harmlessly to earth.

The female tested him first.

Incredibly fast, she darted, fangs bared, for Oates' feet. He quickly drew up his knees, but the coyote changed her angle of attack and bit at his left thigh. The animal's teeth closed on Oates' pants and tore free a strip of the thin cloth.

Frustrated for now, the female retreated, growling as she shook the cloth in her mouth.

The dog coyote had watched the attack with keen, knowing eyes. The prey had moved slowly and that suggested an injury of some kind. It was weakened so much it had made little attempt to defend itself. This could be an easy kill.

The dog moved to its left, positioning itself for a flank attack. Dropping the scrap of cloth, the female advanced a few steps, then stopped. Head lowered, the animal kept its amber eyes on Oates' face.

"Get the hell away from me!" Oates yelled. He threw another handful of sand.

This time the coyote attack was coordinated. The dog rushed in from the flank and the female ran straight at Oates. Oates tried to rise to his feet, failed, and the dog sank its teeth into his right forearm, immediately drawing blood. The female had sprung for the man's throat, but he had raised himself enough to upset her aim. Her fangs closed on his belly and tore at him.

Oates screamed. He kicked out at the female and the hard sole of his right foot took her full on the snout. The coyote yipped in pain and backed off, snarling. The dog, hearing his mate's cry of hurt, was startled and he too bounded back a few steps.

The first round to Oates. But, wiser now, the coyotes attacked again.

This time both of them jumped on Oates and he collapsed under their weight, falling on his side. He smelled the feral stench of the animals and felt their fangs rip into his back and thighs.

Desperately, Oates tried to sit up, striking out with his right arm. He hit the dog a couple of times, but his punches were weak and ineffective. Blood sprayed around him and dripped like rubies from the muzzles of the coyotes.

Oates was done, and he knew it.

The flat statement of a rifle shot racketed through the hollow quiet of the evening.

The dog coyote shrieked and fell away, landing on its back, its legs twitching.

Another shot.

The female dropped without a sound, her deadweight suddenly heavy on Oates.

He felt the coyote being lifted from him and a bearded face with good-humored hazel eyes swam into his view. "You all right, pardner?" a man's voice asked.

Oates tried to answer, but darkness took him and he knew no more.

Eddie Oates opened his eyes. He stared up at a low pine roof supported by log crossbeams. He smelled meat and onions, the faint tang of leather and gun oil and the sweet scent of the pine itself.

A faint sound came to him and he turned his head, struggling to place the origin of the noise. There it was, a soft scuffing on the timber floor, like a man wearing boots who was doing his best to be quiet. From what seemed a long way off, a voice spoke to him.

"So you're awake, young feller. An' hungry, I bet."

The tall figure of a man stepped toward him through the gloom of the cabin and stopped in a column of dusty sunlight streaming through a window.

"See," the man said, "I'm nothing to be scared of."

"Where am I?" Oates asked.

"You're in my cabin in a canyon close to Black Mountain. That's the cinder cone you can see from out back—stands about nine thousand feet above the flat." The man stepped out of the sunlight into the shade. "Name's Jacob Yearly, by the way. You mind giving me your own handle?"

"Eddie Oates." He looked startled, a thing Yearly noticed.

"Somethin' I said?" the man asked.

Oates shook his head. "I haven't given a man my name in a long time," he said.

"You on the dodge?"

"No. It's just . . . well, I guess nobody's been interested enough in what I was called to ask me."

"Handy thing, a name," Yearly said. "A man can go far with a good name, not so far with a bad one."

Oates looked around the cabin, rubbing his bearded mouth. "You got a touch of whiskey?" he asked.

Yearly stepped beside the cot where the younger man lay. "I love whiskey. I love the look of it, the smell of it and the taste of it. And I love what it does to me." He smiled. "That's why I never drink it."

An old man dressed in a plaid shirt and canvas pants tucked into mule-eared boots, Yearly sat on the cot, and the springs squealed in protest.

"Right now, I'd say whiskey is the last thing you need, Eddie. You've got a couple of busted ribs and you're all clawed an' bit to pieces. You need food and rest." He rose to his feet. "I got stew on the stove. I'll bring you some."

Oates pushed his pillow up against the cot's iron headboard and leaned back, his eyes lifted to the older man's bearded face. "Why are you doing this?"

"Doing what?"

"Helping me like this."

Yearly shrugged. "I'd do it for any poor, hurtin' critter."

The old man stepped away and returned with a bowl of stew. He handed it to Oates, who suddenly realized he was very hungry. Dipping his spoon into the fragrant mix of meat, wild onions and potatoes was one thing—getting it to his mouth was another.

His hand shook so uncontrollably that he dropped the food, untasted, back into the bowl.

Yearly said nothing. He sat on the cot once again and, taking the bowl and spoon, fed Oates like a father would a sick child.

After the younger man had eaten, Yearly checked the bandage around Oates' chest, then began to spread a salve on his bites and scratches.

"The coyote has a dirty mouth," he said. "There's sagebrush in this and chaparral, so you don't get pizen of the blood. And willow bark for pain." Yearly sat back, looking at Oates. "Sometimes a man has other pains that go deeper, but I can't poultice those."

Sunlight angled brighter through the cabin window where dust motes danced and splashed yellow light on the red and white cowhide on the floor in front of the stone fireplace.

Oates spoke into a breathless silence. "Jacob, I'd like to share my pain with you, but you're wrong, I have none. I've always been a drunk. That's the beginning and end of my life story."

Yearly drew a chair up to the bed. "Tell me about it anyhow, right up to the moment I shot them coyotes off'n you. This is Sunday and I don't labor on the Sabbath, so I've got all day, young feller."

Chapter 8

"Like I told you, there isn't much to tell," Eddie Oates said. "As much as I can remember, my life was hard and always shaped up to trouble.

"I was born over Tucson way in the Arizona Territory. I don't recollect much about my ma, but my father was a drunken, violent brute who made a living as a stone mason, when he worked.

"Then one day when I was about ten, he got into a fight in a cantina over a woman and got shot. My ma died six months later, of a broken heart some said, but I never cottoned to that story. She drank bad water and it killed her. That was all."

Oates shifted position on the cot and Yearly told him to make sure he was favoring his ribs, otherwise they'd play hob and never heal properly.

"So then what happened?" the old man prompted.

"I was taken in by a family who needed a slave who wouldn't eat too much. I was just a little feller, so I fit the bill. Pretty soon they started to beat me, telling me I was a lazy, shiftless and ungrateful wretch.

"Then the local preacher, a man named Stryker, told my foster mother that the trouble was meat. 'I recently read all about it in Mr. Dickens' great novel *Oliver Twist*, ma'am,' he said. 'Give a boy too much meat and you'll spoil him and turn him into a slothful creat'ur who'll give you no work but plenty of sass. That's what Mr. Dickens says. He knows how to deal with boys.'

"I was only being fed table scraps as it was, but pretty soon even those dried up. Then, one day I found a jug of corn liquor in the kitchen, took it down to the creek and got drunk.

"They beat me unmercifully when they found me passed out on the creek bank, of course. But I didn't mind. I knew I had found my calling. That jug was like a passport into a new and better world."

"I've also read Mr. Dickens," Yearly said. "In fact, I have a few of his volumes on the shelf over there. He was holding up Oliver Twist as an example of the cruelty of England's poor laws. Your preacher, Stryker, was a fool."

"Maybe so, but he helped me make up my mind. A few weeks after I found the jug, I stole some money from the house and ran away.

"I drifted east, doing whatever odd jobs I could find, swamping saloons or cleaning outhouses, I wasn't particular. Every cent I earned I spent on whiskey and when I couldn't earn it, I stole it. I figure at one time or another I wrote my name on the wall of every hoose-gow from Tucson to Santa Fe.

"Eventually, I don't know, when, why or how, I drifted into Alma. There was plenty of whiskey in Alma and I drank more than my share. The cowboys would make me play fetch like a dog, sometimes in the saloons, sometimes in the street, but they bought me whiskey, so I'd run and bark all they wanted."

"So why did you leave?" Yearly asked.

"They threw me out. Me, three whores and a simple boy. The citizens' committee said we were useless mouths to feed. After that, I don't remember much. . . ."

Suddenly Oates looked stricken. He sat silent for several long moments, then buried his face in his shaking hands and rocked back and forth on the cot. "Oh my God," he whispered, "what have I done?"

Yearly's voice held a note of confusion. "Son, I don't catch your drift."

"I betrayed them all," Oates said. He dropped his hands and turned his face to the old man. "Sammy Tatum, the three women, I sold them out for a drink of whiskey."

"I guess you better explain that," Yearly said. "You're not making a lick o' sense."

"Before you saved me from the coyotes, I met three men on the trail, big men, wearing buckskins."

"Did they give you their names?"

"No. But the oldest they called Pa, and I heard them call the one who give me this"—Oates' fingers moved to his grotesquely swollen eye—"Clem."

Yearly nodded. "I'd bet my bottom dollar you ran into ol' Mash Halleck and his boys. They're bad ones, so danged mean, even the Apaches ride wide around them." A frown gathered between Yearly's unruly eyebrows. "How come you had dealings with the Hallecks?"

"They had whiskey and I offered to trade a rifle for a drink."

"Pity. A rifle could have saved you grief from them coyotes."

"I didn't have it. The women took it. They left me a note saying they were headed for a town called Heartbreak and that I should catch up when I sobered up enough.

"I told Pa—Mash Halleck—that the women were ahead of me on the trail and he should tell them to give him the rifle."

Oates looked strained as memories returned to him bit by bit, like the pieces of a mosaic coming together.

"They wanted the rifle all right, but they were more interested in the women. . . ."

Oates' voice trailed away into silence. The cabin was warm and outside jays were quarreling in the trees. Finally he said, "Jacob, I appreciate what you did for me, but I have to go after them. Somehow I got to make it right."

"You plan on going up against the Halleck boys?"

"Maybe they left the women alone."

The old man shook his head. "Shame on me for saying such things on the Sabbath, but those women, whores you said, are already in bondage. Mash and his sons will use them hard and when they've had enough, they'll sell them, maybe down to Old Mexico way.

"The only way you'll free the women from the Hallecks is at gunpoint, and even then, you'll have to be mighty slick with the iron. Mash has killed his share, and so has his son Reuben, but Clem's the gun hand, fast on the draw and shoot. Last I'd heard, he'd killed seven men, and the number has probably growed since then."

Oates felt a small sickness rise in him. "I've never even shot a gun."

Yearly nodded. "Figured as much. Then I don't give much for your chances."

The old man trod carefully, choosing his words. "Eddie, you're still a hopeless drunk. I can see it on you. You're only a glass of whiskey away from playing retriever dog for the cowboys again. The Hallecks would stomp you into the ground without breaking a sweat."

Oates shook his head. "No matter, I've got it to do. If I walk away from it, I'll have to crawl into a whiskey bottle and stay there until it kills me. I'm starting to think that I don't want to be a drunken fool ever again." He hesitated, then smiled weakly. "Anyway, that's how I feel today. I don't know about tomorrow."

"Man can lay up troubles for himself by worrying about tomorrow. Hell, boy, today is the tomorrow you worried about yesterday and look at you, lying there all bandaged up an' cozy as a bug in a rug."

Yearly leaned toward Oates, his elbows on his knees. "Now, about them whores. The way I see it, you've got three months, Eddie. That's how long I figure it will be before the Hallecks tire of them. Leastwise, that's been their pattern with the Indian women they pick up."

He rose to his feet, crossed to the stove and poured coffee into two cups. He passed one to Oates. "I only put an inch of coffee in there," he said. "With those hands, I don't want you scalding yourself."

Yearly sat, lit his pipe and said through a cloud of blue smoke, "I've got a proposition for you, Eddie. You work for me the next three months and I'll teach you how to shoot. Can you ride a hoss?" The old man saw Oates shake his head. "Teach you that too. If you can ride an' shoot some, maybe you can meet the Halleck boys on something like level ground. Though I'm making no guarantees, mind."

Oates looked around the cabin, searching for something that would suggest Yearly's occupation. A rusty old bear trap hung on the far wall, but apart from that there was nothing. He said, "What do you do, Jacob? You a cattleman?"

"Hell, no, boy. Cowboying is something a man does when he knows he ain't shaping up for anything else. I cut cinder block out of the side of Black Mountain an' two, three times a year a Mormon man comes from Silver City with a couple of wagons and hauls them away. He brings me supplies and don't quibble none, always pays a fair price."

"What does he do with cinder blocks?" Oates asked.

"He's never said. I heard tell that folks in Arizona use them to decorate gardens an' parks an' sich. But I don't set much store by that."

Yearly thumbed a match into flame and relit his pipe. Talking around the stem, he said, "Well, what's your answer?"

Oates shrugged. "Sure. What have I got to lose?"

The old man smiled. "Eddie, as far as I can tell, not a damned thing."

Chapter 9

Black Mountain was the northernmost sentinel of the Gila. A mile of hilly, broken ground, thick with sagebrush and piñon, lay between Yearly's cabin and the rounded bulk of the peak.

The old man had a remuda of three horses penned up in a pole corral, a paint mustang, a rangy buckskin and a Morgan.

After breakfast each morning, he and Oates hitched the Morgan to a wagon and headed for the mountain, where they cut out red and black lava stones with a pick and shovel. The cinder blocks were stacked behind the cabin, and after three weeks of backbreaking labor were already as high as the top of a tall man's head.

Yearly insisted that Oates take a daily bath in the creek that ran near the house and had him shave off his beard, leaving only a sweeping dragoon mustache that was then fashionable in the West.

Fed on a steady diet of venison stew, bacon and beans and elk steak, Oates put on weight and his shoulders and arms began to show muscle, even as his face thinned into hard, tanned planes.

Yearly was an affable, even-tempered host and employer with an easy way of talking and his rules were few—but for one.

At Oates' insistence, the old man slept in the cot while he spread his blankets on the floor each night. The door to the cabin's only bedroom remained locked at all times.

After their return from the mountain one evening, Oates asked him why. Yearly made a display of lighting his pipe, playing for time as he searched his mind for the right words. Finally he said, "That room is . . . well, it's special to me. I don't want anyone going in there. I don't go in there myself."

"Keep your treasure in there, huh, Jacob?" Oates joshed. He removed one of the oversized shoes the old man had given him and rubbed his aching foot.

"You could say that. I keep memories in there that are precious to me."

"A woman?"

"No, not a woman."

Oates placed a shoe on the floor, then removed the other. "That narrows it down," he said.

Yearly said nothing. Again he made a show with his pipe as a rising night wind rustled around the eaves of the cabin, but for a while only an empty silence stretched between him and Oates.

Finally he said, "Eddie, what's it been, a month?

And already I see a difference in you as the whiskey greed has left. I think you've come so far because you're still a young man and not too old for change. But you still have a ways to go, a long ways."

The old man waved a hand toward the bedroom. "Maybe one day I'll show you what's behind that door, but not today. And not tomorrow or the day after that."

Oates didn't push it. He slipped his feet into his shoes and said, "I'll go check on the Morgan."

"We won't need the Morgan tomorrow," Yearly said.

"How come? We still have lava block to move back to the house."

"I know, but tomorrow I'm going to teach you to shoot."

Eddie Oates hefted the unfamiliar weight of the .44 Colt and looked out over the mesquite flats. "How about that dead cedar near the creek, Jacob?"

"Hell, boy, that's a fair piece. If a man draws down on you from there, you got plenty of room to cut an' run." He stepped toward the cedar and Oates followed. When they were ten feet from the tree he stopped.

"You'll shoot from here." Yearly noted the puzzled look on the younger man's face and said patiently, "Revolver fighters like Clem Halleck will come at you up close an' real personal, especially them as makes fancy moves, skinning the iron fast like he does.

"You shoot the way I'm going to show you and you'll kill your man every time. Don't rush it, Eddie, and aim for the belly. Now, go to it."

As Yearly had demonstrated, Oates took up a duelist's stance, the inside of his left foot against his right heel, the Colt held out straight in front of him.

"Thumb back the hammer, boy, then cut 'er loose."

The triple click of the Colt's hammer was loud in the cool, red-tinted stillness of the morning. Oates squeezed the trigger.

The revolver roared and bucked and the bullet splintered wood dead center from the cedar's trunk.

"Shoot her dry, boy."

Oates did as he was told, firing until the hammer clicked on a spent cartridge. He'd fired five shots at the tree and had scored five hits.

Turning in a drifting gray cloud of gunsmoke, Oates looked at Yearly and grinned. "I'd say that was pretty good."

"I'd say the tree wasn't shooting back at you."

The old man reached into the pocket of the old army greatcoat he wore on cool mornings and passed a cardboard box to Oates. "There's fifty cartridges. It's old stuff that's been lying around for years and it's a mite uncertain, but it's fine for practice. Shoot 'em all and let me see fifty hits on the tree. Cut it down if you can because I'm sick of looking at it."

Yearly turned on his heel and started back to the cabin. "Where you going, Jacob?"

"For coffee. You can come get yours when all the cartridges are gone." The old man stopped and turned. "There are Apaches around this morning, Eddie, so step careful."

Oates swallowed the lump in his throat and managed to croak, "Wha . . ."

But Yearly was already out of earshot.

Oates' mind was not on his target practice and he turned his head constantly for any sign of Apaches. He saw nothing, though every time jays quarreled in the piñons or a jackrabbit bounded across the flat, he jumped.

Despite his unease and the poor quality of his ammunition, which produced a number of duds and fliers, he hit the cedar nearly twoscore times.

Then he lit a shuck for the cabin, his shoes, fitted to Yearly, a much bigger man, flopping and slapping on his feet.

When he ran inside, the old man was sitting in his chair by the fire, smoking his pipe, a volume by Sir Walter Scott in his hands.

"Heard the shooting," Yearly said without looking up. "I'd say, oh, forty-five rounds. You score any hits?"

"Scored with most of them."

"Uh-huh," Yearly said, a comment Oates considered neither approving nor disapproving.

A silence grew between them, then Oates said, almost accusingly, "I didn't see any Apaches, though."

"You won't, unless they want to be seen. But they're here."

"Jacob, shouldn't we be doing something?"

"Like what?"

"Like getting ready to defend ourselves."

"The Apaches never bothered me before."

"Who's to say they won't now?"

"The Apaches, I guess."

The old man looked up from his book. "They're carrying their hurting dead with them. I reckon they've had a bellyful of war for the present."

"I still haven't seen them."

"You will. Coffee's still on the bile if'n you want some. An' clean the Colt while you're at it, Eddie. A dirty gun has killed more than one man. Cleaning stuff in the drawer over there."

The long day was just giving way to evening when the Apaches began to ride past the cabin, heading into the Gila.

Under a sky streaked with ribbons of red and jade, teased by a west wind, they came singly at first, then in groups of three or four. The endurance and fortitude of the Apache were legendary, but these warriors looked like they'd been through it. Many of them wounded, they slumped on their tired ponies, taking no interest in what lay around them. They must have been routed at Alma and it showed.

Oates and Yearly stood outside the cabin in the violet night and watched them pass.

Most of the warriors led ponies burdened by dead men roped facedown across their backs. Oates counted thirty bodies, but probably more had been abandoned along the trail.

"It's too dark to make out faces clear," Yearly whispered, "but I haven't seen Victorio or ol' Nana either."

Asking a question to which he already knew the answer, Oates said, "You reckon they got beat at Alma?"

The old man nodded. "Looks like." He gave Oates a sidelong glance. "Thinking of going back, Eddie?"

"One day, but only to settle some scores."

Yearly nodded. "That can drive a man."

One by one the Apaches melted into the distance and night, leaving only the solitude and silence on the land that God intended.

A match flared as Yearly lit his pipe. Then the old man turned to Oates and said, "Go inside, Eddie. Leave me to study on things for a spell."

A small alarm rose in Oates. "You all right, Jacob?"

"I'm fine. Sometimes a man wants to be by himself, is all."

"Then I'll bring your coat. There's a chill in the air."

Coyotes were yipping somewhere out in the darkness and the wine-dark sky was full of stars.

"I'm not cold," Yearly said. "Now leave me. I'll be in soon."

Oates turned away and started to walk back to the cabin. All his life he'd been isolated, but never alone. There had always been people around, a few friendly, most not, but they were always there. Why a man would stand in the crowding dark and seek out loneliness puzzled him.

He stopped and looked first at the shadowed land, then at the sky, hoping to see what Jacob was seeing and feel what he was feeling. He listened into the night and heard the sigh of the ceaseless wind, the restless rustle of the cedars around the cabin.

Then he began to understand. . . .

The night was coming down on him like a blessing and it had the power to heal the hurt in a man. Now he knew what Jacob knew.

He stepped into the cabin, and for the first time in a long time, the whiskey hunger had completely left him.

Yearly stepped inside an hour later, bringing the memory of the night with him. "Best you spread your blankets, Eddie," he said. "We got a busy day ahead of us tomorrow."

"No more Apaches passing through, huh?"

"Not passing through, no." Seeing the expression on Oates' face, he said, "There are Apaches out there, not many, maybe just a few broncos."

"Why would they stay around?"

"I don't know." He looked at the younger man. "Eddie, there are bad apples in every barrel, and that applies to Apaches as much as it does to white men."

He crossed to his cot, then stopped. "Load the Colt, boy, an' keep it close."

Chapter 10

Next morning Yearly said they wouldn't go to the mountain that day but stay close to the cabin. The old man seemed to have a honed instinct for danger and Oates made no objection.

When Oates went outside to fork hay to the horses, Yearly went with him, his Winchester cradled in his arms. Oates carried the Colt in the pocket of his ragged pants and Jacob had told him to load all six cylinders.

The old man's eyes were never at rest, scanning the land around them and the open ground behind the corral. Now and then he would raise his nose and read the wind, then frown, his knuckles whitening in the rifle stock.

"They still around?" Oates asked.

"Uh-huh. Watching us. They figured I was alone, but now they've seen you and it's making them think."

"Think about what?"

"How best to lift our hair. The Apache is brave, but

he ain't a fool. They'll attack at the moment they figure the odds are on their side. That's why we'll stay together in the cabin."

"I've got the Colt, Jacob. I could bring in the cinder block we've already cut. It will only take a couple of trips."

Yearly shook his head. "You'd be out in the open, boy, an' that's bucking a stacked deck. They'd lift your hair for sure." He smiled. "Hitting a tree with a .44 is one thing. Hitting an Apache is another."

"How many do you figure, Jacob?"

"I don't know any more than I did last night. Enough, I reckon."

"I guess they're pretty mad about the beating they took at Alma, huh?"

"Eddie, an Apache doesn't get mad. He gets even."

Oates threw the paint mustang a last forkful of hay, then followed Yearly back to the cabin.

The place was solidly built of pine logs and had a tar-paper and shingle roof, rare and expensive at that time. But the chimney was of sticks and mud and Yearly said it constantly blew down in gales. There were only two openings to the front, a single window and the door, and none to the back.

The cabin looked as if it could withstand a siege and when the old man barred the door with an oak beam and closed the wood shutters on the window, the building seemed to Oates well-nigh impregnable.

Just before noon, under a blazing sun, the Apaches began to test the cabin's defenses.

Searching bullets thudded into the pine door and

walls. Then a shot shattered the glass of the cabin window and Yearly swore bitterly and long.

Oates stood at the cross-shaped gun port Yearly had cut in the window shutters and his eyes tracked back and forth along the terrain, then drifted back all the way to the Canyon Creek Mountains three miles to the northeast.

The air was sharp and clear, but the hilly ground to the front of the cabin was covered with cedar, piñon and thick stands of prickly pear. The ground rose gradually to a high, rocky ridge dotted with juniper and mesquite that gave good cover for a hidden rifleman.

With idle elegance a black hawk raptor rode the air currents above the ridge, then disappeared to the west and white clouds hung still above the Canyon Creek peaks.

Oates' eyes began to feel the strain of his search. Nothing moved and the oppressive heat of the day lay heavy on the land. Sweat trickled down his cheeks and the rubber handle of the Colt felt slick in his fist.

"See anything, Eddie?" Yearly asked.

"Not a damned thing. You?"

The old man shook his head. He was peering out a hole in the door about a foot square that closed and opened with a hinged panel of pine. The gun port gave fairly good visibility without exposing a defender to enemy fire. "But that don't mean they're not out there," he said.

Oates nodded. They were out there all right, but how many? Two, three . . . a dozen? That many would be too hard to handle for an old coot with milk in his eyes and a drunk.

Oates shifted position to ease a cramp in his leg and waited. Bees droned in the sage outside. A jay flew into a cedar and the branches stirred as it moved from place to place. The silent sky was an inverted, brassy blue bowl and heat waves shimmered along the crest of the ridge. There was no shadow to be seen anywhere and the trees drooped like tired belles after the ball's last waltz has been played.

The hot, drowsy day invited heavy-lidded slumber, but Oates forced himself to stay alert. To sleep now was to invite death.

A sudden movement at the bottom of the ridge instantly attracted Oates' attention. There! He saw him, about fifty yards away, an Apache crouched low, running for a clump of brush, a rifle in his hands. Oates shoved the Colt out the gun slot, sighted on the running warrior, and squeezed the trigger.

The sharp bang of the .44 was loud in the cabin, but Oates was not aware of it. He looked through a drift of smoke but could see no sign of the Indian. The man had vanished.

"Too far, boy," Yearly said. "I seen him my ownself, but before I could draw a bead on him, he was gone."

"Maybe I winged him at least."

"You didn't." The old man's tone of voice was such that it left no room for argument.

A moment later Oates learned the hard way what it meant to fight Apaches.

A bullet chipped wood from the top of the gun port,

then ripped venomously across Oates' neck before thumping into the far wall of the cabin.

Stung, Oates reeled back and slapped a hand to his neck. It came away bloody.

At the door, Yearly fired, sighted, fired again.

"You all right, Eddie?"

"I got shot in the neck. I've never been shot before."

"Stay there."

Yearly crossed the smoke-streaked room and glanced at Oates' wound. "Yup, he burned you pretty good. You'll live, though."

The old man retraced his steps to his post at the door. Oates said to his retreating back, "I never knew Apaches could shoot that good."

"Some can, some can't, just like white men." Yearly looked over at the younger man. "Fire a couple of shots. Let 'em know you're still alive."

This time Oates approached the gun port more warily. He thumbed off a couple of shots in the general direction of the ridge, then ducked behind the cover of the cabin wall.

There was no answering fire.

"Nothing stirring out there," Yearly said.

Oates was feeding shells into the Colt with an unsteady hand. "Maybe they've gone."

He looked out the gun port. A wind strolled through the juniper on the ridge and above the Canyon Creek Mountains the white clouds were tinged with dark gray. Oates thought he heard a distant rumble of thunder.

"They're close, Eddie," Yearly said suddenly.

A whinny came from outside as the mustang reacted to a smell it did not like.

"Damn it, boy, the Apaches are in the corral!"

Without another word Yearly flung out the door, cursing a blue streak. Oates, his belly cartwheeling, went after him.

There were three of them.

One had a rope around the mustang's neck. A second was leading the Morgan out of the corral. The third, a tall Indian wearing a soldier's coat with sergeant's stripes on the sleeves, stood by the corral gate, a Sharps .50 in his hands.

Yearly and the tall Apache fired at the same time. The Sharps bellowed and kicked like a mule. The bullet split the air beside the old man's head. Yearly's shot took the Mescalero low in the belly. The Indian went to one knee, working his rifle.

The Apache leading the Morgan wheeled and his rifle trained on Oates. He had no time to follow Yearly's instruction to assume the duelist's position. Oates held the Colt in both hands, shoved it out in front of him and fired. The Apache fell backward, his rifle spinning away from him.

Yearly was firing. The tall Indian in the soldier's coat was hit again. He rose to his feet and staggered, trying to bring his rifle to bear. Oates shot into him and the man took a couple of steps, then crashed onto his face.

Both men swung their guns, looking for the remaining Apache, but the man had vanished like a puff of smoke.

His ears ringing from the gunfire, Oates stepped

through the smoke drift to Yearly's side. "You hurt?" he asked.

The old man shook his head. "You?"

Oates didn't answer. He looked at the dead Apaches. The tall man was the one he vaguely recalled seeing at the creek, the one who had laughed at Sammy Tatum's drawings. The youngster by the Morgan had a scar on his cheek, and somewhere among the dim recesses of his alcoholic's memory, Oates remembered him too.

Then it slowly dawned on him—he had killed one of them and helped dispatch the other.

Yearly saw the conflict in the younger man. "The first time is always hard," he said.

"They were alive and now they're dead," Oates said. "It's a lot to figure."

The old man smiled slightly. "Would you rather it was you, lying facedown in horseshit? The Apaches knew what could happen and they took their chances."

Oates lifted his eyes to Yearly's face. "I don't feel anything, good or bad."

"That's how it should be. A man should never feel good about killing another human being. But if he kills in a fair fight, when it was either you or him, he shouldn't feel bad about it either." The old man stepped over, closed the corral gate and turned to Oates again. "You catching my drift, Eddie?"

The younger man nodded, never taking his eyes off the dead Apaches, and Yearly said, "You've killed your first man, but I got a strange feeling in my gut that he won't be your last."

"I guess we should bury them," Oates said. He

watched the wind pick up a strand of the tall Indian's hair and blow it across his still face.

"Take their guns and ammunition belts, but leave the bodies where they lay," Yearly said. "The Apaches will come for their dead."

"Damn," Oates said, "but I could sure use a drink."

Chapter 11

At first light Eddie Oates hitched the Morgan to the wagon. The Apaches' bodies were gone.

He and Yearly ate a hurried breakfast, then headed for Black Mountain. Oates carried the Colt in his pocket and the old man kept his rifle close.

They loaded the cinder block they'd cut from the side of the peak earlier, then returned to the cabin. They saw no sign of Apaches.

After several trips that morning, the stack of lava rock was growing and Yearly looked at it with a critical eye. "Eddie, I reckon we've got enough for now. The Mormon man only brings two wagons and I reckon he'll have enough for full loads."

Oates was relieved. Cutting and loading cinder block was hard, dirty work, and pulling down aggregate to get at the rock kicked up choking clouds of red and black dust that worked its way into every crack and fold of a man's hide. Some of the lava rock was razor sharp, and even the thick leather gloves he and

Yearly wore did not protect them from cuts and scrapes.

During the next week Oates practiced constantly with the Colt and Winchester and shot up all the .50-70 ammunition for the Sharps.

Finally Yearly put a halt to it, complaining that if Oates kept this up, there wouldn't be a shell left and the guns would be plumb worn-out.

A few days later the Mormon, a man named Parker, showed up with two wagons, the second driven by a taciturn Texan who wore a long-barreled Colt on his hip as if it were part of him.

By way of introduction, Parker, a large-jowled, affable man, said, "My silent friend here is the Tin Cup Kid. Now, there's a gunman down El Paso way who claims the same handle, but this here is the genuine article, and he's a bad 'un."

Parker grinned. "The Kid don't come cheap, but we're a long ways from Silver City and in this godless country his gun is a great comfort to me."

The Texan showed no reaction to Parker's speech. His thin mouth was unmoving under his mustache, but his eyes were everywhere. He considered Yearly, dismissed him, then looked at Oates, where his hard, blue gaze lingered.

"My associate, Eddie Oates," Yearly said, waving a hand in the younger man's direction. "He's staying with me for a spell."

Parker touched his hat brim. "Pleased to make your acquaintance, Mr. Oates."

"Me too," Oates said. He was unsettled by the Kid's

steady, searching gaze. Did the man know him from somewhere?

Yearly invited Parker inside, but the man politely refused. "Best we get loaded," he said. "I want to make a fast turnaround this trip, with the Apaches out and all." He looked at Yearly. "Had any trouble with them?"

The old man nodded. "Couple of weeks ago, they tried to steal my horses. Eddie and me killed two of them and the third one skedaddled."

For the first time, the Kid showed a reaction. The intensity of his gaze on Oates increased and he looked him up and down, from the shabby shoes on his feet, his ragged pants and the battered, shapeless hat he wore, another of Yearly's castoffs.

The gunman seemed puzzled for a moment, but then his face settled into its usual hard lines and he said nothing.

"I guess you heard what happened at Alma?" Parker asked.

"Saw Apaches carrying their dead," Yearly said, "so I guess the town still stands."

Parker nodded. "A posse of local ranchers lifted the siege, but not before thirty-one whites were killed, including an army sergeant."

"The mayor, a man called Cornelius Baxter," Oates began, "is he still alive?"

"Why, yes, now you ask, he is. Friend of yours?"

"No. We're not friends."

This exchange again attracted the Kid's interest. Oates didn't notice it, but Yearly did.

Parker clapped his hands. "Well, what do you say, Mr. Yearly, shall we get started?"

The Tin Cup Kid took no part in loading the wagons. He stood off to one side, his restless eyes never still. Now and then he took time to build and light a cigarette, a habit to which Texans were much addicted.

Parker saw Yearly give the gunman an irritated glance now and then, and he grinned and said, "Don't mind him, Mr. Yearly. He won't soil his hands with manual labor. Calloused hands are not good for a draw fighter."

After the wagons were loaded, Parker and Yearly settled accounts. The Mormon had brought the old man supplies, and those he deducted from the price of the lava rock.

When their business was concluded to both men's satisfaction, Parker climbed into the seat of his freight wagon.

"See you again in a couple of months, Mr. Yearly," he said. "I trust you'll have another load for me then."

"Count on it," the old man said.

Parker slapped the reins and his mule team started forward. The Kid followed. The gunman gave Oates one last look and to everyone's surprise touched his hat. "See you around, Oates," he said.

Oates and the old man sat in chairs in front of the cabin to catch the flaming glory of the sunset. The lilac evening was cool and a fretful wind searched everywhere for something it had lost. Quail called from among the sage, listened into the silence, then called out again.

"Nice feller, that Mr. Parker," Oates said. He had become much taken by the pipe, though he had not yet mastered the art of keeping the thing alight and was looking into the bowl as though trying to discover the secret there.

"He'll do," Yearly said. He looked over at Oates. "What do you think of the Tin Cup Kid?"

"A gunfighter. He's got the look. I knew one of those in Alma, a gambler by the name of Warren Rivette. He had the look as well."

"The Kid thinks you have it."

Oates laughed. "Jacob, I'm not a gunfighter."

"You're as good with the Colt and rifle as any man I've seen, and I've seen plenty."

"I can't shuck the iron from a holster fast, and I've never even tried."

"A man doesn't need to be fast. He has to be able to hit what he's aiming at, and you do."

Oates sat with the cold pipe in his hand, silent and thinking. The burning sky touched the angles of his face with fire and shadowed the hollows of his eyes and cheeks.

Finally he said, "What is the look, Jacob?"

"I don't know, boy, but whatever it is, you've got it. The Kid knew that, and a man in his line of work can't afford to be mistaken." Yearly shrugged. "Hell, could be it's something inside a man that others sense, danger maybe, a look in his eyes that says back off."

Oates laughed. "Jacob, the only thing inside this man is the town drunk."

"You looking for sympathy, Eddie?"

"Hell, no. I'm stating fact is all."

"Nobody forced you into the whiskey bottle."

"Seems to me that I didn't have much of a choice. What chance does a poor, orphaned boy have to make his mark in life?"

"I knew it. You are looking for sympathy."

Oates' smile was forced. "But I'll get none from you, huh?"

Yearly did not answer that question, but asked one of his own. "That day you stole the jug of whiskey, did somebody come along the creek bank and force it down your throat?"

"You already know the answer to that."

"Tell me again."

"Damn it, nobody forced me."

"And when you stole money and kept on stealing to buy more whiskey and took menial jobs no other white man would take, somebody forced you then?"

Oates did not answer. His jaw set and stubborn, he looked up at the sky where the scarlet was fading to bands of jade and dark blue.

"You crawled into the whiskey jug of your own free will, Eddie, because it was the easiest way. And of your own free will you'll have to crawl back out again."

Oates looked at the old man. He wanted to say, "I have crawled out of the jug and I'll never touch the stuff again." But he knew that was a promise written in the wind. Instead, he smiled and said, "You're a hard and uncompromising man, Jacob Yearly."

"Maybe. But I reckon I'm just a man who tells things as I see them."

Yearly rose to his feet and picked up his chair. "The sky's shading into black, Eddie. Time to have us a bite o' supper."

The old man had rebuilt the bridge between them, and Oates willingly stepped on it. "We cutting cinder block tomorrow?"

"No. Tomorrow I'm going to teach you to ride. A man can't get anywhere in this country without a horse."

"Jacob, you think I'm ready to go after Mash Halleck and free those women?"

"I think soon, Eddie. I think very soon."

"Am I good enough?"

"You asked if you were ready and I told you. Nobody said anything about being good enough."

Chapter 12

By Jacob Yearly's count the paint mustang threw Oates eight times, adding a kick to the shins on the last go-around to reveal his irritation.

After Oates rose painfully to his feet and began to dust himself off, the old man said, "Brace him again, Eddie. He hasn't been rode for a spell and he's feeling his oats." Yearly smiled. "It sure ain't like riding the buckskin, is it?"

Oates had started out on the buckskin. It was an easygoing horse who seemed to know he had a pilgrim on his back and constantly shifted its weight to keep Oates in the saddle.

"Nothing like," the younger man agreed. "He's a demon."

"He's a good hoss, though. He'll keep going all day and be content to eat bunchgrass or cactus come suppertime."

"Sure you didn't slip some o' that cactus under his saddle, Jacob?"

"Nah, I wouldn't do that, Eddie. Hurt the hoss' back. Now climb aboard and show him who's boss."

Again by Jacob Yearly's count, the mustang threw Oates another six times. On the seventh try, the paint settled down and allowed Oates to ride him out of the corral. But as soon as the little horse saw open ground ahead of him, he got the bit in his teeth and took off hell-for-leather.

The old man watched horse and rider disappear into the distance and shook his head. "I guess I should've warned you about that, Eddie," he said, talking only to a cloud of dust. "He will do it, especially after he's been penned up for a spell."

After thirty minutes, Yearly began to worry. An hour passed and he worried even more.

He'd decided to saddle the buckskin and go searching, when Oates and the mustang rode back to the cabin.

The old man looked up at the rider and said, "What in tarnation happened?"

Oates grinned. "He ran me for a spell. Then I got his head turned and we rode in circles. Well, after a while he got tired of that and decided to be true-blue." He patted the paint's neck. "He's a good horse, Jacob, once you get used to his ornery little ways."

Yearly smiled. "This here was a cutting pony and he can turn on a dime. Riding him around in circles like that, he was in danger of disappearing up his own ass."

"I never thought of that," Oates said.

"Well, climb off'n him and walk him around for a

spell. Once he'd cooled down you can put him back in the corral."

Oates swung out of the saddle. "Walk with me, Jacob," he said.

Yearly knew the younger man had something to tell him, but he let Oates do it in his own time. Finally Oates pointed in the direction he'd just come from. "What's back there, Jacob?"

"Well, for one thing, more of the Gila. Then there's canyon country and farther east than that, the Sierra Cuchillo." Yearly gave Oates a sidelong glance. "Somewhere in all that wilderness is Heartbreak, the place where your women and the simple boy were headed."

Oates thought about that, then said, "I don't know exactly. Maybe after three miles, I rode up on a creek. I saw a lot of tracks, cattle and horses it looked like, and they seemed to be heading into the Gila."

"Were the horses shod?"

"I don't know."

"A man would know if he looked close enough." After that mild rebuke, Yearly thought for a few moments, then said, "Could be Apaches driving stolen cattle. There are ranches to the north and west of us could be missing cows."

"I thought it was strange, seeing all those tracks in that empty country."

"Not strange if it was Apaches. But strange enough if it was white men."

"Maybe it's none of our business."

"Everything that happens in this country that's out

of the ordinary is our business, Eddie. We live here, remember?"

"Want to take a ride out there tomorrow?" Oates asked. "I'd like to try the paint again."

Yearly nodded. "Yeah, sure, we'll take a look." The old man shook his head. "Something about all this troubles me, but I'm damned if I know why."

At daybreak Oates and Yearly rode east. The mustang, perhaps tired from its exertions of the day before, decided to cooperate and threw Oates only once before it settled down under saddle.

They rode through heavily forested country and the wind stirred trees not yet drowsy from the heat of the day. Victorio's raids had left no scars on the land and the savage beauty of the high country was enough to take a man's breath away.

Yearly had buckled on the Colt, the first time Oates had ever seen him wear a gun belt, and his Winchester was in the scabbard under his left leg. The old man rode warily, his eyes searching around him, and only after an hour of riding did he speak.

"Getting close, you think?" he asked into the quiet.

Nothing seemed familiar to Oates, but he nodded. "Must be, I reckon."

Yearly drew rein, leaned from the saddle and studied the ground. "No tracks yet." He smiled and pointed to a print in the sand just ahead of them. "Unless you count that."

Oates looked. "Bear?"

"Cougar. There's a few of them in these parts. They

need space because a big male like the one that left that track takes in a lot of range, as much as three hundred square miles."

"A heap of country," Oates agreed, "for one cat."

The old man smiled. "The cougar is no ordinary cat."

A few minutes later they rode up on the creek. Yearly swung out of the saddle and Oates followed him. The older man was already down on one knee, studying the ground.

After a while he rose stiffly and said, "Shod horses all right. I'd say two hundred head of cattle, a wagon and easy thirty riders." He looked at Oates. "Now, why would you need that many men to drive a small herd?"

Oates shook his head. "I don't know, Jacob."

"Heading into the Gila, no doubt about that. As far as I know, there are no ranches in there."

"Rustlers?" It was a word Oates had heard often in Alma.

"Could be. But rustlers work in smaller numbers and they lift only a few head at a time. Why thirty men?"

Oates smiled. The old man had asked that question before and obviously didn't expect an answer.

Yearly looked around him. "Something here doesn't set right with me, Eddie. Too few cattle for so many men. It doesn't make sense. Who would bring an army into the Gila and why?"

"To protect the cattle from Apaches, maybe?" Oates suggested. "Victorio was beat at Alma, but he's still out."

"I hope that's the case," the old man said. He looked at Oates with wintry eyes. "The ranches around this part of the country are all well established and I figured the time of the range wars was gone for good. I'd sure hate to see it come back again. Those were hard times for everybody."

"You think that's why there are thirty men with those cattle? They want to claim some other rancher's grass?"

Yearly swung his horse around. "I don't know," he said. His lined face, the color and texture of old saddle leather, was like stone.

Chapter 13

That night after supper Eddie Oates was quiet, lost in thought. He sat at the fireplace, where Yearly had a log burning against the chill of the night. The old man's head was bent to a book as he smoked his pipe.

Outside in the darkness the silence had come and even the ceaseless wind seemed hushed, spreading its gossip in a thin whisper.

Yearly lifted his head and peered over the top of his book. "Eddie, you're as quiet as a woman's heartbeat tonight. You got the croup, maybe?"

The younger man smiled and shook his head. "I just remembered the names of the three women and I can see their faces clear. Funny that, how my brain's started to work again."

"You mean the three whores?"

"Yeah, Miss Stella, Miss Lorraine and Miss Nellie. As far as they were able, they were good to me."

"Whores with hearts of gold," Yearly said.

Oates laughed. "I wouldn't go that far, but if they were in the chips, they'd always buy me a drink."

The log cracked and a shower of bright red sparks rose into the chimney.

"So, what's your drift?"

"I got to be moving on, Jacob. I have to find them."

"Humph," the old man muttered. Dismissing Oates, he went back to his book.

Slow minutes passed, the only sound the snap of the burning log and puff of Yearly's pipe.

Finally the old-timer looked up again. "When would you leave?"

"Tomorrow, Jacob. It's been almost three months. You've taken care of me long enough."

"I figured we'd start cutting lava rock again tomorrow."

"Jacob, I have to find them."

Yearly nodded. "Well, if your heart's set on it, I won't try to change your mind. You can take the paint."

"Thanks, Jacob. I appreciate this."

"Hell, I can't ride him anyhow. Getting too old for ornery horses."

The old man again went back to his book, but, though minutes passed, he did not turn a page.

He looked up again and studied Oates. Then he cocked his head to one side, thinking, and sighed deeply. "It's time, Eddie," he said. "I've studied on it and I think it's what Pete would have wanted."

"Pete?"

"My son. He died a while back. That was his room and why I keep it locked."

Oates trod carefully, easing into what he had to say. "You never talked about him until now."

"No, no I guess I didn't." Yearly sat quiet for a few moments, then said, "Pete was an ambitious kid, and he wanted no part of his future to be mining cinder block. He was always talking about leaving this wilderness and heading for Denver or New Orleans. Figured he could make his mark in a big city." The old man relit his pipe. "But travel takes money and Pete spent every penny he ever earned."

The smoky fragrance of the log mingled with the musk-scent tobacco odor of the old man's pipe, a down-homey smell that made Oates feel completely at ease. Pete had probably sat in this very chair, smelling that same smell as he looked across at his pa reading Dickens or Scott. But his heart had not been here. In his mind's eye he was seeing Denver with its fine brick buildings, elegant hotels and restaurants and its beautiful, expensive women all got up in the latest Paris fashions.

Denver was a far cry from Black Mountain and this wild, rimfire country that a man either loved on sight or hated with an abiding passion.

Yearly was talking again. "What's it been . . . five years? Good Lord, has it been that long? Pete tried to make a fast score. He held up a stage outside of Alma and the shotgun guard killed him."

The old man was silent for a moment, then said, "Mash Halleck was the guard, back then being more inclined to honest labor. I thought about going after him and killing him, but I couldn't justify it, not in God's eyes or my own. Halleck had been hired to do a job and he did it. You can't fault a man for that."

Yearly let out a long, shuddering sigh, then rose to his feet. He reached into his pocket and produced a key. "Bring the lamp, Eddie," he said.

After the old man unlocked the bedroom door, Oates followed him inside. He placed the lamp on the dresser and looked around. The wooden bed had been made up with loving care and was covered with a bright, patchwork quilt. Pete's hair brushes, pomade and shaving gear were still on the dresser.

A pair of shotgun chaps hung from a nail on a wall and a Winchester stood in a rack along with a black cartridge belt and empty holster.

It looked like Pete had just left and would be back soon, though the room smelled of a place left unused and uninhabited for too long and dust lay thick everywhere.

"Pete was a small man like you, Eddie," Yearly said. "And slender like you."

He crossed to a pine armoire and opened it wide. Without a word he removed a high-button, gray suit and laid it on the bed. A collarless shirt, still folded from the general store, followed, then a wool felt derby hat with a stingy brim.

Yearly reached into the bottom of the armoire and came up with suspenders and a pair of Texas boots with two-inch heels.

"This was Pete's dress-up-go-to-Denver outfit," he

said. "He never got to wear it. I want you to have it, Eddie." The old man smiled weakly. "I'm getting mighty tired of seeing you in them rags you wear."

Oates shook his head, confused. "Jacob, I can't—"

"Yes, you can. It's what I want and what Pete would've wanted. Call it an old man's whim, if you like." He picked up the suit coat from the bed and held it up by the shoulders. "See if this fits."

Oates hesitated and Yearly said, "Try it, Eddie. This once, do as I ask and please me."

Reluctantly, Oates crossed the floor and shrugged into the coat.

Yearly stepped back to admire him. He smiled. "Perfect. A perfect fit."

"I can't take this, Jacob." Oates felt like he'd been backed into a corner. "It doesn't feel right."

"It does to me. Listen, Eddie, when I'm gone, somebody else would wear these clothes. I'd rather it was you. You look . . . like a gentleman and mighty handsome."

Crossing to the gun rack, Yearly took down the Winchester and the gun belt. "In the bottom drawer of the dresser, Eddie. Bring it to me."

Oates did as he was told and found what hefted like a gun, wrapped in an oiled rag. He passed it to Yearly.

"This was Pete's Colt," the old man said, unwrapping the blue, short-barreled revolver. "The Alma vigilantes buried him, then couldn't remember the spot where they'd dug his grave. I searched, but haven't found it to this day. But they did return his guns." He slid the Colt into the holster, then held the gun belt out to Oates. "When you go after the Halleck boys, you'll need this, and the rifle."

Oates took off the coat and laid it on the bed. He did not touch the proffered gun belt. "I can't take all this, Jacob. They're your memories and you should keep them." He managed a smile. "Besides, I've been to Denver and I'll never go back."

Yearly was silent for a long time and all at once he looked grayer and older than Oates remembered.

"Eddie," he said, his voice tired, "at my age a man starts to feel death creep up on him, real close. Sometimes he sees his shadow on the ground and then suddenly there's another one, right beside his. He doesn't have to turn around, because he knows what's there, tapping at his shoulder."

Yearly's eyes sought Oates' in a quiet plea for understanding. "I've been seeing that shadow more often recently, feeling its weight, and I think my time is short. What I got, I want you to have, Pete's stuff, this cabin, my horses and the little money I've set aside. You're the only human being I've cared about since my boy died. It's a hard thing for a man to say, sounds like I'm only talking pretties, but I've come to love you like a son and I never want to see you crawl into the whiskey bottle again."

The less men think, they more they talk, and Oates knew this was a time for thinking. A hollow silence stretched between him and Yearly that neither man seemed inclined to bridge. But finally Oates accepted what fate had thrown at him.

"Thank you, Jacob," he said. "I appreciate it."

The old man smiled. "Damn right, you should. I'm a giving man."

"One thing though, I don't think you're going to turn up your toes anytime soon."

But in that prophecy—portent, augury, call it what you will—Oates was to be proven tragically wrong.

Chapter 14

The sky was on fire as Eddie Oates tightened the cinch on the paint's saddle and the morning air held an edge. Drinking coffee that steamed in the cup, Yearly stood watching him.

"Wish I could go with you, son," he said, "but I'd only slow you down."

"I'll be back soon enough, Jacob. I promise."

The old man nodded. "You've set a task for yourself, Eddie. Mash Halleck and his boys are no bargain."

"I know that going in," Oates said. "But I got it to do."

"Are three whores and a simple boy worth dying for?" Yearly made an apologetic motion with his cup. "Just askin', like."

Oates turned to face him. "I betrayed all of them, Jacob. I reckon that answers your question."

"Like I said, just askin'." A silence, then Yearly said, "You look mighty fine this morning."

Oates was wearing the high-button suit and derby

hat. Pete's stiff new boots were on his feet and fit him well. He wore the store-bought shirt but had forgone the celluloid collar and tie, settling for a faded blue bandanna tied loosely around his neck. The Winchester was in the saddle scabbard and Pete's gun belt was strapped around his lean hips.

"You look the part," Yearly said, as though he'd decided that more praise was needed.

Oates opened his mouth to speak, but the words died on his lips. Following the younger man's gaze, Yearly turned and saw what Oates was seeing.

Three riders were heading toward the cabin at a trot, a purposeful gait that suggested men who knew where they were going and why.

Yearly laid his cup on a corral post and slid the Winchester out of the scabbard on the paint's saddle. His glance at Oates was brief, as were his words. "I sense that mischief's afoot," he said.

He stepped out of the corral to the front of the cabin and Oates followed.

The three riders drew rein and even a less perceptive man than Oates would have realized they added up to trouble. They were young, lean from a lifetime in the saddle, and the faces of all three wore a taunting, arrogant expression, the look of men who knew well how to use the Colts they wore on their hips and were accustomed to lesser men walking wide of them.

They were dressed like punchers, but no cowboy could have afforded the blooded horses they rode or the quality of their firearms.

"Howdy, boys," Yearly said, his eyes wary. "I got hot coffee in the pot."

The oldest of the three men spoke. "You own this cabin, old-timer?"

Yearly allowed that he did.

"Good. Then you got until noon to gather your stuff together and get out."

The old man's smile was not a pleasant thing to see. "To tell you the truth, boys, I ain't much inclined to leave."

That statement hung in the air like smoke on a windless day. The direct gazes of the three men were suddenly cold, hard and calculating, weighing odds. But finally a towheaded youngster with reckless eyes grinned and said, "Mister, you wouldn't want to make our lady boss sleep out in the cold another night, would you? See, she needs a roof over her head and yours is the only cabin around for miles." His smile widened and he lifted his shoulders and spread his hands. "So you see how it is with us."

Oates spoke, drawing the attention of all three men. "Tell your lady boss she's welcome to spend the night here. I'm sure we can make a place for her."

"Ah, but you see, she's coy, modest you might say," the towhead said. "She won't go for that arrangement." He grinned insolently. "Nice hat, by the way."

The rider who'd first spoken, a little older and a lot meaner than the others, leaned forward in his saddle and said, "Maybe you don't hear so good, old man. I said be out of the cabin by noon."

Yearly shrugged. "I hear just fine, but my talking is done. There's nothing we can do for you boys, so ride on afore I forget my manners and start shootin'."

Then the old man made a mistake, the last he'd ever make.

He levered a round into the Winchester. A challenge. A war sound.

All three riders drew, very fast. The three shots sounded as one and Yearly took two of them, one high in his left shoulder, the other, more serious, square in the belly.

The old man slammed back against the cabin wall, trying to bring his rifle to bear.

For an instant Oates had stood rooted to the spot, stunned by the suddenness of unexpected violence. Then he moved.

"You sons of bitches!" he screamed.

He couldn't remember drawing his gun, but all at once it was there, bucking in his hand. The older man shrieked as Oates' bullet smashed away most of his lower jaw. The man went sideways out of the saddle, upsetting the aim of the man on his right who was trying to draw a bead on Oates.

The towhead swung his gun on Oates, fired, missed. Then he was blown out of the saddle as Yearly's Winchester roared.

The third man was fighting his bucking horse, his Colt held high above his head, when Oates shot him. Reeling in the saddle as a bullet slammed into his chest, the man fired at Yearly, thinking he was the danger. Oates' second shot blasted into the man's head. The rider's hat flew off in a scarlet fan of blood and brain and he crashed to the ground. His horse galloped away, the reins trailing, its eyes rolling white.

When Oates kneeled beside Jacob Yearly, the old man was already dead. There was no repose in his features. His face was frozen into a mask of anger, outrage and wonder at the manner and time of his dying.

His heart heavy, Oates rose to his feet. He walked over to the fallen men. Only the oldest man whose lower jaw had been shot away was still alive. He knew the extent and nature of his wound and his eyes were full of terror. Oates shot him, shot him again, then holstered his gun. It was not an act of mercy; it was revenge.

He buried Yearly near the creek, his blackened old pipe in his hands and a volume of Dickens on his chest. Oates had no words, but his whispered, "Thank you, Jacob, for everything," summed up better than prayers how he felt.

After letting the Morgan and the buckskin loose, Oates stuffed supplies into a burlap sack, then set the cabin on fire.

He mounted the paint and rode east. He knew that no matter what happened, he would never come back.

The desire for revenge was a raw emotion new to Eddie Oates, one he had only recently experienced. His first encounter with it had come when he'd thought of returning to Alma and putting a bullet into Cornelius Baxter.

Now a thirst for vengeance fermented in him again.

Three men had died for Jacob Yearly's death and Oates considered that the blood price had been paid. But the person who had sent the gunman here to throw the old man out of his cabin was still alive.

The lady boss who could not sleep another night out in the open and was willing to kill to prevent that happening, was walking the earth.

Oates rode with a face of stone. A fine old man was dead and the woman, whoever she was, continued to cast her vile shadow on the ground.

That could not stand.

For now, his hunt for Sammy Tatum and the three women was pushed to the back of Oates' mind. Jacob Yearly was lying cold in his grave and his soul cried out for vengeance. He would give it to him.

Unbidden, a thought came to Oates, one that suddenly unsettled him.

The Tin Cup Kid had recognized something in him. Oates had thought the Kid was a gunfighter who had met a kindred spirit, a man who shaped up to be good with the iron.

But what if he'd been mistaken and it was something else entirely?

What if the Kid had looked at Oates and saw not a gunfighter, but a fellow killer?

All at once the bright morning seemed darker. And Eddie Oates felt a chill.

Chapter 15

Eddie Oates had revenge on his mind, but no idea how he was going to bring it about.

He was sure the lady boss owned the outfit that had driven the cattle into the Gila. Old Jacob had reckoned she had at least thirty riders, now three fewer, but that still represented mighty steep odds.

The idea of a holing up behind a tree somewhere and bushwhacking her did not appeal to him. If the Tin Cup Kid had been right, and he was a killer, he would still not stoop to cold-blooded murder.

Who was the lady boss? And what was she doing in this country?

As he rode, Oates pondered these questions but could come up with no answers.

The sun was climbing above the ragged peaks of the Sierra Cuchillo, washing out the night shadows. Oates rode close to the wooded hills, windswept mesas and deep canyons of the Gila, riding through forests of ponderosa pine and Douglas fir. Aspen and spruce flourished in the higher elevations, above them gaunt blue cliffs that ended where the sky began.

Around Oates the land lay quiet, the only sound the steady beat of the mustang's hooves, the creak of saddle leather and the chatter of crickets in the grass.

Aware that his wanderings were aimless, apart from a vague idea to follow the cattle tracks he and Yearly had found into the Gila, Oates rode into a narrow arroyo that after a hundred yards opened up into a small, hanging meadow. A creek ran near the base of a fractured ridge and a few cottonwoods and a single, mossy willow crowded close to the running water.

Oates swung out of the saddle, loosened the cinch and let the paint graze. He was wishful for coffee but didn't feel like starting a fire. He settled for cold salt pork left over from breakfast and a couple of Jacob's sourdough biscuits. A small, sharp pain in him, he remembered that these would be the last he'd ever taste.

After he'd eaten, Oates lay in the shade of a cottonwood and tipped his hat over his eyes. Bees buzzed around the creek and close by, the paint steadily cropped grass.

Suddenly he was very tired. Killing in the morning takes its toll on a man.

But Oates' rest was uneasy. His head jerked back and forth as he muttered in his sleep, talking to dead men. He woke, crying out so loudly that the mustang jerked up its head and trotted away from him.

Oates looked around him, his eyes wild. He'd had a bottle. Where was it? Had someone robbed him?

His heart was thumping in his chest and he was covered in a cold sweat. For a moment nothing looked familiar. Where the hell was he?

Gradually, the unknown terrors in him subsided and he grew fully awake. Breathing heavily, he rose to his feet, the dream taste of whiskey still smoky and sweet in his mouth. He stooped, picked up his hat and kneeled by the creek, splashing his face with cold water. After a while he dried off with his bandanna and sat, letting the trembling in him settle.

He'd dreamed of whiskey as vivid and real as a man's dreams of naked women. He touched his tongue to dry lips, the hunger riding him.

Right at that moment, he'd give everything he owned for a drink, the fancy clothes he wore, the paint, his guns. And he would betray anybody, so long as he could get drunk and stay drunk forever. The whiskey oblivion was where he belonged. It was home sweet home to him.

Oates gritted his teeth against the craving in his mind and the pain in his belly. He fell on his side, curling up his knees to his chest.

Then he groaned and slept again.

When Eddie Oates woke, the night had come and the sky was full of stars and the moon was as round as a coin. He rose to a sitting position, his back against the cottonwood, and breathed deep of cool air that tasted of sage and pine.

"How you feeling, boy?" asked a voice out of the darkness.

Instantly Oates was on his feet and he was aware that his gun had appeared like magic in his hand.

"Who's there?" he asked, talking into the moon-bladed night.

"Why, good old Jacob Yearly, as ever was."

Peering into the gloom, Oates saw a red glow that grew brighter, then dulled again. Jacob was smoking his pipe.

"Where are you?" Oates asked.

"Right ahead of you, Eddie. Over this way."

Oates took a few steps, then made out Yearly's tall form. The old man was sitting on a boulder, his pipe in his hand.

"You've had yourself a time, boy," Yearly said.

"I wanted whiskey. I wanted it real bad and I still do."

Yearly nodded. His eyes were full of brilliant blue fire. "Killing a man is easy, Eddie. It's living with it, that's hard. Whiskey can dull the pain for a spell, but it always comes back like a cancer."

"You think I've got a guilty conscience about killing the men who killed you, Jacob?"

"I don't know, Eddie. Conscience is God whispering in a man. Only you know what he's saying."

"I think he's saying that I did what I had to do."

"If that's what you hear, then that's just fine. You got no need to crawl into a whiskey bottle." Yearly stood and put his cold pipe in his pocket. "The trouble is, you don't know what you are, Eddie. Right now your choices are kinda limited—gunfighter, killer, drunk—and you don't know which one to choose."

"Help me, Jacob. Help me do the right thing."

"I can't help you, boy. You can only help yourself, and whiskey isn't the answer and it never was."

"Jacob, why did . . ."

Oates' voice trailed away. . . . He was talking only to darkness.

He became aware of his surroundings, of the gun in his hand. "I'm still dreaming," he said aloud to himself, shaking his head.

Yet, the smell of pipe smoke lingered in the meadow for a long time before it was taken away by the wind.

Chapter 16

The night wind was bending the grass as Eddie Oates scrounged around in the dark and found enough wood for a small fire. He got the coffeepot from his sack, filled it at the creek and threw in a handful of Arbuckle. He set the pot on the coals to boil and sat with his head against the cottonwood, listening into the darkness.

By daybreak the coffeepot was empty and a light rain was falling.

Oates picked up his rifle and walked to the mouth of the arroyo. In whatever direction he looked lay a naked wilderness of trees and rock, modestly veiled by the shifting gray mantle of the rain.

Oates was about to retrace his steps back into the arroyo, when a sound reached out from the distance that made him stop in his tracks. He looked to the east, the direction of the strange noise, but saw nothing.

A minute passed, then another. Oates tightened his hold on the Winchester.

He heard the sound more clearly and now recognized it, the whistles and yips of men driving cattle. A few shorthorns appeared, followed by more, and then a puncher, a man who slapped a coiled rope against his chaps as he rode.

Oates stepped into the shadow of the arroyo wall and kneeled behind the twisted trunk of a maverick cedar. More riders appeared, driving a large herd that began to stream past his hiding place, raising clouds of yellow dust.

He saw her then. She was riding wide of the herd in a flank position, a young, breathtakingly beautiful women sitting sidesaddle on a tall bay Thoroughbred. She carried a riding crop and was dressed in an elegant equestrian costume of gray silk, a top hat of the same color, adorned with tulle, perched on top of her auburn hair.

At one time Oates thought the young belles of Alma parading their huge bustles and tiny hats was the ultimate expression of sophisticated womanhood. He was wrong. Next to this woman they'd look what they were, small-town hicks.

Riding tall and proud, she could only be the lady boss, the woman responsible for the death of Jacob Yearly.

His knuckles white on his rifle, Oates knew how easy it would be to knock her off that high horse. He blinked sweat from his eyes and his hands shook.

"Just aim and fire and it's over," he told himself.

Oates made no move. It would be cold-blooded murder; even a drunk who dreamed of whiskey couldn't stoop that low.

And then it was too late. The woman rode past the arroyo and was lost from his sight.

Despite the rain, the passing herd had kicked up considerable dust and Oates could not estimate how many men rode with the lady boss. At a rough guess, around two dozen, and very few looked to be dollar-a-day punchers.

But then he saw something that made his skin crawl.

A heavily loaded wagon brought up the rear, hauled by a team of four mules. Mash Halleck was up in the box, the ribbons in his hands, and his sons, Clem and Reuben, flanked him as outriders.

There was no sign of the three women and Sammy Tatum.

Oates felt a chill. Were they already all dead? Murdered by the Hallecks before they left the canyon in the Gila?

He pushed any thought of revenge to the back of his mind. His first concern was to find out what had happened to the women.

A few minutes later Oates rode out of the arroyo and swung east. He held to the trees, wary of bumping into more of the lady boss' riders. Rain sifted through the branches of the pines and he untied Yearly's yellow slicker from behind his saddle and shrugged into it.

After a mile he smelled smoke in the wind. Topping a piñon-covered ridge, he rode through a stand of mixed cedar and mountain mahogany and onto a stretch of flat country, covered in feather grass that reached to the paint's knees.

Oates rode warily now, old Jacob's rifle across his

saddle horn. He tried to read the message of the smoke. More of the lady boss' men or the three women? Apaches?

He had no way of knowing. The only thing to do was ride closer and be prepared to fight if he must, skedaddle if he could.

The open ground gave way to timber and the land began to incline upward. Here aspen grew, many of them standing seventy feet high, and the ground was rockier. Through the curtain of the rain, the peaks and mesas of the Gila formed ramparts of blue, garlanded by the gray mist of the low clouds.

Oates pulled up the paint and looked around him. He had come too far. The canyon where he and Yearly had seen the cattle tracks was now behind him and he could no longer smell smoke. A brawling wind shook the aspen and the scattered rain hissed its displeasure.

Swinging the mustang around, Oates rode back down the slope. Had anyone been there to see him, he would have pegged the rider for a man who was lost, or one wandering aimlessly, which amounted to the same thing.

For his part, Oates felt a growing irritation. Jacob Yearly would never have missed the entrance to the canyon. The old man had taught him a great deal, but there are things a man can't teach.

Once he reached the flat, Oates again caught the smell of smoke, stronger this time.

Then to his right, he saw a drift of blue rising above the trees. He levered a round into the Winchester and swung in that direction.

Ahead of Oates was a stand of pine. Beyond the trees rose a high outcropping of rock, shaped like the prow of a ship. From where he was, Oates could make out a narrow stream of water cascading down the rock face.

Alert for any sign of Apaches, he rode into the pines and drew rein.

To the right of the prow-shaped promontory was a shallow cave and he could make out the forms of three women huddled around a smoky fire. A thickset man who could only be Sammy Tatum walked out of the surrounding trees, carrying an armful of wood. He stepped into the cave and disappeared from sight.

A small joy rose in Oates. They were all still alive. His treachery had not killed them.

He kneed the paint forward and rode out of the pines. Instantly one of the women rose to her feet, a hideout gun in her hand.

Oates stopped. "Hello the camp!" he yelled. The rain slanted around him, beating on his hat and the shoulders of his slicker.

"What do you want?" This came from the woman holding the gun.

Oates recognized her. "It's me, Miss Stella."

"Who the hell is me?"

"Eddie Oates." He paused, then added, "From Alma."

A taller, older woman wearing a ragged mackinaw stood beside Stella. "Ride on, Oates. We got no whiskey here."

Nellie Carney stood and angrily rounded on her

companion. "You're such a whore, Lorraine!" She looked out at Oates, the wind flattening her skirt against her legs. "Do you have any grub?"

"I've got grub," Oates answered. "Not much, but enough."

"Then ride on in. We're starving to death here."

Oates rode up to the cave. He studied the women and then Tatum, who stood behind them, shy and awkward and grinning.

The women looked what they were, three saloon whores who had very recently been used and abused. And it showed on them.

"You ladies have been through it," Oates observed.

"We've been through it," Stella said. She looked up at the rider. "Like Nellie said, light and set."

Oates swung out of the saddle. "I'll find a place in the trees for the horse," he said.

"I'll do it, Mr. Oates," Tatum said. He rushed out from behind the women and grabbed the paint's reins. "It's real good to see you again, Mr. Oates."

From chin to forehead, the entire left side of Tatum's face was swollen with black and yellow bruises. "What happened to your face, Sammy?" Oates asked.

The boy looked sheepish and kicked the ground with the toe of his shoe. "Mr. Halleck done that. He said it was because I was stupid."

Anger flared in Oates. "Which Mr. Halleck?"

"Clem," Stella said. She looked at Tatum. "Put the horse up in a dry place, Sam."

"Wait," Oates said. He untied the sack of supplies and slid the other rifle from the scabbard.

"Dry as you can find, Sammy," he said.

"Sure thing, Mr. Oates." The boy grinned.

Oates stepped into the cave, where Nellie quickly relieved him of the food sack. He found a place for himself and propped the Winchesters against the cave wall.

"Your fire's giving off considerable smoke," he said. "You'd better hope there are no Apaches around."

Lorraine laughed. "After what we've been through, the Apaches would be a change for the better." She looked at Oates. "At least you're prospering."

Oates smiled. "An old man by the name of Jacob Yearly took me in, kept me away from the whiskey. I haven't touched a drop in near a three-month."

"I knowed a feller once who stayed off the booze for three years," Lorraine said. "He went back to it though, and it was the death of him in the end."

"Biscuits . . . bacon . . . salt pork . . . oh, and coffee!" Nellie jumped up and down. "Look, Lorraine, we've got coffee!"

"I see it. Now put it in the pot where it belongs."

"I'll get water," Nellie said.

She rushed out of the cave as excited as a girl going to her first cotillion—and she was still smiling as a rifle bullet drove her against the rock wall.

Chapter 17

Oates moved instantly. He grabbed a rifle and threw the other to Stella.

"Get down!" he yelled.

Bullets probed into the cave, whining off the rock walls. Oates saw a puff of smoke among the pine trees and fired into it, then dusted two fast shots to the left and right. He was rewarded by a yelp of pain and a string of curses.

"Nellie!" Lorraine yelled. "Are you hit?"

"I'm hit bad," the woman answered.

"Where?"

"Don't be such a whore, Lorraine."

"Where?"

"In the ass!"

"Stay where you are."

"Hell, I'm not going anywhere with a shot-up ass."

Stella looked across at Oates. "See anything?"

He shook his head.

"You burned one of them. I didn't think you could shoot like that."

"Old Jacob taught me."

"We could do with old Jacob here right now."

"He's dead."

The rain was falling harder and Oates studied the terrain around him. Where was Sammy Tatum? He saw no sign of the boy, or anyone else.

A few minutes passed, and a voice called out from the trees. "You in the cave!"

"What do you want?" Stella yelled.

"Miss McWilliams wants the money you bitches stole from her."

"Go to hell!" Stella hollered. "We earned that money for three months of slavery."

"That was none of Miss McWilliams' doing," the voice yelled back.

"She did her share!"

Bullets whined into the cave again and Lorraine cried out as splinters of rock tore across her cheek. From outside Nellie's voice rose in a terrified shout.

"Help me, somebody! They're shooting at me!"

"Here, take this." Oates passed his rifle to Lorraine.

"Where are you going?"

"To get Nellie."

"You'll get killed if you go out there."

"And Nellie will get killed if I don't."

Lorraine opened her mouth to object, but Oates, Colt in his hand, was already up and running.

Nellie was lying at the base of the ridge, her back pressed against the rock. He kneeled by her side just as a man wearing a black–and-white cowhide vest jumped up from the pines, aiming his rifle.

Oates took a snap shot, fired again, and the man staggered backward, then fell.

"Get up on my shoulder, Miss Nellie," Oates said, his old way of addressing the woman coming to him naturally.

The girl was petite and slim, but she was still a considerable weight. As Oates got to his feet, Nellie over his shoulder, he was grateful for his three months of hard labor at Black Mountain.

He turned and stumbled back to the cave, thumbing off a couple of shots into the pines along the way. Lorraine and Stella opened fire, laying down a covering barrage.

Oates carried the girl to the back of the cave and set her gently on the ground. He turned to Lorraine. "Better see to her," he said.

The woman nodded. "You've come a long way, Eddie. Thank you."

Oates smiled. "I've still got a long road to travel."

He took the rifle from Lorraine and bellied beside Stella. His eyes searched the pines for movement, but he saw nothing but the falling rain.

Minutes passed before Oates turned his eyes to the woman. "Tell me about the money," he said.

"Sure. I took it, all I could grab."

"How much?"

"I don't know. Could be five thousand in gold. We never counted it."

"Why?"

"Wages, if you can put a dollar amount on rape and slavery." Stella read something in Oates' eyes. "Go on, tell me you can't rape a two-dollar whore."

"I wasn't going to say that. I didn't even think it."

As though she hadn't heard, Stella said, "When a man takes pleasure in a woman's pain, it's rape, whether she be a fine lady in a mansion or a whore working the line."

"Now I think that maybe five thousand wasn't enough," Oates said.

"You got that right, Mister."

Oates looked back into the cave. "How is she?" he asked.

"The bullet is in deep," Lorraine said. "We'll have to dig it out of there."

"You're jealous, Lorraine," Nellie said. "Because you got a big ass, you want to cut up mine. You're such a whore."

In a surprisingly gentle voice, Lorraine said, "You hush and lie quiet, child. You've lost a lot of blood and I don't want you losing more."

"I could sure use some of that coffee," Nellie said.

"We'll get you some. Real soon."

"You in the cave!"

"What do you want?" Stella yelled.

"Is that you, Stella?"

"It's me."

"This is Clem, Stella. You know what I can do to you. I can hurt you real bad, honey. Now, throw out the money and we'll ride away from here, and what's done will be done and forgotten and there's an end to it."

Stella threw the Winchester to her shoulder and fired into the trees. "There's your answer!" she yelled.

"I'm coming for you, Stella. And I'll hurt you bad, bitch."

Angrily the woman levered another round, but Oates stretched out a hand and stopped her. "Save ammunition," he said. "If you can't see him, you can't shoot him."

As the morning gave way to afternoon, the rain stopped and the clouds parted. The motionless sun hung in the sky, cobwebbed with rays of blazing yellow, and the day grew hot, the drying rain turning to steam. Only now and then did a stealthy wind blow a cooling breeze into the cave.

Leaving his rifle with Stella, Oates crawled back to check on Nellie. The girl was very pale and an hour ago had ceased to complain about her wound, her words fading into a silence. Now her blond head lay on Lorraine's lap and she looked like a child in sleep.

"The bullet has got to come out and soon," Lorraine said. "If blood poisoning sets in, we'll lose her."

The wound looked bad, red and inflamed against the white of Nellie's hip, a single azure vein showing under the skin.

"Let's get it done," Oates said. "Stella can keep watch."

Oates had carried a Green River knife since his first day at the lava rock workings. He slid the blade from the sheath on his belt and looked at his hands.

"They're steady enough," Lorraine said. "If you're steady enough."

"I've never done anything like this before," Oates said.

"So now you've got it to do, Mr. Oates."

Throwing a couple of pieces of wood on the fire, Oates waited until they were burning well, then shoved the knife blade into the flames.

"I saw a doctor do this one time before a cutting," he said. "I don't remember when or where or why."

"Whiskey is better," Lorraine said. "You pour it over the blade. But we got none o' that."

"No, we got none o' that," Oates said.

The blade was glowing hot. He removed it from the flames and let it cool in his hand. His mouth was dry and his belly was lurching. He met Lorraine's faded brown eyes. "Hold her," he said.

He bent his head to his task.

The knife had to cut deep and Nellie woke, screaming. Oates was aware of the single, horrified glance Stella threw in his direction. He wiped sweat from his eyes with his sleeve and dug deeper.

He felt the tip of the blade scrape bone and Nellie began to thrash, shrieking louder. To add to Oates' problems, bullets slammed into the cave, ricocheting off the walls with a venomous spaaang!

Stella was firing steadily and levered the rifle dry. She immediately reached out and took up the other Winchester. With his left hand, Oates unbuckled his cartridge belt and holster and tossed it to the woman. "Load the rifles from the loops," he said.

He did not wait to see the woman's reaction. He worked his knife again, and, as Lorraine held Nellie down, finally dug out the bullet, bringing gory flesh and skin with it.

It looked to Oates that the wound he'd made was enormous, a huge, gaping hole in the woman's hip that immediately filled with blood.

"I'll see to her now," Lorraine whispered, her voice husky. "You'd better help Stella."

Oates nodded. Then his eyes met the woman's. "I butchered her," he said.

"You did your best."

"It wasn't near good enough," Oates said. He felt sick and exhausted and under his coat his shirt was sodden with sweat. He bellied down beside Stella and took up his rifle.

"It's loaded," the woman said. She did not ask about Nellie. The pain in Oates' eyes told her all she needed to know.

"Did you hit anybody?" Oates asked.

"No, but I came close, close enough that they turned tail and scampered into the trees again, Clem Halleck leading the way.

"They'll be back."

"Count on it," Stella said.

Chapter 18

The long afternoon wore on, but there were no more attempts to rush the cave.

Nellie was awake, but in considerable pain, and Lorraine looked worried. Stella went back to check on the girl and when she returned she too was grim and silent.

"She needs a doctor," Oates said.

Stella nodded. "You got one handy?"

"Hello the cave!"

"We hear you!" Oates yelled.

"Miss McWilliams and her brother want to talk to you. Hold your fire."

"Let her come. We won't shoot."

The woman rode into the clearing in front of the cave, cool and self-possessed, like a fine New York or Boston lady out for an afternoon canter. Beside her, astride a tall, spectacular Palouse, was a handsome young man, an arrogant set to his head and shoulders.

He had the same dazzling good looks as his sister,

but in him her considerable beauty was transformed into effeminacy and petulance.

However, he had taken off his coat against the heat and there was nothing effeminate about the two ivory-handled Remingtons he wore in shoulder holsters over his expensive, brocaded vest.

Stella rose to her feet and Oates did the same.

"As you are by now no doubt aware, Stella, I don't make a habit of talking to whores," Miss McWilliams said, her eyes on fire. "But this once I'm making the exception."

"It takes one to know one, Darlene," Stella said. "Now, say your piece and then be on your way."

Darlene's brother was studying Oates, his eyes lingering on the holstered Colt, making his calculations. Finally, a look of disdain on his face, he looked away.

"This has gone on long enough," Darlene McWilliams said. "One of my men is dead and another is gut-shot and coughing up black blood. He can't live."

Oates was surprised. The term "gut-shot" was the language of cow-town saloons and dance halls, not that of a seemingly well-bred young lady.

"I'm offering you terms," Darlene said. Her bay Thoroughbred was up on its toes, dancing, but she controlled the horse effortlessly.

"I'm listening," Stella said.

The wind walked among the trees and the shadows were stretching longer. The dying sun threw flaming red lances across the sky and the clouds were edged in burnished gold.

"Give me back the money you stole from me and I'll withdraw my men," Darlene said.

"And if I don't?"

"Then we'll starve you out of there, no matter how long it takes."

Oates saw anger flare in Stella. "Darlene, I reckon we earned that money after the months of abuse we took from you and that Halleck trash. The money isn't even yours. You robbed it from a bank in Arizona, remember?"

Darlene looked as if she'd been slapped. "How do you—"

"How do I know? I overheard your brother boasting to Clem Halleck how he'd robbed a bank in Tucson and killed a deputy sheriff while making his getaway. He said you planned and organized that robbery and that after you'd paid off a couple of accomplices, you cleared more than thirty thousand."

Darlene rounded on her brother. "You fool! I told you to never speak of the robbery to anybody."

"Clem had a right to know why what he was guarding in the wagon was so important," the man said.

Spitting venom, Darlene snapped, "I'll deal with you later, Charles." She turned to Stella. "As for you, you little whore, you've just signed your own death warrant."

Stella smiled. "No, Darlene, you've signed yours." She raised her Winchester. "You're not leaving here alive."

"No!" Oates grabbed the rifle barrel. "Not like this, Stella. You'll only bring yourself down to her level."

For her part, Darlene McWilliams displayed considerable courage. She hadn't flinched in the face of Stella's threat. "Wise advice, Mr. Whatever-your-name-is. If she'd shot me, you'd all be dead within seconds."

Charles McWilliams grinned. "I guarantee it."

Darlene swung her horse away and rode out of the clearing and her brother followed.

Stella's cheeks were wet with tears as she rounded on Oates. "What's better," she asked, her frustration apparent in her tone, "to be shot or slowly starve to death?"

Oates had no answer.

The day shaded into night and the coyotes were calling into the darkness. The rising moon had gotten itself tangled in the branches of the pines where the wind teased it unmercifully and tried to shake it loose. Around the cave, the land was lost in gloom, except for the distant glimmer of a campfire.

Occasionally a bullet caromed around the cave, fired by one of Darlene McWilliams' bored besiegers.

Oates was checking on Nellie when Sam Tatum sidled into the cave. He stood in the dim firelight, looking around him, his face puzzled as he tried to assess what had happened.

The boy seemed so disoriented and confused that Oates looked up at him and smiled. "Speak, thou bewildered apparition."

Like someone waking from a dream, Sam swallowed and said, "Your horse is safe, Mr. Oates. After the shooting started, I found a place for him deep in the woods."

"Sam, are you hurt?" This came from Lorraine.

"No, Miss Lorraine. I hid out and only moved after it got dark." His eyes moved to Nellie. "Is Miss Nellie hurt?"

"She got shot, Sammy," Oates said. He saw the boy's stricken expression and added quickly, "But I think she's going to be all right."

He was not trying to spare Sam's feelings. Nellie's wound was still inflamed, but the bleeding had stopped and she was not running a fever. Earlier both Lorraine and Stella agreed that these were good signs.

Nellie was conscious and now she raised her head from Lorraine's lap and smiled. "I'll be fine, Sam. I could use some coffee, though."

"I'll get water, Miss Nellie," the boy said enthusiastically.

"You be careful out there, Sammy," Oates warned. "Those damned bushwhackers are shooting at shadows."

Tatum picked up the pot. "I'll be careful, Mr. Oates."

The boy slipped out of the cave. A few seconds later a racketing fusillade of shots shattered the night into a million shards of sound.

Chapter 19

Nellie screamed as Eddie Oates picked up his rifle and left the cave, fading into the night. He stood close to the wall of the ridge and his eyes tried to penetrate the darkness.

Another shot was followed by a wild, agonized shriek. Then came another flurry of firing that seemed to go on forever. Then silence. Oates heard the water falling from the top of the ridge, splashing into a hollowed-out rock tank at its base.

"Sammy," he whispered, "where are you?"

"Over here, Mr. Oates."

"Are you hit?"

"I'm not hit, Mr. Oates. Wasn't nobody shooting at me."

Oates shook his head. What the hell . . . ?

Sam Tatum emerged from the darkness a few moments later, a large, hulking figure, the coffeepot in his hand. "I got the water for Miss Nellie's coffee," he said.

"Get back into the cave, Sammy."

"Should I put the water on to bile, Mr. Oates?"

"Yes, Sammy. You do that. Now go."

After Tatum left, Oates followed the line of the outcrop, heading wide of the stand of pines in front of the cave. High-heeled riding boots are not built with stealthy walking in mind, and Oates was convinced that every rock he kicked and twig he snapped could be heard clear to Alma.

He stopped often, listening into the night. Once he was sure he heard the distant drum of a running horse, but he wasn't sure. The moon had untangled itself from the pines and was riding high, its bladed silver light deepening the malevolent shadows. He smelled gun smoke and it drifted gray and silent as a ghost among the trees.

Stooping low, his rifle across his chest, Oates stepped into the stand of pines. He looked back at the cave and saw why the besiegers' gunfire had been so ineffective. The cave lay at a slightly higher elevation than the trees, so the only part visible was the roof, now bathed in the flickering orange glow of the fire.

There was little undergrowth between the pines and the ground was carpeted in needles. His heart hammering, he stepped carefully, heading deeper into the trees. A few moments later he found his first dead man.

The body was lying on its back, the eyes wide-open, staring into nothingness. The man had been shot twice in the chest, the wounds so close, Oates could have covered them with a playing card. He was dressed like a puncher, but wore a gold and diamond ring on the little finger of his left hand and his Colt, gun belt and boots were of the highest quality. He may have been a drover once upon a time, but this man hadn't nursed cows for a living in years.

Oates found five more bodies among the trees, all of them with the look of gunmen, their eyes open in the startled stare of the violent dead. The campfire was in a hollow twenty yards away, and a coffeepot still steamed on the coals. Two dead men lay by the fire. The man who had been gut-shot had been dispatched by a bullet between the eyes. The other had managed to draw, but his gun was still clenched in his hand. He'd tried, but he'd been too slow by a mile.

Oates' eyes searched the uneasy night. Had this been the work of Apaches, a hit-and-run raid from out of the darkness?

He immediately dismissed that question. No guns or horses had been taken, prizes the Indians would not have passed up. Besides, Apaches seldom attacked at night. As many dead men could testify, they would, but they were not real keen on the idea.

He and Stella had accounted for one of the dead. Who had shot up the remaining McWilliams riders and killed six men, seven if the apparent mercy shooting of the gut-shot man was counted?

The only man Oates could think of who might have that kind of gun skill was the Tin Cup Kid. But the Kid owed him nothing. Why would he play guardian angel? It just wasn't the man's style.

Oates picked up the pot from the fire and poured himself coffee. He was grateful to whoever had intervened, but now it was time to move. Come daylight,

Darlene McWilliams would be sure to check on the state of the siege and when she found her men dead and him and the women gone, she'd come after them.

Oates finished his coffee and returned to the cave. Replying to the question on Stella's face, he said, "They're all dead."

"Apaches?"

"I don't think so. I'd say a white man . . . or men."

"But who—"

"I've got no idea." He didn't mention the Tin Cup Kid to Stella. The name would mean nothing to her. Instead he said, "We have to get out of here. We've got horses now, if Nellie can ride."

"She'll ride. She'll have to."

Oates smiled. "Then pick a direction, huh?"

Stella did not return his smile. Her face serious, she said, "There's only one direction—east. We were headed for Heartbreak and that's where we're going. All that stands between us and a new life are the miles."

Hesitating, weighing the consequences of what he was about to say, Oates finally suggested, "You could leave Darlene McWilliams' money in the cave, Stella. Then she might let you be."

The woman shook her head. "Not a chance. The five thousand will buy us a fresh start in Heartbreak. We can open our own house and Sam will help us run it. I'm telling you like I told Darlene, we earned that money and we're not giving it back."

Oates nodded. "Well, good luck to you, Stella. I reckon I'll stay around here. I still have a score to settle with Miss McWilliams."

"No, you won't stay around. You're coming with us."

It was pin-drop quiet in the cave and Oates looked around him. Lorraine and Nellie were staring at him, accusation in their eyes. Even Sam Tatum seemed disturbed. Oates' eyes lingered on the two women. Nellie was deathly pale, fragile as porcelain, and Lorraine had aged in the past three months. Her face was lined, tired, the stained, ragged nightgown she wore under her mackinaw covering her like a sack.

"You're all we got, Eddie," Lorraine said. "We can't make it to Heartbreak without you."

"Hell, I'm a drunk," Oates said. He felt trapped, corralled. "I failed you once. I could do it again, anytime, anyplace. All it will take is a whiskey bottle."

"Like I said," Lorraine replied, smiling wanly, "you're all we got. Once upon a time you may not have been much, Eddie Oates, but, Lord help us, we need you now."

Stella laid a hand on Oates' arm. "Darlene McWilliams will be coming after us. Don't you think you'll have plenty of chances to get even?"

Oates' shoulders slumped in acceptance of defeat. Lorraine was right: maybe he still wasn't much, but he owed these people a debt for sentencing them to three months of hell. He had not yet repaid them in full.

He looked at Tatum. "Sammy, bring in my horse and find four others over by the pines. Also, if you see any grub over there, bring that too. And make sure the horses are carrying rifles in the saddle scabbards and pick up any spare ammunition."

The boy bent his head, his mouth moving as he repeated Oates' instructions to himself. Finally he looked up, smiling. "I'll do that, Mr. Oates."

"Good man, then go get it done."

After Tatum had gone, Nellie lay on her side, her chin in her hand, and looked at Oates. "I can't ride," she said. She sipped the coffee Sam had made for her. "There's just no way I can sit in a saddle."

"Yes, you can," Lorraine said. "Let your wounded ass hang off the side."

The girl looked annoyed. "You're such a whore, Lorraine."

"I know. But you'll ride. You want us to leave you here for Clem Halleck and them?"

Nellie shuddered, her eyes shading from defiance to fear. "I guess I can ride," she said.

"I guess you can at that," Lorraine said.

Chapter 20

An hour later, riding through opalescent moonlight, Oates and his charges took to the trail.

He let the others ride ahead of him and he drifted to the rear, the direction of any possible attack.

Here, close to the peaks of the Gila, the night was cool and the wind in the trees made a soft music. There was no defined trail, but to lead the way, he trusted Stella, ahead of him, invisible in the darkness.

Come dawn, if not before, they would have to find a place where they could hole up during the daylight hours, then ride out again after nightfall. He had no doubt that there were competent trackers among Darlene McWilliams' gunmen and they would surely follow close.

After an hour, Stella faded back and drew rein. "We stopped for a spell," she said, her face lost in shadow. "Nellie needs a rest. She's weak from loss of blood."

"She's done well so far," Oates allowed, "but we have to move on soon."

"And we have to find a place to hide out during the day."

"I know that." Oates shifted his weight and his saddle creaked. "While Nellie rests, I'll ride ahead a ways and see what I can see."

"Lorraine is taking care of Nellie. I'll come with you."

When Oates and Stella caught up with the others, Lorraine was cleaning Nellie's wound with water from her canteen.

"How is she?" Oates asked.

"I don't see any sign of infection," Lorraine answered. "There's one good thing to say about the high country—wounds heal faster than they do in towns."

"No thanks to you, Eddie Oates," Nellie snapped. "My butt is all cut to ribbons."

"Sorry, but the bullet was deep."

"Don't worry, Nellie," Lorraine said. "Men will still think you've got a nice ass. Ain't that the truth, Eddie?"

"Hell, yes. As true as I'm sitting a paint hoss."

Oates smiled and rode past. "We'll be back soon," he heard Stella say.

They rode in silence for a few minutes, separated by the pines they were passing through. When they reached a moon-splashed clearing patterned by wildflowers, Stella edged closer. "That was a nice thing you said back there. Nellie worries about her appearance. Looks are important to a whore, you understand."

"I guess they are." Oates sought firmer ground. "How long do you figure until daybreak?"

Stella looked at the stars. "Hard to say. Two hours

maybe. We're at the top of the world and the dawn comes early."

"Then we'll have to find a hiding place sooner than I figured."

They found it ten minutes later, a mesa that Oates figured stood about seven thousand feet above the flat, had there been any flat. As it was, the rocky sides of the butte soared at least a thousand feet above them, the edge of the summit rimmed by moonlight.

Oates searched for a way to the top, and stumbled on a faint game trail. Leaving Stella at the base of the rise, he followed the trail, riding through piñon and cedar. The ill-defined track rose gradually to a height of about a hundred feet, then switched back around a talus slope. As the trees thinned, the route angled more steeply, rising another several hundred feet.

After yet another switchback, the trail widened slightly and climbed at a gradual incline all the way to the summit.

Oates' mountain-bred mustang was sure-footed and made the climb with relative ease. He was not so sure how the others would fare. Their mounts were big American horses, fast and enduring on the flat, but not at home in the high country.

As he reached the top of the mesa, Oates reached a decision. Sammy Tatum and the women would have to make it—there was no other choice.

He drew rein to catch his breath and looked out across the Gila, a fantastic panorama of peaks, saw-toothed ridges and dark, hidden canyons where the moonlight did not reach. Up here the wind gusted stronger and shook the branches of a few scattered cedar and piñon.

Oates swung from the saddle and led the paint, unwilling to take the chance of riding into a hidden crevasse that would plunge him all the way to the center of the earth.

Stepping carefully, aided by the moonlight, Oates stumbled on a shallow depression about an acre in extent. The recent rains had filled the hollow to a depth of several inches, and to his joy he realized that water would not be a problem.

He let the paint drink and looked at the sky. Up here the stars seemed so close he felt as if he could reach, grab a handful and let them trickle through his fingers like diamonds.

Every thought that enters a man's mind is a test, to see what his reaction will be. Now Oates was tested. From somewhere, back in the shadowed regions of his consciousness, the thought of diamonds led to money . . . money to saloons . . . saloons to whiskey . . . whiskey to alcoholic oblivion.

He rubbed a hand across his suddenly dry mouth. A drink would go down well about now. Make him forget his problems, at least for a while.

Oates took a deep, shuddering breath. For a while he had thought the whiskey craving was finally behind him. He was wrong. The hunger lurked in the darkness like an assassin, ready to strike when he least expected it.

How many times would he have to fight this battle? And was it one he could win?

Those were questions without answers. . . .

Behind Oates a shower of shingle rattled down the mesa slope. He turned, his gun up and ready in his hand.

Peering through the gloom, he made out the dark silhouette of a rider, then another. He holstered his gun and led his horse toward them.

"I got tired waiting for you," Stella said when Oates stepped within the range of her vision. "And I brought the others."

"But . . . how did you climb the slope?"

"It wasn't easy," Stella said. She climbed out of the saddle. Then her eyes met Oates' in the darkness. "Despite what you may think, we all ride like Comanches, Mr. Oates. Sometimes a whore needs a fast horse, just like a gambler does."

Stepping to one side, Oates watched as Lorraine and Nellie reached the summit.

"Everybody's here," he said.

That was so patently obvious, no one commented.

Oates tried again. "There's water in plenty and I saw some graze back there on the rim of the rock basin, and some sage. I guess we can hole up here for two, three days if we need to."

"Then what?" Lorraine asked.

"Then I don't know."

Nellie had been leaning against her horse. Her face was a blur of white. "Maybe Darlene McWilliams will just give up. She's got bigger fish to fry."

"Maybe," Oates said.

Helped by the always-willing Tatum, the women

unsaddled their mounts and bathed their faces and necks in the rainwater. The moon was falling now, the stars were blinking out, and the air was shading from purple to dark blue.

Restlessly, Oates took his rifle and sat on the edge of the mesa, his eyes on the timbered country below his lofty perch. After a few minutes Stella joined him. She handed him a thick sandwich of bread and meat.

"Thank you," he said, taking a bite. He hadn't realized how famished he was.

"Thank Sam. The boy is a forager." She produced tobacco and papers. "Look, he even found me this. There must have been a Texan in that bunch."

Stella built a smoke and scratched a match into flame on the rock beside her. She lit her cigarette, then after a while said, "Where do you suppose they are?"

"Down there somewhere, looking for us. Or they will be soon." He turned to the woman. "What do you know about Darlene McWilliams?"

"Only what I heard around her camp after the Hallecks threw in with her. I know that she and her brother fled Arizona just ahead of a hanging posse. The ranchers down in the Bryce Canyon country are a hard bunch and they'll string up a woman for rustling as readily as they'll hang a man. Along the way, Charles McWilliams robbed a bank for a road stake and killed a deputy in the process."

Stella drew deeply on her cigarette. "Happily for Darlene, the robbery brought in a bigger haul than she and Charles expected, and that gave her an idea. She hired a bunch of hard cases and drove a rustled herd into the Gila country. The girl is ambitious and she plans to be the biggest rancher in New Mexico. She'll buy what she can, steal what she can't."

Oates smiled as he chewed on his sandwich. "I reckon Miss McWilliams will find the ranchers in this part of the state just as tough as they are in Arizona. They won't sit on their gun hands as she rustles cattle and takes over their range."

"Maybe so, but ol' Charlie is a named revolver fighter. Clem Halleck told me he's killed four men. Come to that, Clem is mighty fast with a gun his ownself. Darlene figures that between them both they can handle any little problems that might arise."

"They won't be little problems," Oates said. "I think the young lady will have her hands full."

Stella stubbed out her cigarette butt. "Small problems, big problems, Darlene can hire all the gunmen she needs. Money talks."

"And that's how come she wants the five thousand you took."

"Yeah. Darlene knows that right now she has to hold tight on to every cent she's got."

The night was fleeing the morning light and far off, the sky to the east was a pale blue tinted by scarlet. A single star still lingered, hanging like a lantern to illuminate the path of early travelers.

Oates looked down into the aborning day, seeing it arrive clean. Nothing moved among the pines, but higher, the aspen were in a state of constant agitation. The air was cool and smelled of sage and the mountain freshness of the high country.

Stella rose. "I'm going to check on Nellie."

Oates nodded. "Thanks for the sandwich."

For the next half hour Oates studied the terrain below, but saw no sign of life.

Then, as the morning brightened, a movement caught his eye. A solitary horseman was riding past the mesa, his head turning constantly as he checked his back trail.

The man rode a fine black and had a rifle across his saddle horn. Oates looked closer, but the rider vanished into the trees and was gone from sight.

Did the man look familiar? Oates racked his brain. There had been something in the way he carried his head that struck a chord with him. Where had he seen the mysterious rider before, and was he one of Darlene's gunmen?

Somehow he felt that the man added up to trouble. But for whom?

Angrily, Oates slapped the rock beside him.

Damn it! Who was that man?

Chapter 21

As the women and Sam Tatum stretched out in the meager shade of a twisted cedar and slept, Oates maintained his lonely vigil at the mesa rim.

Less than twenty minutes after he'd sighted the mysterious rider, Darlene McWilliams and her brother had led a dozen men through the trees, following in the man's tracks. The Halleck boys, father and sons, were among them.

She'd brought her wagon with her. The big freight with its huge, iron-rimmed wheels was slowing her down, but she seemed unwilling to be separated from her ill-gotten fortune by leaving it behind with the herd.

Oates shook his head in frustration. Now Darlene and her gunmen were ahead of him, cutting off the route to Heartbreak.

Maybe, once he and the others cleared the Gila, they could swing north and go around their pursuers. But there was a problem: Where exactly was Heartbreak?

Stella had only a vague idea, and it was possible they could wander in the wilderness forever, or at least until they starved to death or were overtaken by winter. They might end up hoping the Apaches would arrive and put them out of their misery.

Oates rose to his feet. Tired as he was, he no longer wanted to watch helplessly from the mesa while events unfolded below him. He made up his mind. It was time to find out where Darlene was headed and see if there was any way of avoiding her.

Quietly, Oates saddled the paint and filled his canteen, then kneeled and gently shook Stella awake.

He quickly told her what he'd seen from the rim. Then, fearful of waking the others, he whispered, "I'm going after Darlene and her boys. I need to know where they're headed." He smiled. "Once I find out, we can take a different route."

Alarm showed on Stella's face. "You'll come back?"

"Of course I'll be back. I'll return before dark."

Stella laid her fingertips on the back of Oates' hand. "Be careful, Eddie. The Hallecks are a handful just by themselves. You might be riding from one kind of trouble into something a lot worse."

Oates' smile grew. "Don't worry, Stella. I'm not that brave, you know."

Oates headed east along a confused trail of horse and wagon tracks left from the morning. The land began a steep ascent and he rode through forests of fir, spruce and aspen. Once a huge black bear watched him from the dappled shade of the trees, then shrugged, deciding that he was nobody of importance.

After a mile the wagon tracks turned northeast, along the rim of a canyon that Oates guessed carried the unquiet waters of the Gila River. Riding closer, he saw that the walls of the bluffs were at least two hundred and fifty feet high, and, as Darlene McWilliams and her men had done, he gave the canyon a wide berth.

Now the terrain abruptly sloped downward and Oates rode through a high desert woodland of cedar and piñon, with sycamore growing closer to the creeks near the canyon.

The day was very hot, the burning sun well up in a sky the color of washed-out denim. The wind felt like a dragon's breath, and under his high-button coat Oates' shirt was sticking to him with sweat. He drew rein, shrugged out of the coat and draped it over the back of his saddle. Then he wiped the damp brim of his fancy plug hat and settled it back on his head.

He was jumpy, on edge, not liking the situation. By rights he should go back, get the others together and convince them to return to Alma. Now that the Apache menace was over, Cornelius Baxter and his vigilantes might welcome them with open arms. He could forget Heartbreak, forget avenging the death of old Jacob Yearly and resume his career as . . . what? Town drunk?

Back at the mesa, he'd more or less told Stella that he was a coward, and maybe he was. That thought was always at the back of his mind, keeping company with the whiskey bottle.

Oates' shoulders slumped in the saddle. Returning to Alma was a way, and once he would have accepted its path. But it was his way no longer. He must keep telling himself that. . . .

He kneed the paint into motion and again followed the trail.

Oates crossed several shallow creeks as he headed northeast, parallel to the canyon that seemed to go on forever. He was riding through a stand of mixed piñon and cedar when he stopped suddenly and faded into the shadows.

Coming directly toward him was the hammering sound of a running horse.

Oates had left the trail at this point, though he'd kept it in sight. The big wagon needed open ground and had kept away from the wooded areas as much as possible. But, uneasy as he was, Oates had no such luxury. He preferred to stay to whatever cover he could find.

The rider, a man bent over in the saddle astride a tall, black horse, galloped past Oates' hiding place. The running horse was kicking up such a cloud of dust that Oates caught only a single, fleeting glimpse of the rider; then he was gone. A few tense seconds passed; then four other horsemen rode into the dust, trailed by their own billowing, yellow cloud.

Whoever he was, the man on the black horse was

the same rider he'd seen from the mesa that morning and Darlene McWilliams' men were pressing him close.

Oates heard shots. Then the sound of the running horses faded into the distance.

Riding out of the trees, Oates considered his options. But since the enemy of his enemy could only be a friend, he knew what he had to do. He swung the paint around and set his heels to its flanks.

Dust swirled over him as Oates followed on the heels of the McWilliams riders. Now he heard a steady volley of shots ahead of him and he slowed the mustang to a walk. After a few hundred yards, the shooting grew louder and he swung out of the saddle and led the paint into the trees. He slid his Winchester from the scabbard and went ahead on foot.

The McWilliams riders had the man treed somewhere and were closing in for the kill. Oates' mouth was dry and he was as nervous as a whore in church. He gulped down his fear like a dry chicken bone and walked forward, his rifle slanted across his chest. Four against one was not good odds. But four against two wasn't a whole sight better.

A massive granite boulder blocked Oates' path, a stand of prickly pear growing at its base. He rounded the rock and took in the situation at a glance.

The mysterious rider was holed up at the top of a shallow saddleback ridge. Dust still drifted in the air, so he'd obviously ridden up there. Scattered cedars grew along the hollow of the saddleback, and among them Oates saw the outline of a man's head. He had removed his hat, or had lost it, and now and then he picked a target and fired his rifle. As far as Oates could determine, he had made no hits.

Falling away from the ridge was a gradual slope, covered by the rocks of an ancient lava flow. Here and there pines grew and the McWilliams riders were scattered behind the rocks and trees, shooting steadily. Their concealed positions allowed for movement, and as Oates watched, they advanced slowly up the hill, taking advantage of any cover.

Time was running out for the lone rifleman.

Oates considered opening up from where he was, but that would immediately attract the attention of four guns and, out in the open as he was, he could end up being shot to pieces.

Ahead of Oates the trail curved around two massive boulders, a grotesquely twisted pine growing in the notch between them.

Making up his mind, he covered fifty yards of flat ground and dived behind the rocks. Beyond was what he had hoped to see—four horses standing head-down at the edge of the trail.

He rose to his feet and levered a round into his rifle. When he was a few yards from the horses he fired between them, kicking up dust at their feet. The animals stood, ground-tied, right where they were.

Cursing, his hands shaking, Oates fired again—with the same result.

Outlaw mounts were trained to stand, no matter what, and these four were no exceptions.

"There's somebody at the horses!" came a cry from the slope.

Suddenly a man was running toward him, a rifle in his hands. Oates levered a round and he and the man shot at the same time. A bullet drove Oates' hat from his head, but the gunman was hit hard. He staggered back a step, crashed to the ground and his Winchester rattled down the slope.

Oates heard a shot followed by a shriek from somewhere higher up the slope; then he was running for his life. He plunged headlong into the trees, turned and dropped to one knee.

Two men came down the slope opposite, one sliding all the way on his rump, and ran for the horses. They mounted quickly, threw a quick glance at Oates, then slapped spurs to their mounts and galloped away.

Oates sprinted from the piñon and fired a couple of parting shots to keep the fleeing gunmen honest. Then his eyes lifted to the ridge. He saw no one and nothing stirred up there but the wind.

He climbed the slope and checked on the man he'd shot, a lean, hawk-faced youngster whom Oates recognized immediately. He was Mash Halleck's son Reuben.

His face grim, Oates understood the implications. He had no doubt that the McWilliams riders had recognized him. By all accounts Mash was a vengeful man and there was no backup in him. He'd avenge the death of his son and keep on a-coming until he did.

Mash had been an enemy before; now he'd be a nemesis from hell.

Oates didn't recognize the other dead man sprawled on the slope. He climbed up to the crest of the ridge and looked around. The mystery man was gone, his passage marked by a cloud of dust that was now sifting to the ground.

Whoever he was, he'd been wounded. He'd been hit during his fight on the ridge or sometime before. Blood spattered the rocks where he'd lain and a trail of scarlet spots in the sand led to where he'd mounted his horse.

How badly was the man hurt? There was little blood, but that didn't mean much. He might only have been winged. But then, a gut-shot man doesn't bleed out either.

Oates made his way back down the slope. He picked up his hat and wiggled a finger through the bullet hole in the crown. That had been too close. He set the hat on his head and mounted the paint, sitting the saddle for a few moments, undecided on his next move.

Finally he swung east again. He'd left the mesa to discover Darlene McWilliams' whereabouts and that's what he would do.

The sun was directly overhead and the land slumbered in the heat. Flies buzzed around Oates and tormented the mustang so that it constantly shook its head, making the bit chime. Among the trees the clear light changed constantly, shading from burnished gold to pale blue where the shadows pooled.

For a while Oates rode in the wagon tracks near the canyon rim, but then he swung wider, the heavily forested peaks of the Black Range just ten miles ahead.

There was always a chance that grim old Mash Halleck would search for his son's body, and Oates had no desire to meet him and Clem on open ground with iron in their hands.

After thirty minutes Oates turned toward the canyon again, riding through aspen, ponderosa pine and then woods of cedar, piñon and sycamore as the high country fell away rapidly.

The air was crystal clear, spangled by shafts of sunlight, and after a mile the wide scar of the canyon came into sight. And something else became apparent— the smell of wood smoke. But this was not the scent of burning pine or creosote bush, but the harsh, acrid tang of old wood, probably oak and hickory.

Oates drew rein, looking into the quiet day. Ahead of him lay a gently sloping meadow of about ten acres, bright with the white and purple flowers of fleabane, verbena and Apache plume.

Where the meadow ended, a wooded area began and Oates was sure he saw a wisp of smoke rise above the trees.

He was not a man born to carefulness, but in this hard, dangerous land it was a trait Oates was rapidly acquiring. He scanned the meadow and the trees beyond, rested his eyes, then searched again.

Grass rippled in the breeze, tree branches stirred, but he saw no sign of humans. Sliding his rifle from the scabbard, he levered a round and kneed the paint into the meadow.

Wary now, his head moving constantly, Oates rode through the pasture and with a sense of relief reached the tree line. He swung out of the saddle and advanced on foot, leading the horse through the underbrush.

The trees thinned and to his left he saw the canopies of several cottonwoods. He turned in that direction, then stopped dead in his tracks.

What he saw horrified him.

Chapter 22

Eddie Oates took in the scene with a single appalled glance.

Near a narrow creek stood the burned-out remains of Darlene McWilliams' wagon. But what drew Oates' attention were the two men hanging from a cotton-wood branch, their bodies gently swaying in the breeze.

He led the paint out of the trees and walked to the creek.

As he drew closer he recognized the hanged men. They were the two gunmen who had fled the fight at the ridge. Both had been badly beaten before they were strung up as their swollen, bruised faces testified.

Oates looked up at the bodies, remembering the hanging of the Hart brothers back in Alma. But the brothers hadn't been beaten like this. The older of the hanged McWilliams men had been battered so severely, one of his eyes hung on his cheekbone

Mash Halleck had begun to take his revenge, starting with the men who had abandoned his son.

At that moment, Oates knew he could expect no mercy from the Hallecks and could expect even worse torture. Both dead men had recognized him at the ridge and no doubt had spilled the beans to Mash, perhaps trying to bargain for their lives.

Leaving the mustang, Oates stepped over to the wagon. The treasure box was gone. The money sacks were probably now in the saddlebags of Darlene and her brother.

Had she tried to stop the hanging? Oates doubted that. Darlene was a cold, ambitious woman and the deaths of two of her hired hands would mean nothing to her.

Carefully, Oates scouted the area. There were no horse tracks beyond the creek and it was plain that Darlene and her riders had turned back at this point. Heading where? Oates hoped it was all the way back to the rustled herd, but somehow he doubted that.

Suddenly he was fearful for Stella and the others. If they'd left the mesa, even for a minute . . .

Oates ran to the paint and swung into the saddle, filled with a sense of panicked urgency.

Something was wrong, very wrong. He could sense it.

The day was dying as Oates headed back toward the mesa.

Only when he left the trees and rode across open

ground was he aware of the enormous breadth of the sky. Shooting stars were falling to earth in a constant trail of sparks, and Oates thought that if he held his breath and was quiet enough, he'd hear them thump onto the grass and lie there, smoking like cinders.

Around him as he urged the paint forward at a trot, coyotes were talking in the darkness and once an owl swooped over his head and vanished among the moonstruck pines like a gray ghost.

There was an eerie, ethereal cast to the night and Oates felt he was being watched by eyes hidden in the trees that, full of moonlight, gleamed like opals.

He wiped damp palms on his pants, thinking of ha'ants and boogermen. Oates forced himself to smile. Fear has a way of making the wolf bigger than he is and it quickly changes the man back to the boy.

He had no reason to fear the night . . . only the all-too-mortal humans who stalked its caves of darkness.

The mesa revealed itself as a massive, hulking shape that blacked out a galaxy of stars. The moon bathed the land in silver light, but created shadows everywhere.

It took Oates ten frustrating minutes to find the faint thread of the switchback game trail, but once he did, the sure-footed mustang climbed willingly enough.

He reached the summit, let his stunned eyes read the scene before him, then swung out of the saddle and tried to piece together the disaster that had befallen his companions.

A blackened, burned-out cedar was his first clue.

The tree had been set ablaze, accidentally it seemed, because the ashes of the small fire that could have caused it lay close to the trunk.

The blazing tree would have been a fiery beacon that would have been seen for miles. Had it attracted the attention of Darlene McWilliams and her riders?

Oates looked around and the flutter of something white caught his attention.

A sheet of paper had been pinned down by a rock. Next to it, wrapped in a scrap of cloth, were meat and bread. Oates made a sandwich and as he chewed, he held the paper up to the bright moonlight. Only one word had been scrawled on the paper: *HEARTBREAK*.

But under that, Sammy Tatum had made a quick sketch that showed five riders on a pine-edged trail.

Five riders!

Oates looked more closely. The three women were obvious, sitting their saddles with their skirts tucked up over the knees. But there were two men. One was Sammy, riding like a sack of grain, the other a tall man on a horse that the boy had shaded black.

The mystery man had seen the blazing tree and had persuaded the others to leave the mesa, probably pointing out that if he'd seen the fire, so might Darlene McWilliams.

They were now headed for Heartbreak, wherever that might be.

Oates finished the sandwich, then realized he was dog tired. He told himself that any decision he might make could wait until he had some sleep.

He led the paint to the patch of bunchgrass, loosened the girth, then stretched out on the bare rock and slept. The night closed around him and the smiling moon blanketed him in white light.

The dawning daylight woke Eddie Oates.

He rose to his feet and worked out the kinks in his back, grimacing. The mustang was grazing, though there was little grass left. But the little horse was used to making do and doing without and seemed none the worse for wear.

"Wish I could say the same thing about myself," Oates groaned, rubbing at a persistent knot in the small of his back.

To the east, the sun had not yet risen above the mountains, but it was already doing its best to banish the night. The lemon sky was tied up with red ribbons and the topmost peaks and ridges of the shadowed Gila glowed with a halo of gold.

Stretching, Oates stepped to the edge of the mesa and his brown eyes studied the country below. There was no movement, no sound.

His immediate concern was not with Stella Spinner and the others. Whoever the mysterious rider was, he was good with a gun as he'd proven at the siege of the cave and later on the ridge. They were safer with the tall man on the black horse than they'd be with him.

As for Darlene McWilliams, she'd been hurt. She'd lost men and was still missing five thousand dollars of her money. But, thinking of old Jacob Yearly, Oates decided she had not been hurt enough.

Suddenly a plan came to him.

It was time to take the fight to Darlene, by a round-about means certainly, but it might just work.

Of course, the plan hinged on his living long enough. And that was a mighty uncertain thing.

Oates tightened the cinch on the paint and mounted. He was wishful for coffee, a gallon maybe, hot and strong and sweet as sin, but he had none of that and dismissed the thought from his mind.

Where he was going there was plenty of coffee—if a man survived long enough to drink it.

Chapter 23

Eddie Oates rode west for five miles through wooded, hilly country, then swung due north. When he was directly opposite the eastern slopes of the Canyon Creek Mountains, he turned directly toward them. Several miles later he was among the foothills and calculated that Black Mountain and the scorched ruins of old Jacob's cabin were now directly south of him.

Was Darlene McWilliams still holding her herd there?

Oates' plan depended on her staying put. He doubted that she'd yet had time to move against other ranches where she could find better grass, more water and a supply of winter feed.

She might also want to hire men to replace the ones she'd lost, and that would take time, even in the high country where there was no shortage of footloose outlaws and gunmen looking for work.

Oates rode south until the conical bulk of Black Mountain loomed large in front of him. Remembering the ridge opposite Jacob's cabin where a man could observe the country concealed, he swung out of the saddle and ground-tied the paint on a patch of tufted grass among the pines.

Taking his rifle, Oates headed for the ridge. The sun had begun its slow climb into the pale sky and the morning was already hot. Sweat trickled down Oates' cheek, down his neck, and he wished he'd left his high-button coat with the horse.

A gradual slope, covered with prickly pear, sage and a few piñons, led to the ridge. Bent over, he made his way to the top, then looked out into the land spread before him.

Darlene's herd was still there, strung out for a mile or so along the flat in front of the cabin. A few cows were grazing among the cottonwoods lining the creek where Jacob had made him take a bath, and Oates smiled at the memory.

To his surprise, the cabin had been repaired, the string and baling wire, make-do mending of gunmen, not carpenters, but it had a roof and new pine door. The corral had been extended to hold more horses, and a ramshackle bunkhouse and an equally rickety cooking shack had been built.

It was obviously the abode of transients. Darlene had her heart set on grander quarters and she'd no intention of living there for long.

A man left the cabin and walked to the bunkhouse where he stepped inside and left the door wide against the heat. After that, there was no other movement of man or animal.

Oates had seen all he needed. He backed away from

the ridge and walked to his horse. He removed his fancy coat, folded it carefully and draped it over the saddle, then mounted.

He swung the paint west again, keeping close to the cliffs and mountain slopes of the Gila. By noon, riding through a forest of ponderosa pine, he reached Iron Creek Mesa, then headed northwest.

As he rode, Oates admitted to himself that he had very little idea where he was going. He desperately reached back through the alcoholic mists of his memory, remembering laughing, easygoing Tom Carson, one of the biggest ranchers in the state.

On his rare visits to Alma, Carson had always bought Oates a drink or three. Although his punchers made him play the fetch game, Carson never had.

Now, where was his ranch?

Oates recalled being told that Carson's Circle-T lay to the northeast of Alma and that his ranch house was built in the shadow of Bear Wallow Mountain.

Was he even headed in that direction?

Trusting to memories as flimsy as gossamer in a wind, Oates crossed a creek lined by huge cottonwoods, then rode into forested hill country cut through by shallow arroyos.

Even a man born under a dark star can get lucky now and again, and Oates' good fortune came in the shape of a lanky, loose-geared puncher who was sitting his pony in a stand of ponderosa, building a smoke.

As Oates rode up on the man, the cowboy showed no surprise at meeting another human being in the middle of a wilderness at the top of the world. He lit his cigarette and said through a cloud of blue smoke, "Howdy."

"Howdy," Oates said. He drew rein. "I'm looking for the Circle-T ranch. Ever heard of it?"

"I should say."

"Can you point the way?"

"Goin' that way my ownself."

"I'd appreciate if I could tag along," Oates said.

"Suit yourself."

The puncher, a lantern-jawed man with sad, hound-dog eyes and a drooping mustache, fell in beside Oates and for the next half hour they rode in silence.

Amused, Oates broke the silence. "You're not a talking man, are you?"

The cowboy shrugged. "I got nothing to say."

"You could ask me why I want to find the Circle-T."

"None of my bidness."

After another ten minutes of silence, the puncher spoke without turning. "One time down in the Panhandle, a foreman says to me, I'm a man of few words. When I say come, you come.' I said, 'I'm a man of few words my ownself. When I shake my head, I ain't comin'.'"

Now the cowboy looked at Oates. "Mister, that's the longest speech I've made in a twelve-month, an' I don't plan on making another. So, no offense, but don't ask me no more conundrums."

Oates smiled and nodded. "No offense taken."

An hour later, after riding the foothills between a pair of mountain peaks, Oates and the puncher came up on the Circle-T ranch.

The ranch house was a sprawling timber building with a sod roof. Behind it lay a corral, barn, bunkhouse and other outbuildings. Unlike Darlene McWilliams' shabby headquarters, everything Oates saw was built solid, to last.

As far as he could remember, Tom Carson had been in the country for six years. Despite his place being an affront to the Apaches, the rancher still had his hair, which said much about the toughness of the man.

Outside the cabin, the puncher swung out of the saddle. "Wait here," he said.

He stepped to the door and knocked. The door opened, but whoever stood behind it was lost in shadow.

"Somebody to talk to you, boss," the puncher said.

As the cowboy led his horse to the corral, Carson stepped outside, wearing a gun. His eyes lifted to Oates. "You hunting a job or ridin' the grub line?"

"Neither, Mr. Carson, though I could sure use coffee and a meal."

"I can supply that. But if you ain't hunting a job, why are you here?"

"I need to talk with you, Mr. Carson. It's all-fired important."

Carson's eyes had been searching Oates' face. "Don't I know you from somewhere?"

Oates nodded. "Name's Eddie Oates, Mr. Carson." When that didn't seem to register, he added, "Most recently, from Alma."

The big rancher smiled. "Now I recollect, the town dru—" Carson let that go quickly. Taking in the gun on

Oates' hip and the rifle under his knee he said, "You've changed."

"Some."

"Go down to the cookhouse. Tell the cook I said to feed you and then come back and talk to me. I swear, if you were much skinnier you'd have to stand up twice to cast a shadow."

Oates badly wanted to say his piece there and then, but he knew better than to try to push it. Besides, Carson was already in the cabin and had closed the door behind him.

He swung out of the saddle and led the paint toward the cookhouse. The puncher he'd met on the trail directed him to put up his horse in the corral, where there was a supply of hay.

The cook was a small, rotund man who apparently did not share the short-tempered, sour demeanor of the breed. After Oates told him that Carson had sent him, he smiled and waved him to a table that was big enough to seat a dozen punchers.

"Set," he said, "an' I'll bring you coffee."

The man returned a few moments later with a pot and a tin cup and set them on the table. "Scrawny little feller, ain't you," he said.

Oates nodded, pouring himself coffee. "That's already been noted."

"Well, son, I'll fatten you up on a thick beefsteak and maybe half a dozen eggs. You like eggs?"

The food was good and after he'd eaten, Oates pushed himself away from the table. He rose and found the cook at the stove.

"I appreciate the food," he said. "That was mighty good eatin'."

The fat man looked pleased. "Not too many say that around here."

Oates smiled. "Well, they should."

He walked back to the cabin, feeling on edge. A lot was riding on what he was about to tell Carson and how the man took it.

Would he even believe him?

Despite its rough exterior, the cabin was luxuriously furnished with heavy leather chairs and tasteful works of art on the walls, including a framed portrait of George Armstrong Custer, draped in black crepe. The polished wood floor was covered in Navajo rugs and the huge, fieldstone fireplace boasted ornaments of burnished brass.

It was a masculine place with bedrooms leading off the main cabin and showed little female influence. But it was comfortable and built tight and snug against the harsh winters of the New Mexico high country.

Carson ushered Oates into a chair, then asked if he'd eaten well. Oates allowed that he had, and the rancher said, "Now, tell me why you're here, Eddie."

Using as few words as possible, trying to get his point across clearly, Oates told Carson about Darlene McWilliams' ambitions to be the biggest rancher in the state by fair means or foul. He described the killing of Jacob Yearly and then told how Stella Spinner had taken five thousand dollars and how Darlene had tried to get it back.

"Darlene still has a war chest of twenty-five thousand from the bank robbery in Arizona, Mr. Carson," Oates said. "And she's hired gunmen, including Clem Halleck. And her own brother, Charles, is a well-known killer."

Oates realized things were going badly when Carson sat forward in his chair and said, his face stiff, "Stella Spinner. I remember her. She was a two-dollar saloon whore in Alma, was she not?"

Without waiting for an answer, Carson rose to his feet, opened the cabin door and roared, "Somebody!"

A puncher must have answered, because the rancher yelled, "Bring me Garcia!"

Carson regained his seat, his face like thunder.

Oates, feeling uncomfortable, said, "Every word I've told you is the truth, Mr. Carson. Darlene Williams means to take over the whole range, yours included."

A few minutes passed, the only sound the ticking of a tall grandfather clock in the corner and the distant squeak of a waterwheel.

Then someone scratched at the door, and Carson yelled, "Come in!"

A slim, handsome Mexican stepped inside. He wore two Colts low on his thighs and a wide sombrero dangled in his hands.

Carson turned to the vaquero. "Garcia, if it came down to it, could you shade Clem Halleck with the iron?"

"*Sí, Patrón.*"

"How about Charles McWilliams?"

Garcia hesitated a heartbeat, then said, "*Sí, Patrón.*"

"That will be all," Carson said, "but stay close."

A look of relief flashed across the vaquero's face. Then he turned and fled.

Carson smiled without humor. "It would seem that I have little to fear from gunmen."

"Mr. Carson, you have everything to fear from Darlene McWilliams," Oates said.

The rancher smiled. "Harsh words, Mr. Oates, about the woman I intend to marry."

The door to Oates' bedroom had been left opened, and Darlene McWilliams, wearing a pink, embroidered nightdress, stepped beside Carson and laid her hand protectively on his shoulder.

She looked breathtakingly beautiful . . . and she was smiling.

Chapter 24

Tom Carson reached up and placed his hand on Darlene's.

"Mr. Oates, you've been lied to by a whore," he said. "You see, shortly after she arrived, I met Darlene in Alma. She told me she'd sold her ranch and was looking to buy a new property. Of course, what she and I did not count on was that we'd fall in love at first sight. That very night in Alma, I asked her to marry me and she consented."

"The best and easiest decision I ever made in my life," Darlene said.

Oates was stunned. "How did she explain her long absences, the time she spent chasing after Stella?"

"She wanted her money—"

"Our money," Darlene corrected.

Carson smiled. "Yes, our money. She wanted it back from the woman who stole it from her. I can't blame Darlene for that."

"But the gunmen . . . Clem Halleck and his pa. The others . . ."

"Mr. Oates," Darlene said sweetly, "I hire drovers, not gunmen."

The woman had spoken softly, smiling, but her suppressed rage was almost like a malevolent physical presence in the room.

His voice choking in his throat, he knew he was losing. "Mr. Carson, this woman hid out in a canyon in the Gila, maybe fearing the hemp posse that was after her would not stop at the border. Was that the act of an innocent person?"

Carson opened his mouth to speak, but Darlene beat him to it. "I was a stranger in a strange land and the Apaches were burning and killing everywhere. I was very afraid and I had to protect my men and my herd." She raised an eyebrow. "Under those circumstances, wouldn't you have hid out in the Gila, Mr. Oates?"

"Damn it, you killed my friend, old Jacob Yearly, a man who wouldn't hurt a fly."

"I did try to buy his cabin, yes. But that was before I met Tom. You and that insane old man threw down on my cowboys and killed three of them." She hesitated. "That was murder, Mr. Oates."

"Darlene," Oates said with great finality, "Stella Spinner might be a whore, but I'd take her word over yours for anything. You're a damned liar."

Carson jumped to his feet. "I've heard enough. Oates. I said you'd changed, but you're still a damned drunk. By rights I should gun you right where you stand for the insults you have leveled at my future bride. But I won't kill a man I invited under my roof and who ate my food."

He strode to the door and opened it wide. "Garcia, see this man to his horse and escort him off my land."

Oates rose and walked out the cabin door. Garcia was waiting for him.

"Mr. Carson," Oates said, "be careful. She will try to kill you."

The door slammed in his face and Garcia said, "Please, this way, senor."

The vaquero rode with Oates back to the hill country between the mountains. Before he turned and rode away, he said, "Best you don't come back here, senor. It is for your own good I'm telling you this."

"Everything I said to your boss was the truth," Oates said. He couldn't understand why he was doing that, trying to justify himself to this man.

Garcia shrugged. "The *patrón* doesn't take me into his confidence, so I don't know about these things."

Without another word, the vaquero swung his horse and headed back the way he had come.

Oates watched the man leave, then headed east, a sense of utter defeat weighing on him. Love at first sight . . . marriage . . . she'd done it all so quickly.

Darlene McWilliams had won.

The day was waning and darkness would soon find him as Oates saw Black Mountain rise against a rose-colored sky tinted with gold and scarlet.

Acting on a sudden hunch, he rode toward old Jacob's cabin, and as he'd expected, the herd was gone. Darlene McWilliams must have given orders to move her cattle onto Circle-T range that very day. She was losing no time in her bid to take over Tom Carson's ranch.

Oates approached the cabin warily, fearful that a few of Darlene's riders might have stayed behind. But there was no sign of life and every staring window was a rectangle of blackness.

He stepped out of the leather, let the mustang's reins trail and opened the door, his gun in hand. His mouth was dry and his heart thudded in his chest.

But inside he saw only gloom, the last of the afternoon light seeping through the cabin window, forming a tracery of misty gray where shadows lurked.

Everything pointed to a hasty exit. An empty whiskey bottle was tipped over on the table, dirty dishes lay everywhere and the blanket that had covered the door to the bedroom was torn down and trampled underfoot. Jacob's old leather chair was gone, and in its place was a rickety bench that had been hurriedly cobbled together.

But the fire he had set had not done the damage to the bedroom Oates had expected.

Darlene had slept on Pete Yearly's bed and the dresser in the room was scorched but had still been usable, as some spilled face powder attested. Apart from that, she had taken everything she owned with her, and only the powder suggested that the woman had ever been there.

Oates left the cabin and walked down to the cookhouse. Greasy pots and dishes were scattered all over the rough pine table and rats scurried at his approach. But to his joy he found an unopened sack of coffee, a coffeepot and cans of beef, peaches and vegetables.

Throwing his finds into an empty flour sack, Oates returned to the cabin.

It was now fully dark and he lit a lamp against the gloom, then stepped outside again to take care of his horse.

Oates was not hungry, but he was tired from the long riding of the day and the reception he'd received at the Carson ranch. Yawning, he stretched, then carried the lamp into the bedroom. He removed his boots and hat and hung his gun belt on the bed, close to hand.

That done, he blew out the lamp and stretched luxuriously on the protesting cot and was asleep almost instantly.

The horned moon rose, nudging at the stars that filled the sky, and the night crowded close around the cabin. Out in the corral, the paint lifted its head, listening to the yips of hunting coyotes. It whinnied softly and stomped a foot, made restless by the wind that explored among the trees and set the open cookhouse door to creaking. Somewhere an owl asked its question of the witching hour, then looked around with luminous eyes, seeking an answer.

Eddie Oates slept on, wandering in darkness.

The moon dropped lower in the sky and the brilliance of the stars grew in intensity. A big dog coyote, old as sin, trotted toward the corral. But the mustang threw up its head and reared, and the coyote turned and slunk away like a shadow.

Oates stirred and his eyes flew open, staring into a black wall. Then he turned and saw firelight cast a scarlet, flickering rectangle on the floor.

He rose and padded on sock feet into the cabin.

The room had changed. Everything was back to what it was, and Jacob Yearly sat in his chair, smoking his pipe, an open book on his lap. Without turning, the old man smiled and said, "Howdy, Eddie. It's been a spell."

Oates stepped closer. Jacob's eyes shone like rubies as they caught and held the firelight.

"I've come to warn you about something, Eddie. Something wicked this way comes."

"It's Darlene McWilliams," Oates said. His voice sounded hollow, as though he was talking in a tunnel.

"It's a man, Eddie. But you're right, she'll still be the worst of them."

"Who is this man?"

"You'll know him when you see him."

"Jacob, I'm having a dream. Isn't this a dream?"

The old man nodded. "Yes, this is a dream. But the man I'm telling you about will be a nightmare."

"How will I know . . ."

Eddie Oates woke, lying on his back on the bed. He stared up at the rafters where the spiders live. Daylight streamed through the door to the cabin and outside he heard the song of morning birds.

He swung off the bed and stepped through the door. The room was as he'd found it the day before and the ashes in the fireplace had many days ago gone cold.

Oates slumped onto the bench, his face in his hands. He'd had a bad dream, was all. Drunks like him had them all the time. They saw and spoke to things that breathed and hissed and moved but weren't there.

He rose and stepped to the table and picked up the whiskey bottle. On the label it said KENTUCKY STRAIGHT BOURBON, but inside the bottle was as dry as mummy dust. Oates held the neck to his nose. The odor was still there, the vibrantly complex, buttery aroma of oak, sherry wine, leather, creamy vanilla and dried fruit. Saliva jetted from back corners of his jaws and his head swam.

He held the bottle at arm's length, his eyes again caressing the label. Then he threw the bottle against the far wall, where it exploded into a thousand fragments.

Oates turned and he saw the open book on the bench. It had not been there before. He couldn't have missed it. He picked up the volume and looked at the title, William Shakespeare's *Macbeth*.

The book had been opened to act 4, scene 1. His eyes quickly skimmed over the lines but stopped abruptly when he read the words of the Second Witch: "By the pricking of my thumbs, something wicked this way comes."

A vague, unfocused fear spiked at Oates. Despite the

warmth of the morning sunlight streaming through the cabin window, he shivered. He carried the book back to the bedroom, where he threw it on the cot.

Old Jacob had warned him. But about whom . . . or what?

Chapter 25

Jacob Yearly's cabin had afforded Oates, for the first time in his life, a measure of, if not happiness, then contentment. And he was reluctant to leave.

The old wagon was still there, and after a struggle during which he was kicked three times and bitten once, he hitched up the mustang to the traces and spent the rest of that day at Black Mountain cutting and loading lava rock.

He had no idea if the Mormon trader would be back, but if he did return, he'd expect to see a supply of cinder block.

That evening he bathed in the creek, then mended gear and worked around the place. After a supper of chili made with canned beef, beans and spices he'd found, he went to bed just after dark and slept soundly.

Next morning, still groggy from sleep, Oates sat on the stoop of the cabin door and drank coffee in the cool dawn air.

He saw the rider from far off.

Oates laid his cup on the stoop, went inside and buckled on his gun belt. He returned, sat once again and took up his cup.

As the rider came closer, Oates studied him, and was unimpressed.

He was a small, frail-looking man sitting a worn saddle on a moth-eaten, one-eared mule. The rider wore a high-button suit, a plug hat and looked uncomfortably hot in a celluloid collar and red-and-black striped tie. Chinless, he had a top lip that overhung a small, prissy mouth. Perched on a prominent, thin nose, very red at the tip, were a pair of pince-nez spectacles. As he rode up to the cabin, Oates saw that the little man's eyes were pale green, the whites shot with a tracery of scarlet veins.

Hung from his saddle were a carpetbag and a rectangular leather case, carved with the initials PJP.

The man drew rein on the mule and smiled, revealing widely separated teeth the size and color of pinto beans. "Good day to you, sir," he said. "A fine morning, is it not?"

Oates allowed that it was, then said, "Passing through?"

"Oh, deary me, yes. Passing through."

"The Apaches are out. A thing you should have been told."

"Not any longer. I was assured by an army officer in Alma that the cavalry have driven the savages out of the Gila and back into Arizona."

"He should know."

The little man sat back in the saddle. "My name is

Peter Jasper Pickles, by the way. I travel in ladies' undergarments of an intimate nature." He patted the
leather case. "My products tend to be of a practical
rather than ornate nature. As Mrs. Pickles once told me,
speaking of bloomers, 'Peter Jasper, the costume of
women should be suited to their wants and necessities.
Bloomers should conduce in a trice to their health,
comfort and usefulness. And while bloomers should
also not fail to conduce to their personal adornment,
they should make that end of secondary importance.'"
Pickles bobbed his head. "A very wise woman, my
wife, and quite the expert on ladies' undergarments.
Oh, deary me, yes."

Oates saw no evidence on Pickles of a hideout gun
and the man looked exactly what he claimed to be, a
small, timid, henpecked drummer who traveled in
practical, cotton bloomers.

"Something wicked this way comes . . ." but surely it
couldn't be Peter Jasper Pickles.

"Name's Eddie Oates and I've got coffee on the
stove," Oates said.

"Thank you, Mr. Oates, but I don't indulge." He
tapped his stomach. "Dyspepsia, you understand. Mrs.
Pickles always says that the sovereign remedy for dyspepsia is three tablespoons of warm cow's milk taken
night and morning. As in all things, she is correct, for
the milk sweetens my stomach and keeps the dreadful
ailment at bay."

"Where you headed, Pickles?" Oates asked.

"A town named Heartbreak. It's to the east of here."

"I've heard of the place, but I've never been there."

Oates wondered if he should be heeding the alarm bell ringing in his head. "It's a fair piece."

Pickles smiled. "Everyone says exactly what you do, Mr. Oates, that they've heard of the town but never been there." He tapped a forefinger to the side of his beaky nose. "But I've heard on good authority that the place is full of women, attracted by the lure of rich silver miners. Where there are females, there is a market for bloomers, Mr. Oates. And I go where the customers are."

He leaned forward in the saddle, as if he were about to impart a great secret. "I've heard that many of the marriage-minded young ladies who flock to Heartbreak go partway by barge up the Gila River. If you'll forgive a little salesman humor, the miners call the barges 'the Fishing Fleet.'"

Pickles slapped his thigh and laughed, a thin, high-pitched wail. "I told that to Mrs. Pickles as a good joke, but somehow she failed to appreciate its drollery."

Oates nodded and managed a smile. "Yeah, it's funny."

The little man lifted his hat, revealing a bald head thinly covered by strands of combed-over hair from just above his left ear. "Well, I have a long journey ahead of me and I must be on my way. It's been wonderful talking to you, Mr. Oates."

Pickles looked over Oates' shoulder to the open cabin door. "That is, unless you have any ladies to home?"

"Nary a one," Oates said, shaking his head. "I'm all by myself."

"Ah, too bad." Pickles swung his mule away. "Well, good day to you, sir."

Suddenly Oates was chilled to the marrow of his bones. It had only been a fleeting glimpse, an impression he'd caught for just an instant.

He rose to his feet, looking after the man. What had he seen in Pickles' face?

Chapter 26

Eddie Oates leaned on the corral fence in the bright morning light, looking at but not seeing the mustang. For its part, the little paint had retreated to a far corner, recalling the wagon and the hot, dusty misery of Black Mountain. It had no desire to go back there ever again.

But cutting into lava with pick and shovel was far from Oates' mind. He was trying to visualize Pickles' face again, the way it was for that instant. It was as though the man's mask had slipped and . . .

No, it wasn't that.

Then he remembered. It was his eyes. Slanted in his direction, for a single moment they'd gleamed green, feral, menacing, the untamed eyes of a dangerous hunting animal. They were the eyes of a man who could kill coldly and professionally, without hate.

Oates shook his head. He was being ridiculous. The little, inoffensive man sold bloomers, not his gun, if he even had a gun.

What was in the leather case?

The man had tapped the case when he spoke of his merchandise, but it was long and narrow. How were bloomers packed? Oates allowed that he was not an expert on women's fixings, but surely they were folded and not rolled lengthwise.

Was it a rifle case, for a high-powered weapon?

P. J. Pickles, a sure-thing killer hired by Darlene McWilliams to get her money back and murder those responsible for its theft? Or Peter Jasper Pickles, drummer and expert on female garments of an intimate nature?

What was he?

Oates pushed away from the corral. He was being ridiculous. A bad dream about Jacob Yearly had him spooked, was all. Pickles was what he seemed, a traveling drummer.

Then he remembered the man's eyes ... and he wasn't sure of anything.

His indecision made Oates remain close to the cabin that day, but he was careful to stay away from the door and window after the lamp was lit.

That night he slept with a gun close at hand, and he was awake before first light. He made a quick breakfast of canned meat and coffee, saddled the paint and was on the trail east just as dawn was breaking.

He had reached a decision in the night. If Pickles was really a hired killer, then he must warn Stella and the others. They were with the man who freed them from the siege at the cave, but if he was still alive, he might trust an inoffensive little man who sold bloomers for a living. He might even turn his back on him. . . .

Oates kicked the paint into a trot. He had already lost too much time by hanging around the cabin yesterday and he cursed himself for being an indecisive fool.

He'd let Pickles lure him into a false sense of security. He'd heard it said that Billy the Kid was a harmless-looking fellow, and so were lawmen Bat Masterson and Texas John Slaughter. Small, quiet-spoken men, none of them seemed likely killers, but they were.

Around the saloons, Oates had often heard men talk of hired, sure-thing assassins and bounty hunters.

If Pickles was indeed one of those, his looks were deceiving. No doubt he depended on them as a cover when he rode into a place, killed someone and then quietly left.

There was nothing about the little man that would draw attention to him. In his guise as a bloomers drummer, he would make sure to stay away from saloons where rotgut whiskey often led to offense when none was intended and then to war talk and gunfire.

Men like Pickles did not seek fame or a reputation as gunfighters. He'd consider it the height of folly to engage a man in a gunfight when there was no profit in it. That was not good business. Manhunting was his profession and he'd be good at it.

The more he thought about it, the more Oates became convinced that Pickles was the nightmare Jacob Yearly had talked about in his dream.

"Something wicked this way comes. . . ."

And it came, not in the shape of a ferocious gunman, but in the guise of a small, dyspeptic drummer riding a one-eared flea-bait mule.

Oates rode alert in the saddle, his eyes constantly searching the trees and high, rocky ridges. The trail east from Black Mountain was becoming more familiar to him and wherever possible he kept close to the ponderosa pine and aspen forests where a man could find cover fast if he was put to it.

But when the day was just beginning to fade, Oates again entered unknown country, the pine-covered slope of Lookout Mountain rising just ahead of him. To the northeast lay the Sierra Cuchillo and to the west the waterless, desert badlands began.

Oates sat his horse and looked around him. He saw no evidence of a town.

Then something to the south caught his eye.

Behind a shallow ridge, smoke was rising straight as a string into the air, a smudge of black against the red and lilac sky.

Was that where Heartbreak lay?

Keeping the paint to a walk, Oates rode across a hundred yards of flat ground, then urged the mustang up the sage and piñon slope. At the top he drew rein and felt a pang of disappointment.

Below, next to a thin ribbon of creek, lay a ramshackle, unpainted shack and beside it a sorry corral, cobbled together by baling wire and whatever crooked rails were easily available. A shed that did duty as a barn was drunkenly lopsided and was supported by slanted poles. Muddy black pigs rooted close to the cabin and the grounds were dirty and unkempt, littered with discarded food cans and whiskey bottles. Even from his lofty perch on the ridge, Oates caught the vile stench of the place.

There were three horses in the corral, all of them good-quality animals.

It was a spot to avoid, but whoever lived there might know where he could find Heartbreak.

Oates came off the ridge and reined up outside the shack.

Suddenly a huge, bearded man with ugly, piggy eyes loomed in the doorway.

"What the hell do you want?" he said. His right hand was out of sight.

It was an unfriendly greeting to be sure, but Oates let it go. No one knew better than he that not everyone in the West was a paragon of hospitality.

"I'm looking for—"

"Be off with you," the big man snapped. "There's no bed and grub for you here."

Oates opened his mouth to speak again, but stopped when a young Apache girl, carrying a water jug, brushed past the man and headed for the creek.

The girl, barely a teenager, was dressed in the Mexican fashion in a shirt and long skirt, a leather belt decorated with conchas around her slim waist. Her swollen, bruised face testified to a recent beating and she walked with a limp, favoring her left leg.

When Oates looked back to the door, two men were now standing there. The bigger man had stepped aside and next to him was a towheaded runt wearing a dirty undershirt and long johns. He'd buckled a Colt around his waist and had also strapped on an insolent grin.

"What's the saddle tramp want?" he asked the big man.

"A bed an' grub probably. I've told him to git, an' he better git fast."

The towhead stood on tiptoe and whispered something into the bearded man's ear and Oates saw his expression change. He'd been surly before; now he looked sly.

"Dallas here has just reminded me of my bounden duty to be hospitable to strangers," he said. "I most profoundly apologize. Why don't you step down, Mister, and come inside, like you was visiting kinfolk?"

The towhead put space between him and the big man, and he grinned as he studied Oates thinking things over.

Oates had no illusions over what was going to happen. The Winchester under his knee, the Colt on his hip, his horse and saddle represented more than three months wages to trash like this. They were not about to let him ride out of here alive.

The Apache girl was returning to the cabin. When she heard what the big man said, the eyes she lifted to Oates were bright with alarm . . . and warning.

Oates remembered the horses in the corral. Was there a third man?

His skin crawling, he looked around him. There he saw it! A quick flicker of shadow behind the shack's open window. It was there; then it was gone.

Playing his hand close to his chest, Oates smiled and said, "Thank you for the offer, but I got to be moving on. But if you could direct me to the town of Heartbreak, I'd be right obliged."

Every nerve in his body tingling, Oates' perceptions were sharpened, as if he were looking at the scene before him through the wrong end of a telescope.

He noticed a slight turn of the big man's head toward the window, a subtle movement Oates might have missed a few moments before.

He drew and fired in the same instant, then fired again.

There was the sound of shattering glass. Then a man screamed, followed by a high-pitched, bubbling shriek that ended in a drawn-out wail.

"Damn you!" the towhead yelled. His hand was dropping for his gun, but he froze when he saw Oates' Colt already covering him. The man's fingers opened and his revolver dropped back into the leather.

"Hell, I never took ye for a draw fighter," he said, his face incredulous. "You don't hardly look the type."

"Unbuckle the belt, let it fall, then step away from it," said Oates.

The towhead did as he was told, studiously taking three sliding steps to his right. He looked up at Oates. "Inside," he said, "I think ye done fer ol' Meacham."

"He had his chance," Oates said.

The big bearded man was rooted to the spot. A Colt dangled from his right hand but he'd made no attempt to use it.

Oates looked at him. "Drop it."

As the towhead had done earlier, he opened his fingers and let the gun drop as if it were suddenly red hot.

"Mister," he said, "we was only funnin' you. We took ye fer a pilgrim, like." He turned to the man called Dallas. "Ain't that the truth?"

"Truth, lie, I don't think he's gonna believe us anyhow, Jake," Dallas said.

"Now we're all acquainted," Oates said, "I'd still like to know—"

He stopped as the Apache girl suddenly dived beside Jake and picked up the gun he'd dropped. She took a step back, looked into the man's eyes, then fired into his crotch.

Jake screeched and fell to the ground. His knees drew up and he clutched at his bloody groin. After a while he sat up, and, as his kicking heels gouged runnels in the dust, he slipped his suspenders off his shoulders and dropped his pants.

He looked down and what he saw horrified him. It horrified Oates as well.

"Dallas," Jake hollered, "the Apache bitch has done fer me. She's blown it all away."

The towhead seemed less than sympathetic. "Jake, you was always goin' at her with that thing, mornin', noon an' night. What did you 'spect?"

Oates' couldn't muster much sympathy either. Stella had told him that a man can rape a whore. He can also rape an Indian girl.

"Dallas, you better get something to bandage what he's got left. He's bleeding like a stuck pig."

The man shook his head. "Mister, he ain't got nothing left."

"Bandage him anyway."

Dallas turned to go into the cabin, but Oates stopped him. "Use his shirt."

Oates swung out of the saddle. The man inside the cabin was still unaccounted for.

The Apache girl stood next to him, her black eyes on Jake, who was rolling around, wailing, resisting Dallas' attempts to staunch the flow of blood.

She turned to Oates. "Serves him right." She spat in Jake's direction. "Dirty, rutting pig!"

Oates smiled. "I guess you're the one to know about that."

He stepped toward the shack, but the girl stopped him. "I go. The one inside is just as bad as this one."

Before he could object, the girl swept past him and walked into the cabin. Oates heard two shots, then a scream. A few moments later she appeared at the door, the smoking Colt at her side.

"He was still alive," she said. "Now he's dead."

Dallas had heard enough. His face wild, he sprang to his feet and ran for the ridge.

The Apache girl sent a couple of bullets after him, but Dallas quickly disappeared over the rise. She shook her head. "He is not a warrior. There would have been no honor in killing him."

Jake looked up at Oates, his face twisted in agony, his eyes pleading. "You ain't just gonna ride away an' leave me here."

Oates shrugged. "Not much else I can do. You sure as hell can't fork a bronc."

"Take me inside." Jake cast a fearful glance at the girl. "An' don't let that Apache bitch near me."

"She sure don't like you much, Jake. Look at her, seems like she cottons to cutting you up some."

"She's done enough already. I ain't gonna be much use to the whores no more."

Oates nodded. "I was going to say times are hard all over, but with you in your present condition I won't."

The big man groaned and fell on his back, clutching at himself.

Remembering old Jacob's instructions, "Always reload after a desperate action. An empty gun ain't nothing but a chunk of iron," Oates punched out the empty shells from his Colt and slid fresh rounds into the chambers.

He holstered his gun and stepped into the shack. The dead man could have been Jake's twin, only dirtier. It looked to Oates that the bullet he'd fired had grazed the man's head. But he had two other, deadlier wounds to the groin and chest.

Oates shook his head. Apache women were not ones to forgive and forget.

Chapter 27

Oates dragged the dead man outside, then helped Jake into his bed, a filthy cot that stank even worse than the rest of the shack.

He lit a lamp against the growing darkness and said, "After we're gone, Dallas will come back and take care of you."

"I paid twenty dollars in silver for that squaw," Jake groaned. "Worst investment I ever made. Damned Mexicans didn't tell me she was plumb crazy."

"Apaches are notional," Oates said.

He turned to leave, but Jake's voice stopped him. "You got to stay close. I'm bleedin' to death here."

"You should've thought about that before you planned on robbing and killing me," Oates said. "And before you treated the girl so badly. What is she? Fifteen maybe?"

"You go to hell," Jake said. He was fixated on his bloody, ruined groin and didn't look up.

Oates smiled. "I'll save you a place by the fire, Jake."

Ignoring the curses Jake hurled in his direction, he searched around the shack and took what supplies he could find, a side of bacon, cans of beans, coffee and a small pot.

Studiously, Oates stepped around a corked, earthenware jug. He knew only too well what it contained and he heard its siren song. After a battle with himself, he gave in enough to lift the jug. He shook it and let the whiskey talk to him, promising him the world. After a while he set the jug down again and walked away from it, turning his back on the only friend he ever had. It was a betrayal . . . and it hurt him bad.

Oates sacked what he'd found and when he stepped outside again, the Apache girl was already sitting a rangy black with a white blaze and four white socks.

"This is Jake's pony," she said, then added proudly, "He doesn't need it anymore." Her black eyes dropped to Oates. "You are a great warrior. I will go with you."

Oates shook his head. "Girl, I'm riding a dangerous trail with an enemy behind every bush. I have to ride alone." He smiled, trying to reassure her. "You can go back to your own people now."

"I am Lipan. My people are far to the south. You are my people now."

The girl saw Oates' hesitation. "I am a good girl, a Catholic girl. I was taught at the mission by the holy nuns and I say my prayers to the Virgin every night. I did that even when Jake was grunting on top of me like a hog."

Her eyes misted. "My name is Nantan, and I don't understand why you wish to send me away. I'll be a good wife to you."

Oates tied the sack to his saddle, then swung onto the paint. "Nantan," he said, "if you want to buy into my troubles, then you're welcome to ride along." He shook his head at her. "By the way, my name is Eddie Oates and I sure don't want a wife."

The girl looked as though she hadn't heard. "I'll be good to you, Eddie," she said.

Oates let his shoulders sag. He wanted to talk sense to Nantan, but obviously she wasn't in the mood to listen. He tried a different tack. "I'm looking for a town called Heartbreak. Do you know where it is?"

"Once I heard Jake and the others talk of it, but they said they'd never been there."

"Did they say where it was located?"

Nantan stared, then shrugged. "No. They did not say."

A small disappointment in him, Oates said, "Let's find a place to camp well away from here before it gets much darker."

The girl nodded, her eyes downcast, suddenly the dutiful, obedient, Apache wife.

Oates groaned inwardly. Given all the difficulties he was facing, the last thing he needed on God's green earth was a woman problem.

As they rode away from the shack, Oates heard a despairing wail from inside.

He smiled and turned to Nantan. "I guess ol' Jake just tried to take a piss," he said.

Guided by moonlight, Oates found a place to camp among a group of boulders near a seep surrounded by a few pines and a single cottonwood.

After he tended to the horses, Oates built a fire and put water on for coffee. He speared strips of bacon on twigs and hung them over the fire to broil.

After he and Nantan ate and finished the last of the coffee, Oates put out the fire, then spread his blanket roll and stretched out. Nantan immediately snuggled beside him and Oates shook his head.

"You know, for a good Catholic girl, you're certainly bold," he said.

"I am tired, Eddie."

"I thought Apaches never got tired."

"Only the Catholics do."

The girl's eyes were closed and she fell asleep almost at once.

Oates lay awake for a while, looking up at the stars, listening to the coyotes talking into the night. He spent some time worrying over Peter Jasper Pickles, the whereabouts of Heartbreak, Darlene McWilliams' next move and the well-being of Stella and the others. He searched his mind for other things to trouble himself with and found plenty. . . .

But then he too slept, and the only sound was of his and Nantan's breathing and the distant cry of the coyotes.

When Oates woke to a hazy morning, Nantan was gone.

He rose and checked on the horses. The black was no longer there.

Oates felt a conflict of emotions.

Apaches were notional and it seemed that Nantan

had taken the notion to ride off and go back to her own people. That removed the wife problem, but still, he experienced a sense of loss. The girl had sand, as she'd demonstrated at the shack when she'd gunned Jake. She was also right pretty and might even be beautiful once the swollen bruises on her face healed.

He recalled the rhythmic pulse of her back against his and the soft whisper of her breathing in the night. Now the only voices he heard were echoes of his own thoughts, the sound shadows of a lonely man.

Under a gray sky that threatened summer rain, Oates made a hasty breakfast of coffee and bacon, then saddled the paint. He planned to sweep north in his hunt for Heartbreak, riding the high country parallel to the Sierra Cuchillo. If that failed, he'd turn south again.

The rain that had threatened earlier was falling and Oates buttoned into his slicker as he swung the paint north, heading into a rugged wilderness of dizzying, sawtoothed peaks, rocky ridges and dense forests of aspen and pine that prospered mightily eight thousand feet above the flat.

After an hour, the weather grew worse. Lightning scrawled across above the misty summits of the mountains like the signature of a demented god, and thunder crashed.

Oates found his way blocked by a wide canyon. Not trusting a slippery descent in a hammering downpour, he swung into a stand of pines where there was some shelter from the rain. He stepped out of the leather and

let the mustang forage on whatever it could find among
the trees.

Wet, miserable and lost, Oates looked out at the rain-
lashed landscape, a vast panorama of mountains and
black, fractured sky. He would not attempt to cross the
canyon until the weather cleared, though when that
might be he had no idea.

As to what lay beyond the gorge, he couldn't even
guess. More high desert country he suspected, that
went on and on and never stopped. Maybe the land
stretched clear to the roof of the world where traveling
men said snow-white bears hunted with great, blue
whales.

Discouraged, cold drops of water trickling down the
back of his neck, Oates stood and waited, like a man
with all the time in the world. . . .

Nantan saved him.

She came up from the south, riding the black
through the raging storm.

Oates saw her and yelled, and the girl swung toward him. She was soaked to the skin, her shirt clinging to her breasts, her long, dark hair hanging in wet
strands over her shoulders.

She rode into the trees and sat the horse, looking
down at Oates. "Why did you not wait for me?" she
asked.

He saw anger in her eyes. "I thought you'd gone,"
he said, then added lamely, "back to your people."

"I told you, Eddie, you are my people now. Nantan
is your wife."

Oates let that go. Now was not the time to discuss his marital status. "Where did you go?"

"I did what an Apache wife does. I went out early to search for your town."

Hope flared in Oates. "Did you find it?"

The girl nodded. "I met a man. He told me where it was. It is south of here, west of the Salado Mountains, a place well-known to the Apache."

"A man? What manner of man?"

"A small man on a donkey."

"Nantan, was it a donkey or a mule?"

The girl shrugged. "Donkey, mule, what is the difference?" She reached behind her. "He gave me these as a present."

Nantan held out a pair of frilly bloomers, threaded through with pink ribbon.

"I have not ever had such a present." The girl smiled. "*Nunca un tan bonito*: never one so pretty."

Oates felt a chill. "You spoke to this man. Did he say where he was going?"

"Yes, I spoke to him because we were strangers in the rain. He said he was going home to his wife." She held up the bloomers. "He said he'd sold many of these to the white women in Heartbreak."

"How did you find me?" Oates asked.

"Eddie, you are easy to follow, even for a Catholic Apache."

Oates shook his head, more a gesture of despair than disgust. In an empty land, two people meet by chance, one a sure-thing killer and dangerous enemy, the other an abused Apache girl who called herself his wife.

Was it fate? Or some twisted, cruel destiny that was even now mocking him?

Oates realized it was neither.

Pickles was headed out of Heartbreak and Nantan was searching in the same direction. Even in this wilderness the chances were fairly good that they'd meet.

Had the man already found Stella and the others and killed them?

When he reached the town he'd ask around and try to get a lead on them. Three whores, a gunman and a simple boy traveling together might be a happenstance that would stick in memories, especially if there was a lawman around.

Oates looked at Nantan. In the manner of Apache women, she'd known her man was contemplating something and would not interrupt his thoughts.

With a sudden pang of guilt, he saw that the girl was soaked through, getting wetter and shivering. He shrugged out of his slicker and held it up. "Come down," he said, smiling.

Nantan slid off the horse's back and Oates helped her into the coat. "Keep you a little drier and warmer."

The grateful, adoring glance the girl gave him made Oates feel even more guilty. "Let's hit the trail," he said gruffly.

With a cupped hand he helped the girl mount again. Then he swung into the saddle of the paint. "We'll find a nice, dry hotel in Heartbreak," he said. "And some decent grub."

Then Oates thought of P. J. Pickles out there on the trail somewhere, heading back to tell Darlene Mc-Williams with a smile that the job she'd paid him for was done.

If Stella, Nellie, Lorraine and Sammy were dead, he would not let Pickles live.

He'd go after the man and kill him.

Chapter 28

Oates and Nantan rode through driving rain. The day was as dark as night, black clouds hanging low over the treetops. Thunder roared and blustered, content to let the savage, lancing lightning do its dirty work.

A searing white bolt struck a ponderosa not fifty yards from Nantan, who was taking up the rear. The tree split with a loud crack and burst into a column of fire. The blaze lasted for a couple of minutes until the rain pounded the inferno into submission. Soon only a few flames fluttered like scarlet moths on the charred trunk.

Oates turned in the saddle and said, "That was way too close."

Nantan heard, but did not answer. By the shocked look on her face, she also thought it was close.

By noon Oates and the girl were riding parallel to the south bank of Cuchillo Creek, past lofty cottonwoods and a few hardwoods. There had been no letup in the rain and thunder still growled in the distance.

Nantan kneed her horse beside Oates, water running down her face. "If we follow the creek, we'll come to a stage station," she said. "Maybe we can get out of the rain for a while."

"How far?" Oates asked.

"An hour's ride, less. That is, if Victorio didn't burn it."

Oates nodded. "I could sure use some coffee."

"Jake took me there one time," she said. "He was meeting Dallas at the stage." She rode closer. "Jake killed a man that day."

"Why did he do that?"

"They played poker and Jake lost, so he killed the man."

Oates smiled. "Nantan, I hope they don't remember you."

"I was not inside. Jake tied me by my wrists to a tree. He said they didn't let Apache squaws into the station."

Oates waited until a peal of thunder passed, then said, "If you'd told me this back at the shack, I'd have put a bullet into ol' Jake my ownself."

Nantan smiled. "Now Jake must squat like a woman. It is enough."

The Cuchillo stage station was a low, squat, timber building with spacious corrals and a large barn. There were several other outbuildings, but as the two riders approached, these were lost and invisible in the rain.

A man stood in the shelter of the portico running the length of the cabin, smoking a cigar. His eyes were on

Oates and Nantan and, as they rode closer, the expression on his lean, leathery face was not particularly friendly.

Oates drew rein and said, "Howdy."

The man nodded. He wore a Colt on one hip and a huge bowie knife on the other.

"We were looking for coffee and a dry hour to drink it."

"Then you came to the right place." The man motioned with his head. "You can put your horses up in the barn. The hay is free, two bits for oats."

"You go inside, Eddie," Nantan said. "I'll take the horses."

"No need, I'll go with you."

The girl shook her head. "It is a wife's duty. You go inside."

The man on the porch was looking at Nantan curiously, and rather than create a scene, Oates stepped out of the saddle.

"Come inside," the man said. "Name's Bill Daley. I'm in charge of the station." He smiled. "And, Mister, you look like a drowned rat."

"Feel like one too," Oates allowed. "And the name's Eddie Oates."

The inside of the station was cramped but warm and dry. A couple of tables and benches took up much of the floor space, and a large, cast-iron cooking stove stood against one wall.

To Oates' left a couple of barrels and a pine board served as a bar and there was another, smaller table, where five people sat.

Oates' jaw dropped and he took a step back, bumping into someone standing behind him. He turned, then his eyes lifted . . . lifted again. He'd stepped on the toes of a man who stood at least nine inches over six feet from his miner's boots to the top of his battered plug hat. The look in the man's ice blue eyes was not encouraging.

"It's all right, Shamus," Stella Spinner said, rising from the table. "He's a friend."

The woman ran to Oates and hugged him close. "Eddie, I'm so glad you're here."

For the first time in Oates' life someone was happy at his coming, and it affected him deeply. He had trouble finding the words and later would not be able to recall what he said, but he did remember Stella leading him to the table.

And the shock that followed.

Lorraine, Nellie and Sam Tatum, grinning like a delighted possum, were there, and another man, his chest heavily bandaged.

Handsome as ever, though looking drawn and pale, was the riverboat gambler Warren Rivette.

The man took in Oates' gun, his soaked but good clothes and his fashionable dragoon mustache. "Pleased to see you again, Eddie," he said. "I'd say you've changed since the last time I saw you."

"Some."

Rivette waved a hand. "Take a seat."

Confused, Oates sat beside Stella. He looked at the gambler closely as he tried to grapple with the fact of his being there.

Rivette read Oates' eyes and smiled. "I don't quite know either, Eddie. The truth is that a man doesn't have a conscience. The conscience has the man. I thought you and Sam and the ladies had been roughly handled in Alma, so after the Apaches left, I went looking for you."

"As simple as that, huh?" Oates said.

Rivette shook his head. "No, nowhere near as simple as that. Why does a man do what he does? Sometimes he can't explain it." All eyes were on him and the gambler decided to lighten up. "Besides," he said, "I was getting mighty bored in Alma. All the interesting folks had been hung, shot by Apaches or banished."

Rivette pushed a bottle toward Oates. "Daley calls this whiskey. I call it something else. But you're welcome to make a trial of it."

Oates shook his head. "I'll pass, but thanks anyhow."

By the nature of his profession, a gambler needs to be a perceptive man and Rivette read the signs. "Shamus," he said to the big man who was hovering close by, "take this vile swill away. I'm deeply ashamed to offer it to my guests."

"Sure, Mr. Rivette," Shamus said, suspiciously eyeing Oates. He picked up the bottle and glasses and returned them to the bar.

Oates eased into conversation again. "I have someone with me," he said, "an Apache girl." He heard the door open and turned. "And here she is. Her name is Nantan."

Rain dripping from her slicker, her hair plastered

over her face, Nantan stepped to the table. Rivette, raised to be a gentleman, got to his feet and a blushing, grinning Sam Tatum did likewise.

Oates made the necessary introductions. Then Lorraine rose and rushed around the table. "You poor thing," she said to Nantan as she began to unbutton her slicker, "you're soaked through."

Her eyes moved past the girl to Daley who was lifting a sooty coffeepot off the stove. "Hey, Daley," she yelled, "after you've done that, move your lazy ass and bring me a towel."

"I've only got two hands, Lorraine," Daley said, setting the pot and cups on the table.

"Nobody knows better than me how many hands you got, Daley."

Nellie, looking prim, said, "I declare, Lorraine, you're such a whore."

"Takes one to know one, Nellie," Lorraine said.

Daley looked at Nantan as all three women now fussed over her, then to Oates. "First time I've ever had an Apache in here. Usually they're outside whoopin' and hollerin', if you catch my drift."

"Sorry," Oates said.

"Lipan, ain't she?"

"Yes. How did you know?"

"A man spends enough time around Apaches, he knows." Daley shrugged. "I've never had no trouble with Lipan."

The man turned away and walked behind the bar. Oates was uneasy. While he'd been talking to Daley he was sure he'd heard Nantan say the word "wife."

Now Stella confirmed it. "Well, congratulations, Eddie," she said, grinning. "I never took you for the marrying kind."

"I'm not married and she's not my wife," Oates protested. "We didn't have a churchin' or nothing like that."

"You could do worse, Eddie," Rivette said. "She's a right pretty girl."

Then Shamus, the big, ugly, broken-nosed Irishman, did something strange. He stepped to the table, dropped a huge ham of a hand on Oates' shoulder and said. "I can't say it in Apache, but a Mescalero woman taught me their wedding chant—"

"Damn it all," Oates said, "I told you, I'm not married."

"If Nantan says you're married, you're married," Lorraine said. She looked at Shamus. "Let the happy couple hear the wedding chant, Irishman. That ought to seal their bond, like."

Shamus took a breath and, his hands pounding a drumbeat on the table, chanted.

Now you will feel no rain,
for each of you will be shelter for the other.
Now you will feel no cold,
for each of you will be warmth to the other.
Now there will be no loneliness,
for each of you will be friend to the other.
Now you are two persons,
but there are three lives before you: his life, her life and
  your life together.

Go now to your dwelling place to enter into your days
together,
and may all your days be good and long upon the earth.

After Shamus was finished speaking, there was a round of applause. Rivette bowed and said, "Please sit at the table, Mrs. Oates, and have some coffee. It will warm you."

Stella made a place for the girl beside Oates and he was freed from commenting on the wedding issue when Rivette said, "Eddie, I guess that was you back at the ridge when I was pinned down by the McWilliams riders."

Oates poured coffee for him and Nantan, then nodded to the gambler's bandaged chest: "You took a bullet."

"It could have been worse. You saved my life that day."

Oates looked around the table, still hardly able to believe what he was seeing. "How did you all end up here?"

Rivette spoke up. "After I left the ridge, I knew I was hurt bad. Then at nightfall I saw a blazing fire on top of a mesa. I figured only you could be that dumb, Eddie. Anyway, I needed help, so I was willing to take a chance."

Sam Tatum said, "It was my fault, Mr. Oates. I lit a fire too close to the tree." The boy looked miserable. "I do silly things sometimes."

"We all do silly things, Sammy," Oates said. His eyes angled to Rivette. "Especially someone as dumb as me."

Rivette caught the look and smiled. "Sorry, Eddie. Like I said, you've changed considerably, so being dumb doesn't apply anymore."

The gambler pulled the coffeepot and a cup toward him. He inspected the inside of the cup before he poured, then said, "The ladies here patched me up as best they could, but they knew I needed rest. We set out for Heartbreak, but I couldn't make it, so I told them to detour here and we'd hole up until I recovered my strength."

Rivette found a cigar in his shirt pocket, bit off the end and Stella lit it for him. Through a cloud of blue smoke he said, "Bill Daley used to have a clip joint on the San Francisco waterfront and one time I helped him out in a shooting scrape. He wrote me a letter before I drifted to Alma and told me he'd gone straight and was running the Cuchillo stage station with Shamus here. I figured he owed me a favor."

Daley overheard and grinned. "Helping me out in a shooting scrape means he killed two men and wounded a third. They were trying to roll me in an alley, but made the mistake of drawing down on Rivette." He nodded. "I'll say I owe him a favor."

"You're lucky you found us, Eddie," Stella said. "We're heading for Heartbreak tomorrow."

Then Oates told them the bad news.

Chapter 29

Warren Rivette stayed his hand as his cup was halfway to his mouth. He set the cup back on the table without tasting the coffee.

"Pete Pickles took a contract on Stella?" he asked, his handsome face stiff with shock.

Oates nodded. Earlier he'd told the others about Darlene McWilliams' plan to marry Tom Carson and how she'd already moved her cattle onto the rancher's grass. Then he described his meeting with Pickles and how Nantan had met the man on the trail to Heartbreak.

"Warren, do you know this man Pickles?" Nellie asked.

"I know about him," Rivette answered. "I've heard some named guns, no pushovers themselves, say he's the most dangerous man west of the Mississippi. When Pete Pickles accepts a contract to kill a man, from then on in that man is as good as dead." He looked at Stella with bleak eyes. "Or woman."

Nantan spoke for the first time. "He seemed such a nice man. He gave me a present of"—she turned to Oates—"what do you call them, Eddie?"

"Bloomers." Oates looked at Rivette. "He's posing as a bloomers salesman."

The gambler's fingers moved to the Colt in his shoulder holster, as though it brought him a measure of comfort. "Pete Pickles can be what he wants to be. He's what the Navajo call a shape-shifter, a man who can himself turn into any animal he chooses. Now, Pete can't become a wolf or a coyote, but he can present himself as a preacher, a frail old woman, a bloomers drummer . . . anything that will help him get the job done. He's the original wolf in sheep's clothing.

"He offers a money-back guarantee, but he's never yet had to forgo his fee, no."

"How many men has he killed?" This came from Lorraine, who looked strained and more than a little frightened.

"I don't know exactly, but he set himself up in business at the end of the War Between the States and by this time the number of his victims could be in the hundreds. Most times Pickles kills with a rifle, but he'll use a garrote, knife, poison, fire . . . whatever suits his purpose."

Lorraine touched the back of Stella's hand with the tips of her fingers. "Honey, there will be law in Heartbreak," she said. "We'll be safe there."

Rivette said, "Eddie, can you and Nantan leave with us tomorrow at first light? There's safety in numbers on a watched trail."

Oates nodded. "Sure we will, though a man like Pickles will tend to be sudden."

"That's a chance we'll have to take. We'll have four women riding with us and the only description he'll have of Stella is the one Darlene McWilliams gave him."

"Pickles will recognize me all the same," Stella said. "He'll know I'm the one that's doing the trembling."

After a breakfast of elk steak and eggs provided by Daley, Oates and the others saddled up in the thin, predawn light. The rain had stopped for now, but the black sky showed no promise of a brighter afternoon.

Daley stood beside Rivette's horse and looked up at the gambler. "I wish I could send Shamus with you, Warren," he said. "He's a good man in a fight, but I need him here when the stages arrive." His eyes pleaded for understanding. "You see how it is with me."

"You've already done enough, Bill, and I'm beholden to you," Rivette said. "We'll meet again soon."

"*Buena suerte, mi amigo,*" Daley said. "And ride careful."

Rivette was still weak from his wound and Oates took the point as they rode into a glowering morning that offered nothing but a keening wind and the prospect of rain to come.

They rode directly south, across rolling land forested with ponderosa pine and juniper, here and there passing ridges of bare, granite rock. Nantan caught up with Oates and told him it was here that she'd met Pete Pickles.

Oates looked around him and nodded. "It's bushwhacking country, no doubt of that," he said. "Stay with me, Nantan, and keep your eyes skinned."

After an hour they left Mud Spring Mountains behind them, then swung to the southwest and headed for Palomas Creek. Farther to the west lay the deeply gouged breaks of the Salado Mountains, a bastard child of the vast Black Range.

The rain started as Oates and Nantan rode up on the creek. They sheltered under the cottonwoods and waited for the others.

"You know the first thing I'm going to do when we reach Heartbreak?" Lorraine said as she huddled against the trunk of a tree.

"No, what?" Stella asked.

"Have a hot bath, then head down to the nearest ladies' shop and buy me a new dress and shoes. Oh, and a hat with flowers on it."

"I hope you do, Lorraine," Nellie sniffed. "You've been traipsing around the country long enough in a shift that's all in rags and a coat not even a tramp would wear." She looked around at the others, huge raindrops falling over them from the cottonwood branches. "You know what I'm going to do?"

"Do tell," Lorraine said. "You're such a dear."

"Check into the hotel, have a bath, then roll into a soft bed with feather pillows. I plan to stay there for a week at least."

"How will you eat?" Stella asked.

"Lorraine will bring me food, won't you, Lorraine? You can wear your nice, new dress so you don't lower the tone of the place."

Stella smiled. "We're all looking pretty shabby. If we're to open our own house, each one of us needs new clothes."

"I'm gonna get more paper and pencils," Tatum said. "Then a peppermint candy stick." He looked around at the people watching him and added defensively, "Well, I like candy sticks."

"How about you, Eddie?" Lorraine asked.

Oates shrugged. "I don't rightly know," he said.

"Buy a dress for Nantan, to match her new bloomers," Nellie suggested.

"That's a thought," Oates said. He looked at Rivette. "How about you?"

"Belly up to a poker game. Who knows? Maybe I've finally outrun my losing streak."

Nantan said nothing, looking a little lost, prompting Lorraine to ask, "What about you, honey? What do you want to do in Heartbreak?"

"Just be with my husband," Nantan said, "as a good Catholic girl should."

Oates was surprised. This time Nantan's words didn't trouble him a bit.

Stella looked up through the tree branches at the leaden sky. "Well, since we all have urgent reasons to be in Heartbreak, I suggest we hit the trail."

"Right! Rain or no rain," Tatum said. "We're not made of sugar and we won't melt."

Stella smiled. "Sam, you're as smart as a whip."

Oates mounted before anyone else. "I'll scout the country beyond the creek," he said. "We think Heartbreak is right ahead of us, huh?"

Rivette said, "Yes, it is. Bill Daley said he rode past it one time, but never stopped there. He says once we clear the creek and head due south, we'll ride right into Main Street, and Bill isn't a man to lie, no."

"I'll take Nantan with me," Oates said. "She's a better scout than me."

Helped by wide sandbars, Oates and the girl splashed across the creek and rode south under a roof of thunder, their heads bent into a slogging rain.

Nantan's eyes were everywhere, on the way ahead and their back trail. She seemed uneasy, on edge, and Oates caught her mood.

He guessed that she had the same thought he did: when would Pete Pickles make his move?

The rugged hill country around Oates and Nantan was hemmed in on both sides by forested mountain peaks and rugged crags. The Rio Grande lay just five miles to the east, its often-turbulent waters making their way toward Texas and the Gulf of Mexico, and beyond the river lay the desert badlands.

Oates figured the elevation was about four thousand feet above the flat, but the land was rising sharply and forests of mixed juniper and aspen were becoming more common.

Nantan lay back, her head turning constantly as she searched the gray, rain-lashed land.

Oates knew the girl sensed danger, but was it here, now, or stalking their future? If he asked her, she wouldn't be able to tell him. He knew that. Apaches had an instinct that warned them of hostile country, but they were seldom able to pinpoint a cause. They felt the threat deep in their being, like a man who turns and stares into the darkness, hearing soundless footsteps behind him.

Despite the rumble of thunder and the rattle of the downpour, Nantan was hearing something that deeply disturbed her ... and Oates felt a coldness in his belly he recognized as fear.

Ahead of him the rocky crest of a hogback made a break between stands of aspen and he rode in that direction, hoping for a better view of the terrain.

Oates reached the top of the hill and his face split into a delighted grin. "Nantan," he yelled, waving the girl close. "Look!"

A town lay at the bottom of the rise, a single street with a row of buildings on either side. To the west of town ran a fair stream, bordered by spreading cottonwoods, spanned by a well-constructed timber bridge. A cluster of outlying shacks lay to the west and north, several grander houses among them.

Even from a distance, the place looked worn and weather-beaten, the still, shabby buildings silver gray behind the shifting veil of the rain.

But to Oates this was a great city, every bit as fabulous as glittering Dodge City, a welcome, warming sight for the weary traveler.

"Heartbreak," he said, taking Nantan's hand. "Girl, we made it."

Nantan's black eyes searched into the distance. "The women of this town do not cook, or light fires against the chill of the morning?"

Oates looked at her. "I'm not catching your drift."

"Where is the smoke?"

His gaze shifting to the town again, Oates studied the rooftops. He saw plenty of chimneys, but no rising smoke. Uneasily, he checked each window that was visible. All were in darkness. Surely, in a dreary, gray day, the town merchants would have lit lamps to banish the gloom, and so would the saloons.

There was no one on the street or boardwalks, not so unusual in itself as the townspeople would try to avoid the rain, but the very absence of human activity added to the desolate, forsaken atmosphere of the place.

Oates did not want to face the stark truth, but the proof was down there, forcing him to accept it.

Heartbreak, their goal for so long, was a ghost town.

Chapter 30

"Maybe," Stella said, "everybody's still asleep."

"It is early yet," Nellie said, "and people do like to stay late in bed on a rainy day."

Lorraine's eyes were bleak. "It's a dead town. There's nothing there for us."

"It seems to me we should ride down there and take a look," Rivette said. "Not much point in talking about it up here, no."

"At least we can shelter from the rain, huh?" Nellie said, smiling.

No one answered, bitter disappointment tugging at all of them.

Oates and Nantan in the lead, they crossed the bridge and rode into the street. Windows stared at them with cold, unfriendly eyes and somewhere a forlorn door banged incessantly in the gusting wind.

The stores were empty of goods, and many of their doors stood open, as though their owners had left in a hurry and had never returned. A single hat, frilled with white net and decorated with red flowers, stood askew on a stand in the window of the New York Chapeau Shoppe.

Lorraine urged her horse onto the boardwalk, rode into the store through its open door and grabbed the hat. When she emerged, her battered old sombrero was gone and the fancy chapeau was on her head.

"I declare, Lorraine," Nellie said, "that's stealing. You're such a whore."

"It's not stealing when nobody owns it," Lorraine said. "And it takes one to know one, Nellie."

They rode past a blacksmith shop, its forge long gone cold, then the Alamo, Sideboard and Last Chance saloons. All their windows were smashed and the roof of the Last Chance had fallen in along with one of its walls.

Set back from the street behind what had once been a well-tended lawn, now overgrown with cactus and bunchgrass, was the Bon View Hotel. It was a two-story timber building with fine balconies on both floors and it seemed to be largely intact, apart from a few broken windows and a front door that was off one of its hinges. But the place looked lost, as though it had wandered away from the town and couldn't find its way back.

The doors of the livery stable were open, but the stalls were empty, and a soaked coyote slunk away as they rode up on the burned-out hulk of Solly Diamond's Burlesque Theater and Dance Hall. Next door the First Bank of Heartbreak was also a charred shell, like the theater, probably the result of a lightning strike.

Beyond lay a few shacks in varying states of disrepair, then an endless vista of forested hills that invited the riders to share their somber loneliness.

Oates pulled up and without looking at the others, said, "Welcome to Heartbreak, the end of the trail and the ass end of everything."

Nellie was snuffling back tears and even Nantan looked numb, as though she'd looked around her and decided to retreat to a distant place.

"We'll put the horses up in the barn, then head back to the hotel," Oates said.

"Anything to get out of this rain," Lorraine said. "My new hat will be ruined."

There was still a supply of hay in the barn and a couple of sacks of oats that had been attacked by rats but still held enough to last their mounts a few days. The livery had a good, solid roof and was dry, and the horses seemed glad to be finally out of the weather.

"It feels good to be in a dry place," Nellie said as she stood in the middle of the hotel lobby, looking around her. "I wonder if there are still beds in the rooms?"

"Let's take a look," Lorraine said.

After the women went upstairs, Oates, Tatum and Rivette searched the rest of the hotel. There were no signs of hurried departure, half-eaten meals on the dining room tables, a newspaper dropped to the floor in the lobby or carbonized steaks on the grill that had continued to cook until the stove fire went out.

It looked as if the people had just abandoned the town and gone somewhere else.

"Apaches?" Oates asked Rivette.

The gambler shook his head. "I don't think so. Apaches would have burned the place."

"Mr. Rivette," Sam Tatum said, "why would the people leave?"

"Why does any town die? There could be a number of reasons. Most likely a prospector staked a silver claim, then others arrived hoping to strike it rich. When the claims didn't pan out, there was nothing to keep the miners here any longer."

He smiled at Tatum. "I think the name of the town should give you a fair clue to what folks ended up thinking about their prospects here."

"Two saloons, a theater and dance hall, and a fair-sized hotel," Oates said. "Somebody invested money."

Rivette nodded. "There are always people willing to take a chance, hoping for a boomtown. It just didn't happen. When the cards fall that way, all a man can do is pick up his chips and try somewhere else."

"But where did the people go?" Tatum insisted.

"I don't know, Sam, but I'd guess south to Silver City or Lordsburg." He looked around him, at the cob-webbed ceiling and dust lying thick everywhere. "It all happened a fair spell ago, maybe before the stage station at Cuchilla was built."

The kitchen had been stripped bare of supplies, which was bad news. Now finding grub would become a priority.

Lorraine came downstairs and stood at the door to the dining room. "There are beds upstairs, but no mattresses. Nellie is distraught."

"No food either," Oates said. "As soon as the rain clears, we'll have to move out."

"Move out to where?" Stella asked, pushing past

Lorraine. "We came to Heartbreak to start a new life, and that's just what we're going to do."

"Stella, it's a ghost town, or haven't you noticed?" Lorraine said.

"I've noticed, but we're going to bring Heartbreak back to life. We'll open our own house as we planned, maybe hire some more girls, and hang out a Welcome sign at both ends of town. The men will come and bring money with them."

She looked at Rivette. "Warren, you can start a saloon. Lord knows, you've spent enough time in them to know the business."

The gambler smiled. "Stella, I greatly admire your spunk and determination, and I admit that opening my own saloon has its attractions, but Eddie is right, we don't have any paying customers or food to sustain us until we get some. My dear, plenty stays right where it's at, but hunger moves on."

But Stella would not be deterred. "There's plenty of game in the hills and we can shoot our own chuck to keep us going. Unless I'm mistaken, Silver City is less than sixty miles to the south and we can go there for supplies. Say a week there and back with a pack-horse."

She turned on Lorraine and Nellie. "In the meantime we'll search every store, house and shack in town. I can't believe that the good citizens of Heartbreak took every scrap of grub with them."

"There might be rats." Nellie shuddered. "I'm awful afeerd of rats."

"I'll go with you and hold your hand, Nellie,"

Lorraine said, grinning. "I won't let the big, bad rats git you."

"I declare, Lorraine, you're such a whore."

"Then go by yourself."

"No, you can come with me."

Stella said with an air of finality, "Right, then it's settled." She looked at Rivette, then Oates. "Warren, Eddie, is it settled?"

The gambler shrugged his acceptance and Oates said, "Hell, we'll give it a try, why not?"

"Pete Pickles is out there someplace and he's a handful," Rivette said. "Are we forgetting that?"

"I'll hunt and take Nantan with me," Oates said. "She'll be able to sense Pickles' presence well before I see him." He looked at the girl. "Does that set well with you?"

Nantan nodded. "You are my husband. I will go where you wish me to go."

Rivette grinned at Oates. "Maybe I should have stayed away from the fancy ladies on the riverboats and married an Indian girl."

"Or maybe you should have married one of those fancy ladies," Lorraine said archly, "and made an honest woman of her."

The gambler smiled and gave an elegant little bow. "Touché, dear lady."

"All right, let's start a search," Stella said. "Eddie, bring us back an elk."

"A real big, fat one," Rivette said. "And see Nantan keeps you well clear of Pete Pickles."

Chapter 31

Helped by Nantan's skill as a tracker, Oates shot a deer eight miles south of Heartbreak, on the near bank of Seco Creek. In a teeming rain they skinned out the buck, wrapped the meat in the hide and loaded it behind Oates' saddle.

"You see any sign of Pickles?" he asked the girl.

She shook her head. "He does not like the rain, I think. But he's close."

Uneasily, Oates looked around him, at the far bank of the creek where there were wide, grassy areas, and at the forested foothills to the west. All he saw was the wind moving among the pines, the only sound the rush of the creek and the hiss of the deluge.

"We'll take the meat back," Oates said, swinging into the saddle. "We can hunt again tomorrow."

Nantan's disturbed black eyes were fixed on his. "There is evil . . . here."

Oates felt a wild spasm of fear. His head turned this way and that, searching into the gunmetal day. "I don't see anything!" It was almost a shout. "Nantan, I don't see a damned thing!"

"It comes . . . this way," the girl said, shivering inside a slicker that was several sizes too large for her.

Pete Pickles came down out of the Salado Mountains riding his one-eared mule, a black umbrella spread like bat wings over his head.

Oates watched him come, then slid the Winchester out from under his knee.

Pickles rode on, and when he was close enough he smiled. "Eddie Oates, as ever was," he yelled. "How are you my dear, dear friend?"

Oates said nothing.

Pickles rode closer and when he was a few yards away he reined up the mule. "Ah, the young native girl I met on the trail," he said. "How unfortunate that we must always meet in the midst of a torrent." He looked at Oates. "How are you, my friend?"

"Pickles," Oates said evenly, "I'm not your friend."

"Ah, but I am yours, Eddie. As dear Mrs. Pickles always says, a friend is one who knows you as you are, understands where you've been and accepts what you've become. By those criteria, I am your friend indeed."

Pickles had a drip at the end of his large nose and looked like an inoffensive drummer who traveled in ladies' intimate undergarments.

"Tell me what you want, Pickles, then give us the road," Oates said. His knuckles were white on the stock of his rifle.

"Ah, as I tell Mrs. Pickles, the art of conversation is

dead. It's, 'How are you, Mr. Pickles? How's the missus? Now let's get down to business.'" The little man shook his head, a movement that made his pendulous lower lip shake. "I believe people today lack contentment and that's why the simple pleasantries of life are so often ignored." He looked at Nantan, the rain drumming on his umbrella. "What is your opinion on that, my dear?"

Nantan straightened. "Leave us," she said, her eyes frightened. "You are evil."

Pickles nodded. "Oh well, I see there is no conversation to be had here, and just as I was about to invite you young people to share tea with me, had we been able to find a dry spot for our little tête-à-tête."

He leaned back in the saddle. "First a little demonstration of my sincerity, then we'll talk more."

The man was fast, faster than Oates ever expected.

His hand went inside the yellow, oilskin slicker he wore, and then a short-barreled Colt was in his fist, belching fire.

The bullet hit the receiver of Oates' rifle, stinging his hands, then ranged upward. The mangled .45 gouged a furrow along the front muscle of Oates' shoulder, then hit the brim of his hat, jolting it off his head.

When the bullet hit the rifle, Oates' numb hands let it fall. Now he grabbed for his belt gun.

"I wouldn't," Pickles said. His eyes were very green, slanted, like a wolf's.

The muzzle of the man's Colt pointed unwaveringly at Oates' chest. His own gun had not even cleared leather and he let it slip back into the holster.

The sudden gunfire had spooked Nantan's black pony, and she battled the horse, her bared thighs clamped to its sides.

"Unbuckle the rig and let it fall, Eddie," Pickles said. He smiled. "Left hand, if you please."

Oates knew he couldn't buck the drop, and did as the man said.

Nantan had the black under control and Pickles smiled at her. "Are you all right now, dear? My, my, but you did give me a start."

He was still smiling when he pulled the trigger and his bullet smashed Nantan from the back of the horse.

Oates screamed his rage and kicked the paint toward Pickles, reaching for the skinning knife on his belt. The gunman's mule sidestepped like a prize cutting horse and as Oates swept past, Pickles smashed his gun down on his head.

Later, Oates would remember the world suddenly going dark. But he would not remember the sickening impact of his unconscious body hitting the ground.

Eddie Oates felt uncomfortable, cramped. He tried to move his arms, but they were held stiffly down at his sides. His legs wouldn't work either.

Had he been buried alive? Panicked, he opened his eyes—and saw Pete Pickles' face close to his own.

"Ah, the dreamer awakes." The gunman smiled. "Tut, tut and tut, Eddie, that was a very foolish thing you did, viciously attacking me like that. Now look at yourself. All you've got to show for your impetuous behavior is a very sore head."

"You son of a bitch," Oates gritted, "you killed Nantan."

He tried to move, to grab the little man around his scrawny neck, but the ropes that bound him to the trunk of a cottonwood held fast.

"The native girl is not dead, Eddie. A high shoulder wound is seldom fatal." He turned and waved a hand. "Look."

Nantan lay on her back, her head resting on Oates' saddle. She was covered by the slicker and her eyes were closed . . . but she was breathing.

Pickles stared into Oates' face again. "I abhor violence, Eddie, I really do. But this little demonstration was necessary. I very much need to conclude my business here and get back to my dear wife. I long to return to the bosom of my family, as you surely understand."

"You're dirty, low-life scum, Pickles. A woman shooter and a yellow-bellied coward. Untie me and give me an even break and we'll have at it."

The gunman shook his head. "And where is the profit in that, Eddie? No, here's what we're going to do. You and Nantan will go back to Heartbreak and tell that vile Stella person to hand over Miss McWilliams' five thousand dollars. Say to her that Peter Jasper Pickles does not want to kill her, but that you and the native girl are proof of my determination to get back the money . . . ah yes, by hook or by crook."

Pickles smiled. "Do you understand so far?"

"Go to hell," Oates snapped.

"Good. Then we do understand. Two days from

now—see, I'm allowing you plenty of time—you will return here and hand over the money to me. Then I'll leave this country forever and you'll be rid of me."

The little gunman glanced at Nantan. "Now, Eddie, we can do this the hard way, if that pleases you. Simply put, I can take the native girl with me to guarantee your compliance in this affair. Of course, I won't feed her or tend to her wound, so two days from now she'll probably be dead."

Pickles shook his head. "Must it come to that? Please tell me now, Eddie."

He leaned over Nantan, looked at her closely, then straightened and addressed Oates again. "She's sleeping peacefully, and that is a good sign."

"What did you do to her, you—"

"I gave her a mild opiate, Eddie, that's all. She will sleep for a while and feel no pain." Pickles laid a hand on Oates' wounded shoulder and squeezed hard, the wolf gleam in his eyes. He grinned when Oates winced.

"Now, dear Eddie, I could also complete this task by killing everyone in Heartbreak and simply taking the money. But all that blood and death becomes tedious and above all, time-consuming. And time is not really on my side. To tell you the truth, Eddie, Mrs. Pickles says I'm getting too old for this profession and really should retire soon." He looked wistful. "She's such a caring woman, my lady wife."

Oates' mouth was dry, but he made an attempt to spit in Pickles' face. The effort was a failure. But the revulsion and contempt that drove it were clear.

"That was ill-mannered and crude, Eddie," Pickles said. "And I'm so very disappointed in you."

Pickles took a step back, measured the distance between him and Oates and lashed out with the back of his hand. The man had unexpected strength, and the power of the blow snapped Oates' head to the left, then to the right as another slap smashed into his cheek.

Growling deep in his chest, Pickles continued to punish Oates, almost slapping him into unconsciousness. When it was finally over, Pickles was smiling again. Oates tasted blood in his mouth and a veil of scarlet shrouded his left eye.

"Eddie, that is how I discipline a recalcitrant child. I beat the defiance out of him . . . or her."

Pickles shook his head. "I'm sorry it had to come to that, but you were so naughty, Eddie, you forced me to it." He studied the other man's face. "Now, tell me what you have to do when you get back to Heartbreak."

Oates stared at the man, uncomprehending.

"Eddie, concentrate. You know, I can wake the native girl and I can hurt her really bad while you watch. Oh dear, don't tell me that will be the way of things." The man's tone suddenly became harsh, grating, a voice from the lowest reaches of hell. "Tell me, you pathetic little wretch."

"Get the money," Oates whispered.

"Louder!"

"Get the money! Bring it here."

"When, Eddie?"

"Two days from now."

"At what time?"

"Now. This time. Morning, I mean."

"And if you don't?"

"You—you'll kill everybody."

Pickles smiled. "Oh, well done, Eddie. Mrs. Pickles would be so proud of you, a chastised child who has at last seen the light."

He turned and looked at Nantan. "She will wake soon and you two can be on your merry way," he said, turning to Oates again. "I'll keep you bound to the tree, Eddie, but I'm sure you'll soon work yourself loose. Oh, by the way, I helped myself to the choicest cuts of your venison. I knew you wouldn't mind."

Pickles reached under his slicker and produced a candy stick. "Now, sweets for the sweet, a treat to enjoy while you're freeing yourself from your bonds." The gunman broke off a large chunk of the candy, stepped closer to Oates and rammed it forcefully into his bloody mouth.

Oates gagged as the stick stuck fast in his teeth and throat. He tried to spit it out, but the candy was jammed tight and he felt blood and saliva trickle down his chin.

Pickles laughed. Suddenly the gunman's face was transformed, no longer the weak-chinned features of a harmless drummer but something else . . . something demonic, frightening, without compassion or a shred of human empathy.

"Your little Indian whore called me evil, Eddie," Pickles said, grinning as he watched Oates choke, writhing against the rope that held him to the cottonwood. "And you know, she's right. I am evil, and I do so enjoy it."

He stepped away. "Until two days hence, then. And Eddie, don't try to eat the candy so fast. I declare, you'll make yourself sick."

Pickles was laughing as he swung onto his mule. And he was still laughing as he opened the umbrella over his head and rode into the tumbling rain.

Chapter 32

Eddie Oates knew he was in danger of choking to death.

The jagged chunk of stick candy had been driven so hard and deep into his mouth that he could only take thin breaths through his blood-filled nose.

His chest heaving, he twisted against the rope, trying to free himself, but it had been looped around his chest and waist several times and then tied tight.

Oates bent his head, trying to spit out the candy, but it was stuck fast.

Again and again he felt himself drift into unconsciousness, but each time he forced himself to stay awake. If he passed out, he'd suffocate.

Blood filled his mouth, now sticky with melted sugar, and trickled thickly down his throat. His chest on fire, he coughed and gagged, struggling to breathe. But Oates knew he was fighting a losing battle. The day crowded in on him like a black fog and he surrendered to darkness. . . .

Oates felt his head being jerked upward, someone's fingers yanking roughly on his hair.

He opened his bulging, bloodshot eyes and Nantan's face swam into view, hazy and indistinct. The girl thrust two fingers into his mouth and hooked the candy stick. She jerked it out, looked at the candy in disgust as it trailed saliva, then angrily threw it away.

Oates frantically gulped air into his lungs, like a drowning man who is suddenly shot to the surface of the sea. "Thank you," he gasped. "You saved my life."

Nantan made no answer. She had stepped behind the tree and untied the knotted rope.

Oates fell forward onto his hands and knees where he dragged at the air, his wet hair falling over his face. He stayed there for a long while, spitting blood from his mangled mouth, then rose unsteadily to his feet.

Nantan leaned wearily against the cottonwood, the right shoulder of her shirt crimson with blood. Oates picked up the slicker and draped it around her. He held the girl close, whispering meaningless words, telling her she was going to be fine . . . going to be all right . . . even though he didn't know the extent of her injury.

Around them, clouds hung low in the sky and shrouded the mountains and trees in somber gray, as though they were wearing mourning garments, grieving for the dead sun.

Gently, Oates sat Nantan at the base of the cottonwood. The canopy provided little shelter from the rain, but he didn't want the girl walking around until he found a dry place to check on her wound and if need be, spend the night.

As far as Oates could tell, there was no shelter anywhere and, despite the cottonwoods, the creek seemed to offer nothing.

"Stay there and don't move," he told Nantan. After the girl nodded in reply, her wounded eyes lifted gratefully to his, he walked to the water's edge. And what he saw pleased him.

At a shallow bend in the bank the floodwaters of the spring snowmelt had gouged deeply, creating a space about four feet high and half that deep, roofed by a tufted overhang. At that point the tumbling creek was separated from the hollow by a sandbank that was at least ten feet wide.

It would do, but Oates knew he was going to have a devil of a time transforming the crumbling gouge in the bank into a rainproof shelter.

He checked on Nantan again, then searched the ground where he'd lost his knife during his wild charge at Pickles. After a few minutes he found the knife and stuck it in the sheath on his belt.

Fortunately there were plenty of fallen branches scattered along the creek and Oates roughly sharpened their butt ends and carried them to the hollow. He drove the pointed branches deep into the sandy edge of the overhang, and when he decided he had enough, he went in search of leafier specimens.

After thirty minutes of steady work with his knife, Oates had found enough branches to thickly roof the overhang. He tested the interior of the hollow and it seemed snug and dry enough.

Oates got Nantan and helped her inside. He removed the slicker from her shoulders, then unbuttoned her shirt.

"It's not so bad, Eddie," the girl said, attempting to smile. "I don't have too much pain."

Oates studied the wound and decided that Nantan's statement was just Apache bravado. Pickles' bullet had hit high, as he'd said, but it looked as though Nantan's collarbone was broken at the point where it met her shoulder. The round had gone all the way through and had nicked her shoulder blade as it exited.

It was a painful but not a killing wound, though it was serious enough and infection could be a problem. Oates recalled that Nellie's injury had been worse and had healed well, though she walked with a slight limp that Lorraine had told him was probably permanent.

He made a crude sling from Pickles' rope to immobilize Nantan's right arm and take stress off the collarbone, padding it where necessary with strips cut from his own shirt.

After he finished, Oates asked, "How do you feel, Nantan?"

"It's good to be out of the rain, Eddie."

Oates smiled as he buttoned his shirt. "I mean, do you hurt?"

"Not much." The girl had seen the bloody gouge on his shoulder. "You're wounded," she said.

"I got burned by Pickles," he said. "It's not deep and it will heal."

Tears glistened in Nantan's eyes. "Oh, Eddie, we're all shot to pieces."

Despite his aching head, the pain in his shoulder and the discomfort of being soaking wet, Oates managed a laugh. "I thought Apaches never exaggerated stuff like that."

The girl blinked back the tears and smiled. "The Catholic Apaches do."

Oates squatted on his heels. "I have to see to the horses. Sit still and keep as warm as possible, huh?" He spread the slicker over Nantan. "I'll be right back."

The paint had stayed close to the creek where the grass was sweeter. Oates stripped the saddle and led the horse deeper into the trees. He did the same for the black, then spent the next few minutes venting curses on Pickles.

The man had pulled the hide-wrapped bundle of deer meat off the mustang's back, took what he wanted and scattered the rest. Oates repacked the venison and left it by the creek bank. Later he'd take the meat into the hollow, where the coyotes would not get at it.

He found his hat, now with a second bullet hole in the brim, and then the Winchester. Pickles' bullet had damaged the receiver so badly, only the attentions of a skilled gunsmith could save it. Since there was none of those around, Oates tossed away the useless rifle.

He found his gun belt and buckled it around his waist. His eyes searched the distance to the west. The blue mountains looked like a still-wet watercolor behind the shifting screen of the rain. Pickles had gone that way, and Oates planned to go after him and kill him.

If—and it was a big if—Nantan could make it back to Heartbreak on her own.

Oates searched among the cottonwoods and found enough wood to build a fire. The fallen branches were wet, but not all the way through. His fire would smoke, but with luck it would burn well enough.

He filled his pockets with twigs and tree bark, picked up the deer hide and returned to the hollow in the bank. Nantan was sleeping, probably from the lingering aftereffects of the sedative Pickles had given her, and Oates was careful not to disturb her.

He chose a corner of the hollow for his fire, feeding it carefully with shredded bark and twigs. After the flames caught, he gingerly added tree branches. As he expected, there was smoke, but the fire began to blaze and after a few minutes showed glowing red coals.

Selecting a thinner branch, Oates skewered pieces of venison and propped the stick above the fire to broil. He would have preferred fattier meat that would have dripped and sizzled and kept the blaze strong, but deer was what he had and recently he'd learned to make do.

After a while Oates shook Nantan awake. "Eat," he said. "It will help you regain your strength."

He and the girl shared the broiled venison and then sat close to the fire as the long day darkened into night.

Nantan slept again, but Oates stayed awake, listening to the night sounds, the rustle of the wind in the trees, the whisper of rain and the cries of the coyotes.

Finally Oates drifted into sleep and dreamed wild dreams of Pete Pickles.

Come the morning light, the rain was gone and his fire was out.

Oates crawled out of the hollow and stretched the knots out of his back.

Today he would kill Pickles or the gunman would kill him. He had no other choice because there was no other way.

Chapter 33

"Nantan, Pickles thinks he's got me running scared, that I've shown yellow and will do anything he asks," Oates said. "He's wrong, and all I can do now is prove to him how wrong he is. And the only way to do that is by killing him."

He had just told the girl about Pickles' demand that he bring Stella's five thousand dollars to the creek or he'd kill everyone in Heartbreak. Now he waited for her reaction.

The teaching of the good Mexican nuns may have given Nantan a veneer of civilized behavior, but in her heart and soul she was still Apache. She listened to what Oates had to say, then nodded. "My husband, you must do what you feel is right. If that is to take the warrior's path, then so be it."

She sat in silence for a while, watching the ripples in the creek, then turned to Oates and said, "Even if you brought him the money, he would kill you anyway." Her black eyes met his. "He is evil, and evil is the absence of good, just as darkness is the absence of light. All you can do with a demon like Pickles is destroy him."

"Can you make it back to town and wait for me there?"

"I would rather go with you, but I fear I would slow you down." The girl nodded. "Yes, I can ride to Heartbreak."

Oates was anguished, an emotion new to him. "Nantan, I got to be riding."

"I know. Get me to my feet, Eddie."

After he helped the girl onto the back of her horse and placed the venison behind her, Oates looked up at her and said, "Ride careful. Tell the others I'll return soon."

Nantan said nothing. She reached behind her neck and untied a rawhide string. Attached to the cord was an almost-translucent black stone. She held it out to Oates and said, "Wear this. It will bring you luck. The Lipan call it Apache tears, because the stone was formed from the tears shed by generations of Apache women for their dead warrior husbands."

Oates took the stone and hung it around his neck. "You must leave now, Nantan," he said.

The Apache have no word for good-bye. The girl merely nodded, then swung her horse to the south.

Oates watched the girl go. Then he called out, "Nantan! My wife!"

If she heard, she gave no sign.

Fifty miles to the west the new-aborning sun was washing out the night shadows from the San Andres Mountains as Oates left the creek under a flaming sky dappled with jade and gold. The wind that only the day before had gleefully joined the rain to do mischief had fled to the Salado peaks, where it sullenly stirred the trees and shredded the petals of the wildflowers.

The day was coming on clean, smelling of sage and pine and vast distances, and Oates rode directly toward the mountains, trusting that Pickles had kept going in a straight line.

There was no guarantee that the man would be in the Salado Mountains, but since they were only five miles due west of Heartbreak, they were an ideal spot for the gunman to hole up.

Keeping to the pine and juniper forests as much as possible, Oates followed Seco Creek to the Salado foothills, then, as the morning grew brighter, swung north at a walk, constantly eyeing the arroyos and rock ridges.

He deeply felt the loss of his rifle. If Pickles opened up on him at a distance, he'd be in a world of hurt. By all accounts the man was an expert with the long gun, and the revolver riding high on Oates' hip brought him little comfort.

As the sun rose higher, light streaming through the trees made a play of dappled shade and around him bees were already buzzing among the blossoms of the wildflowers. Once he spotted a buzzard quartering the sky above him and several antelope passed him at a distance, on their way to the creek to drink.

After thirty minutes Oates rode up the south fork of Palomas Creek, and beyond to the north, the high-shouldered bulk of Panther Peak was outlined against the mist blue sky.

There was no sound, no sign of life, and it seemed that even the animals had already sought shelter, prepared to drowse through the coming heat of the day.

Oates drew rein, suddenly beaten. Trying to find one man in this wilderness was an impossible task. He also had the uncomfortable feeling that Pickles could be playing with him, letting him come on while his rifle sights were squarely on his chest.

Oates made up his mind. He would cross the creek and head north as far as the craggy peak rising more than six thousand feet above the flat. If he saw no sign of Pickles he'd head back to Heartbreak.

But to turn tail would be a disappointment, to say the least. The man owed Oates for what he had done to Nantan. That was something he would never forget or forgive. If he didn't track down the vicious little gunman, if the man killed and then rode free with no retribution coming down on him, Oates would regret it for the rest of his life. Already it seemed that Darlene McWilliams, now safe behind the guns and fences of the Circle-T, had licked him, and the death of Jacob Yearly would go unavenged.

After yet another defeat, inevitably he would seek solace, perhaps in Nantan, but more certainly in a bottle. It was a bitter pill, but Oates figured he might have no option but to swallow it.

But that morning Pete Pickles would reveal a weakness ... one that was destined to ultimately seal his fate.

After years of success as a manhunter, Pickles had grown arrogant, and arrogance diminishes wisdom.

A less confident man, preparing to make a kill in hostile country, lies low and waits his chance. He does not build a large fire in the indigo light of early morning, sing at the top of his lungs and fry smoking bacon.

In his immense conceit, Pete Pickles did all these things.

And Oates smelled and heard him.

The creek ran through a narrow, treed canyon to the west and Oates rode cautiously. When he reached the mouth of the gulch, he stepped out of the leather and advanced on foot.

Swollen by rain, the creek babbled loudly over its pebble and sand bottom and the wind was softly sighing among the pines. Treading on cat feet, Oates entered the canyon, walking among cottonwoods and sage. Higher, along the rim, ran a wall of aspen.

Now, deeper into the canyon, there was little sound. The hushed morning held itself still, tense with the moment. Insects made a small whirring in the grass at Oates' feet, stirring the flowers.

He stopped, wary now.

Pickles was very close, just twenty yards away in a grassy, hanging meadow that sloped gradually down to the creek.

The man stood at a fire close to the bank, his back to Oates, who was now close enough to hear the man sing.

" 'Bringing in the sheaves, bringing in the sheaves.' "

Pickles took a knee and lifted the lid of his teapot, checking the contents.

"'We shall come rejoicing, bringing in the sheaves.'"

He rose to his feet and stared out at the creek.

"'Bringing in the sheaves, bringing in the sheaves.'"

The man turned and looked directly into the tree shadows at Oates.

"'We shall come rejoicing, bringing in the sheaves.'"

Pickles smiled. "Hello, Eddie. You're just in time for tea."

The man was wearing a Colt in a shoulder holster. The leather rifle case was closed and propped against a tree.

"I'm here to kill you, Pickles," Oates said.

"Oh dear. And, silly me, here was I thinking you'd already brought me the money."

Oates stepped out of the cottonwoods and onto the meadow. Pickles' green, cat eyes were luminous, watching his every move.

"Did you like the hymn, Eddie?" the gunman asked. "It's the very latest thing, written by a Mr. Shaw and a Mr. Minor, not papists I hasten to add. Dear Mrs. Pickles has become so exceedingly fond of that particular song of praise, she demands that it be sung in church every Sunday, especially on those rare occasions when I'm to home."

Oates walked closer until ten yards separated him from Pickles. He was confident of hitting his target at that range. "Shuck the iron, Pickles, and get to your work," he said. "I mean to kill you."

The gunman shook his head. "I do dislike scenes,

Eddie. They upset me. Now, why would I draw down on you? There's no profit in that, is there?" Pickles kneeled by the fire and picked up the pot. "Please, come over here and have tea and we'll talk about this. Fault finding is not for us, Eddie. Mrs. Pickles always says that only vulgar people take delight in pointing out the faults and follies of great men."

"You're not a great man, Pickles. You're a yellow-bellied, bushwhacking skunk who shoots down unarmed women."

Laying the pot carefully at the edge of the coals, Pickles got to his feet.

"Harsh words, Eddie, but I'm not going to fight you. I like you too much for that."

"Fill your hand, Pickles, or I'll gun you right where you stand," Oates said.

"Then you'll have to shoot me in the back, Eddie. And I know you're too much of a gentleman to do that."

Pickles turned away. But when he crouched and then suddenly swung around, he was already shooting.

Way too fast.

Pickles was a sure-thing killer, an expert with the rifle, but not really a practiced revolver fighter. Had he planned ahead for this battle, he would have picked Oates off at a distance at little risk to himself.

Now the expression on his shocked, unbelieving face revealed that he knew he was a dead man.

Oates heard Pickles' bullet split the air beside his head. The man steadied, then raised his Colt to shoot again. But Oates was already firing. His first shot hit the gunman in the shoulder, his second missed, but his third, a solid chest hit, punched Pickles' ticket to hell.

Pickles stepped back, his mouth twisted in a snarl. But his legs would not support him. They went out from under him, like a man skidding on an icy sidewalk.

Oates fired again, another miss, but Pickles crashed onto his back and lay still.

Before he approached the fallen man, Oates reloaded his Colt. He recalled Jacob Yearly telling him to never trust a dead wolf until it's been skun.

Pickles was still alive, but the death shadows had gathered in the man's cheeks and in the hollows of his eyes.

"Dear me, Eddie," he said. "I guess God wasn't listening to my hymn singing. He didn't help me much."

"Pickles, even God can't help you if you try to run a bluff when your poke's empty."

"Who taught you to shoot like that, Eddie? If I'd known you were so good with a gun I'd have handled this scrape differently."

"An old man by the name of Jacob Yearly taught me. He was worth a thousand o' you."

"And what happened to this paragon?"

"Your boss, Darlene McWilliams, ordered him killed."

Pickles groaned deep in his throat. "I'm dying, Eddie. Damn it, man, I can't quite believe that a little runt like you has done for me."

"Good riddance," Oates said, no pity in him.

"I always thought it might come to this, Eddie, me

dying like a dog in the middle of nowhere." He turned his head. "Over there, beside my rifle at the base of the tree, in my coat pocket there's a letter to my dear wife. I've kept it on my person for many years, telling how much I love her and not to grieve for me when I'm gone."

He raised his head, his fading green eyes on Oates' stone face. "The address is on the envelope. It's—it's in Denver. See that she gets it. . . ."

Then life fled Peter Jasper Pickles and only his empty carcass was left.

Oates looked down at the man for a while, then stepped to the tree. He found the letter, returned to the fire and threw it into the flames where he watched it curl, turn black and burn to ashes.

He had not opened the letter, nor did he look inside the rifle case. To Oates, the case and the weapon that lay inside were things of evil. He tossed the case into the creek where the rifle would rust at nature's pace.

That done, he kneeled by the fire and poured himself tea. He ate the bacon, deer liver and wild onions Pickles had cooked and found it good.

Chapter 34

"I left him where he lay," Oates said. "By this time he's probably poisoned all the coyotes for miles around."

"Lucky Pickles didn't see you coming, Eddie," Rivette said. "He'd have laid for you."

Oates shrugged. "Well, I gave him an even break. He shot too fast."

"You never know how a man will stack up until he's faced with it," Rivette said. "Seems to me Pickles should have put in more practice with the Colt's gun."

Oates turned and smiled at Nantan. "I'm glad you're feeling better."

"No thanks to you," Lorraine snapped. "Tying up the poor thing's arm with rope!"

"It's all I had," Oates said mildly. Nantan now had a proper sling, made out of what looked like an old sheet. "You did a good job, Lorraine," he said.

"Don't thank me; thank Stella. She's the one played doctor."

"When you've been around punchers as long as I

have, you get to bind up a heap of broken collarbones," Stella said. She looked at Oates. "She'll heal up nicely, but she'll always have a scar."

"No more bare shoulders for me come fiesta time." Nantan smiled.

"Oh for heaven's sake, just brush your hair over it," Nellie sniffed. "No one will notice. If it's men you're thinking about, they won't be looking at you that close anyway."

"You're such a bitch, Nellie," Lorraine said.

"It takes one to know one, Lorraine."

They were sitting in the dining room of the Bon View Hotel, a single lamp burning the last of the precious oil they'd found. On an adjoining table lay a few cans, a small package of coffee, another of salt and a box of iron-hard army biscuit, all the food they'd been able to find in their search of the town.

However Lorraine had unearthed a worn, cotton dress that fit her poorly, but she had at last ditched her ragged nightgown and mackinaw.

Stella rose and returned carrying a large tin box that she set on the table.

"Eddie, can you leave tomorrow for Silver City?" she asked. "We badly need supplies."

Oates nodded. "Sure, but I don't like to leave Nantan alone."

"I won't be alone," the girl said, speaking through a yawn because the hour was late. "I'm going with you."

"But—"

"No but, Eddie," Nantan said firmly, "I'm going."

Rivette laughed. "Eddie, never argue with a woman

when she's tired. Never argue with her when she's rested either."

Stella said impatiently, "Eddie, that's something you and Nantan can work out for yourselves. Right now, I want to talk about what we need. And be careful in Silver City. They'll take you for a rube and try to charge you three prices for everything. That's why I've made you this list and the price you should pay."

She opened the box and handed Oates a scrap of paper. "Read that," she said.

Oates scanned the list of items.

Salt pork 11 cents/pound
Bacon 15 cents/pound
Salt beef 9 cents/pound
Fresh beef 5 cents/pound
Flour (extra fine) 5 cents/pound
Hardbread 10 cents/pound
Beans 10 cents/quart
Rice 8 cents/pound
Coffee 12 cents (Rio) or (Java) 15 cents/pound
Sugar 8 cents for Louisiana brown/pound
Vinegar 6 cents/quart

"Looks like you've got it covered, Stella," Oates said. "I won't let them cheat me."

"There are a few more things I didn't write down," the woman said. "Butter, cheese, eggs, apples, soda crackers—whatever looks good and is reasonably priced. Oh, and bring me a few sacks of tobacco and smoking papers." She looked at Rivette. "Cigars?"

The gambler nodded. "Cubans, if you can find them. If not, whatever is available."

Stella opened the box again, coins clinking as she searched through it, and finally produced a gold double eagle. "This is for the supplies and your expenses, Eddie. Use my mare for the packhorse. She'll stand."

"We need ammunition," Rivette said. "A few boxes each of .44-40s for the rifles and .45s for the revolvers."

"Warren," Lorraine said, "Eddie's just got through telling you that Pete Pickles is dead."

"Yes, he did at that. But Darlene McWilliams is still alive."

"What does that mean?" Stella asked.

"I don't know what it means, maybe nothing, maybe a lot," Rivette said. "I just don't believe we've seen the last of her."

"She's about to marry the Circle-T," Oates said. "Tom Carson has more money than God, and what's his is now Darlene's. I don't reckon she'll ride all the way out here for five thousand dollars. I figure Carson carries that amount in his billfold when he goes into town on Friday night."

"We should be on our guard anyhow," Rivette said. He glanced around the table. Stella and Nellie looked a little frightened. Sam Tatum and Lorraine were merely interested and Oates seemed on edge. He couldn't get a read on Nantan, who was part of all this, but detached from it at the same time.

"Back in the Louisiana bayous where I was raised, I remember my grandmother and all the other old, black-eyed swamp witches always knowing what was going to happen weeks or months before it did," Rivette said. "Births, deaths, marriages . . . they knew.

"My mother was the same way. She had the gift. Some call it second sight, and I think maybe she passed it on to me."

"What do you see?" Lorraine asked eagerly.

Rivette smiled and shook his head. "I don't see, Lorraine. I feel. And the feeling I have is that Darlene McWilliams shares the same weakness as Pete Pickles. She's an overly arrogant and ambitious young woman in a hurry, and she'll make a mistake, overstep her mark.

"After that happens, she'll want her five thousand in a hurry and she'll come after us."

"When?" Stella asked.

"I don't know. But it might well be sooner rather than later."

Oates had been silent, lost in thought, and now he said, " 'Something wicked this way comes . . . ' "

Rivette looked at him, surprised. "*Macbeth*, right?"

"Yes. The witches of *Macbeth*."

Looking around the table, as the wind howled around the eaves of the building and the lamp flame guttered, the gambler said, "I can't put it any better than Shakespeare. . . . 'Something wicked this way comes.' We can expect it soon. And we should be ready."

"Do you think Rivette is right, Eddie? Will that McWilliams woman come here?"

Nantan was whispering in the darkness, her mouth close to Oates' neck.

"Yeah, I think she will. Warren Rivette doesn't air out his lungs often, but when he does, what he says is worth listening to."

They had chosen a bedroom on the first floor of the hotel and Oates had spread his blanket roll on the rough timber planking. Moonlight, as thin as mist, filtered through the naked windows and cast elongated crosses that rose from the floor and stretched up the far wall.

"Eddie, is she a danger to us, this woman, to you and me?"

"She's a danger to Stella, so she is an enemy of all of us."

Nantan nodded, her soft lips brushing Oates' skin. "That is how it should be. It is the Apache way."

The girl was quiet for so long, Oates thought she was asleep, but she whispered, "Eddie, we are not truly man and wife until our bodies have joined. Do you believe that? Nellie told me it is so."

"Nellie doesn't have the sense God gave a goose. But when your shoulder heals, we will join. You're the last person in the world I'd want to hurt, Nantan."

Another long stretch of quiet; then she said, "Sleep well, my husband."

"You too, Mrs. Oates. You too."

Chapter 35

Three months passed and during that time Oates and Nantan made four trips to Silver City. On his last visit he arranged for a brewer's dray to deliver whiskey, beer and a French glass mirror to Rivette's saloon. Oates and Sam Tatum had helped the gambler renovate the Sideboard, now renamed the Riverboat. And Rivette placed an optimistic painted sign outside the premises that promised patrons FINEST CIGARS, CORDIALS AND LIQUORS.

Stella took over the best gingerbread house in town, and she, Lorraine and Nellie imported furniture, carpets and bedding from Silver City. It took the better part of two months, but when the Golden Garter opened for business, all agreed that the place must rival the best cathouses in Denver or Dodge City.

Miners and even a few cowboys began to drift into Heartbreak and by their fourth month, Stella and Rivette saw their business pick up. The attractions also attracted the rougher, outlaw element, and several times

Oates and the gambler were forced to run them out of town.

But, with paying customers at a premium, the high-rolling hard cases were usually told they could come back when they were prepared to act like gentlemen, and most did.

The lack of a proper eating house was a problem, but that was solved by the arrival of Hermann the German, his fat wife and two even fatter daughters.

By Oates' estimate, Hermann Schmidt would skin out at around three hundred fifty pounds and his wife and daughters a few ounces less.

Schmidt said he was headed north to Socorro, where the Buffalo Soldiers stationed at Fort Craig would be a regular source of customers for his steaks, sausages and pies. He winked at Rivette and told him that he might also be able to find husbands among the officers for his daughters.

But when Schmidt saw that the restaurant in town had been abandoned more or less intact, he parked his wagon and declared that he was willing to make a trial of it.

The big German wanted to name his place the Aschaffenburg, but wiser heads prevailed and he agreed to change it to the more manageable Hermann's Kitchen.

A steady stream of supply wagons now regularly blocked Heartbreak's only street and the stagecoach drivers regularly stopped to allow passengers to sample tastier fare than Bill Daley's fried elk and beans.

Fall came and went and Heartbreak prospered.

Stella hired three new girls, a man named Fallon took over the hotel and a second saloon opened. There was now a general store and talk of a ladies' dress and hat shop arriving soon.

Sam Tatum found a new career, painting portraits of miners to send home to loved ones, for which they paid handsomely. Using Nellie as a model, Tatum also did naked lady pictures for Rivette's saloon and the Golden Garter and was well on his way to becoming a well-to-do artist.

Oates and Nantan found a house on the outskirts of town and he made a living doing odd jobs around town and managed to stay away from the bottle.

In November, as winter cracked down hard across the high country, Nantan announced that she was pregnant. Stella and Lorraine were delighted and declared themselves aunts to the unborn they confidently predicted would be a girl. Nellie was unimpressed and told anyone who would listen that Nantan's whole pregnancy thing was probably a false alarm.

After the first snow, many miners decided to winter in town and all twenty rooms in the Bon View were rented. It seemed that everyone was doing a booming business and Stella and Rivette, who were now constantly in each other's company, were getting rich.

For his part, Oates felt out of place in a town he'd helped resurrect from the dead. His odd jobs did not earn him a lot of money and were getting fewer as winter arrived. Nantan needed a comfortable home to raise her child and a husband who could support her.

Oates owned his horse, saddle, guns and the dead

man's clothes he stood up in. There was not much there to build a future around, especially one that involved a wife and child.

As others prospered, Oates grew poorer, and he recognized a danger within himself. Self-pity seduces a man and soon he acts like a victim, a destructive emotion that Oates knew could take him by the ear and lead him to the whiskey bottle.

But one cold afternoon in early December, the attempted holdup of a Wells Fargo stage would be the first link in a chain of events that would change Eddie Oates' life forever.

He was walking back to his house with a few things Nantan needed from the general store when the stage clattered to a stop outside the hotel. A bloody, wounded driver was up on the box, a dead passenger inside and grim old Ethan Savage, the shotgun guard, blistering the air with curses.

Oates looked up at the guard. "What happened, Ethan?" he asked.

"We was attacked just this side o' Animas Peak, that's what happened. Ol' Charlie Grant here took a bullet in the arm an' we lost a passenger when them eedjits started shooting at us as we lit out of there."

A crowd had gathered and Grant was helped down from the box. The dead passenger, an elderly man in black broadcloth, was carried into the hotel.

"Recognize any of them, Ethan?" Oates asked.

"Oh yeah. Mash Halleck was one o' them fer sure." Savage spit a stream of tobacco juice over the side of the stage, then rubbed the back of his gloved hand across his mouth. "He was wearing a bandanna over the bottom of his face, but there's no mistaking them eyes o' his, cold like an ornery snake. I seen ol' Mash up close too many times not to recognize him."

"How many were there?"

"Four—Mash and three others."

Suddenly Warren Rivette was at Oates' elbow. "Can you tell us anything about the others, Ethan?"

"Well, if'n I was a bettin' man like you, Rivette, I'd wager one o' them was Mash's son Clem. All I can tell you about t'other robbers was that one seemed young and well set up, riding a mighty pretty Palouse hoss, and the fourth man looked like a puncher." The old man smiled. "I got a load of buckshot into him."

Oates turned to Rivette. "Charlie McWilliams rides a Palouse horse."

Rivette nodded. "Could be him all right." To Savage he said, "What are you carrying that would make you a target for an outlaw like Halleck?"

"No strongbox this trip. The only money on this stage is what the passengers are carrying. I figure Mash was only huntin' a road stake, sure enough."

"You better see to the driver and your passengers, Ethan," Rivette said.

"Any law around here yet?" Savage asked.

To Oates' surprise, Rivette answered, "You're looking at it."

"The puncher shouldn't be hard to find," Savage said. "A man doesn't ride far with two barrels o' lead shot in his belly."

After the guard had gone into the hotel, Oates

looked at Rivette and smiled. "So we're the law in Heartbreak, huh?"

"Seems like. We don't want a posse of miners riding burros, no, and everybody else is either too old or too fat." Rivette grinned. "Can you visualize Hermann the German on a horse?"

"No, I guess I can't," Oates said. He held up his packages. "I'll take these home and meet you back here in ten minutes." He looked at Rivette closely. "If it was Charlie McWilliams riding the Palouse, then something has happened at the Circle-T."

Rivette nodded. "Yes, something bad for Darlene. I'm willing to bet the farm that she's on the run again and looking for a stake."

"But she has a war chest of twenty-five thousand dollars. Why would she need a road stake?"

"Tom Carson liked his poker and whiskey, but he was careful with a dollar. I guess he insisted Darlene put her money in a safe place, like Cornelius Baxter's bank in Alma. With a Circle-T hanging posse on her trail, Darlene wouldn't have time to make a withdrawal, and she'd know that Baxter would have questioned her and maybe smelled a rat or three."

"You reckon she might come here?"

"Why not? Heartbreak is where her money is and we haven't exactly made a secret about being here. Pete Pickles failed her, but Darlene has three fast guns backing her that won't, or so she thinks."

"Then we should stay right here in town."

Rivette shook his head. "I know we're not going to find Darlene, not with Mash Halleck riding scout for her. But if the cowboy old Ethan shot is still alive, I'd like to talk with him. Maybe we can get enough out of the man to keep Darlene in custody until we can get a United States marshal here."

"It's thin, Warren, mighty thin."

"I'll talk to some of the miners, ask them to keep an eye on Stella. They might not be good on a posse, but here in town they'll be a handful for anybody." He laid a hand on Oates' shoulder. "Besides, worried father-to-be, we'll be back by nightfall. I promise."

The day was bitter cold and Nantan insisted that Oates wear the new fringed, gaily decorated blanket coat she'd made for him and a fur hat with earflaps that she tied under his chin.

She did not mention the dangers he might face, because that was not the way of Apache women, but she kissed him hard and long before he left to get his horse and meet up with Rivette.

As it happened the gambler was at the livery and when Oates stepped inside, he smiled as he looked him up and down. "Well, well, don't you look a sight? Are you going to a wedding or a preaching?"

"It's cold out. Nantan said I had to wear this stuff," he said defensively. He looked over Rivette's expensive sheepskin, fine leather gloves and carefully creased Stetson and couldn't come up with anything damaging to say.

"Just joshing you, Eddie," Rivette said, seeing the fleeting irritation in the other man's eyes. "You look just fine."

Oates saddled the paint and slid his rifle into the scabbard. Then, under a chill blue sky, he and Rivette rode out of Heartbreak and headed south.

The mountains and high ridges were bright with mantles of snow, and patches that had been herded by the wind lay in white arcs among the trees.

They crossed the Seco and Animas, the creek banks frosted with ice as delicate as Irish lace, and rode up on the scene of the attempted stage robbery.

Around them the mountains rose majestically against the clear sky. The rising wind was blowing directly from the north, tossing a few snowflakes, and it was growing noticeably colder.

Rivette was aware of the change in the weather, because he looked over at Animas Peak, his eyes searching, as if he expected to see something of interest. "If he doesn't freeze to death, a gut-shot man can last longer in the cold and a north wind is rising," he said. "If he's still alive he might be close by. Darlene McWilliams isn't the kind to slow herself down by taking along a dying puncher."

Wheel ruts and horse tracks marked the stage route past the Animas foothills. He and Rivette scouted the area but saw no blood trail.

The gambler kneed his horse closer to the hills, his head lifted as he searched the mountain's slope. Suddenly his mount started, then stood straight-legged as it scented something in the wind it did not like.

A rifle shot followed, and Rivette tumbled headlong out of the saddle.

Chapter 36

Oates passed Rivette at a gallop, jerking his rifle from the scabbard. He'd seen a sudden puff of gray smoke from the top of an aspen-covered rise just ahead of him. He threw his rifle to his shoulder and fired as he rode, dusting shots along the top of the ridge.

Still at a flat-out gallop, Oates hit the incline and urged the paint higher. Among the trees a man struggled to his feet, bringing up a Winchester. Oates fired, then fired again. The man staggered, dropped the rifle and crashed backward into the frosted underbrush.

Oates swung out of the saddle, hit the incline at a run and reached the top of the rise. He dived into the aspens, where the man he'd shot sat up and lifted a hand in supplication.

"Don't shoot me no more, Mister," he gasped. "I'm done."

Oates turned, lifting his Winchester as he heard footsteps behind him. When he saw it was Rivette, he relaxed. "I thought you'd been hit," he said.

"Bullet came damned close, that's why I lit out of the saddle," Rivette said. "I was looking for a hole to crawl in. Then I saw you ride past like a Comanche." He looked down at the wounded man. "This the bushwhacker?"

"Yeah, that's him," Oates answered.

"Let me be," the man whispered. "I'm all shot to pieces."

"You should have considered that possibility before you tried to rob the stage," Rivette said.

The puncher looked to be no more than eighteen years old, a redhead with freckles across the bridge of his pug nose. He had a fresh wound in his left shoulder and an earlier one just above his belt buckle. The front of his shirt was covered in black blood.

"Where's Darlene and them?" Oates asked.

"I dunno," the kid said. "They told me they'd be back with a doctor. Then as they walked away, I heard Clem laugh and I knew they wasn't planning on coming back ever."

"What happened at the Circle-T?" asked Oates. "Where is Tom Carson?"

"Speak truthfully boy, your time is short," Rivette said. "You'll meet your Maker soon and this isn't the time to lie, no."

"You two lawmen?"

"Yes, we are," Rivette answered without hesitation. "And we don't take kindly to lying."

"My name is Randy Collins and my ma lives in El Paso, Texas. Her—her name is Agnes." The boy lifted pleading eyes to Oates. "Tell her . . . tell her I'm sorry I was buried in foreign soil."

"I'll tell her," Oates said. "Now, what happened at the Circle-T?"

A flurry of snowflakes landed on Collins' face. Oates gently wiped them away.

"Tom Carson is dead," the kid said. "Charlie killed him. He tried to make it look like an accident, but nobody believed him. He said that Mr. Carson fell off his hoss and hit his head on a rock, but everybody knowed that Tom Carson didn't fall off hosses."

"Darlene wanted it all in a hurry, huh?" Rivette asked.

"Yeah, an'—an' I made the mistake of throwin' in with her. Charlie said once the ranch belonged to Miss McWilliams, I'd be made top hand." A frown gathered between Collins' eyes. "Well, now look at me."

"Why did Darlene and her brother leave in such an all-fired hurry?" Oates asked. "Carson was dead and the ranch was hers."

The boy shook his head. "I'm hurtin' real bad. My belly's on fire. I—I need a drink of water."

"I'll get the canteen," Rivette said.

"Warren, is that wise? I mean giving a gut-shot man water?"

"Do you really think it matters a hill of beans, Eddie?"

"No. No, I guess it doesn't."

Rivette returned with the canteen, lifted the boy's head and let him drink. Collins coughed, then said, "It was the hands that done for Darlene. The only law at the Circle-T is cowboy law. That's how Mr. Carson set it up, and that's how it was with him.

"The boys knowed that Charlie had done for their boss and that Darlene had give the order. About thirty Circle-T hands gathered at the bunkhouse and they're a hard, unforgiving bunch. It didn't take them long to pass sentence on Darlene and her brother They were all for hanging them right there and then."

The light was fading from Randy Collins' blue eyes and as he stepped to the threshold of eternity, he was scared. "You boys will stay with me until . . . until . . ."

"We'll stay," Oates said.

"The pain is getting worse all the time and I don't want to die out here alone."

"We'll be here," Oates assured him. "And we'll see you off in fine style, I promise."

"How did Darlene and Charlie escape?" Rivette asked.

"One of the hands who was agin lynching warned her in time. Darlene and Charlie lit a shuck in a big hurry and me, Mash Halleck and his son Clem covered our back trail. We had a running fight with the Circle-T that lasted most of the day. Then we lost them at night in the Gila. Far as I know, most of them boys are still hunting us. They're fired up."

"Why did you try to rob the stage, boy?" Rivette asked. "Speak plain now."

"A road stake. That was all, just a road stake. We didn't count on the crazy old coot of a guard and his scattergun."

"The crazy old coot was Ethan Savage," Rivette said. "He'd already killed his share before you were born."

"Did you hear Darlene say anything about a town called Heartbreak?" Oates asked.

Collins shook his head. "I don't know nothing about that." He groaned deep in his throat. "I'm hurting real bad," he said. "I can't stand this much longer."

"Take your medicine, boy," Rivette said, his face grimmer than Oates had ever seen it.

"I can't," Collins whispered. His white lips were peeled back from his teeth in a silent scream. "My gut is being torn apart by claws." He looked up at Oates. "Mister, I've told you what I know, so I'm dying clean. He . . . the Man upstairs will take that into account, huh?"

"He'll study on it for sure."

Oates rose to his feet and turned to Rivette. "What do we do with him, Warren? He's hurting more than any man should."

Rivette nodded. He drew his gun and fired once. And the kid's hurting was over forever.

"I didn't mean that!" Oates said, horrified.

"It's all we could do for him. I hope if I'd been lying there, you would have done the same for me."

Oates looked down at his feet and shook his head. "Lordy, but we're living in hard times."

"And there's worse coming down," Rivette said. "We better head back to Heartbreak."

"Darlene?"

"Count on it."

"What are we going to do about the dead kid?"

"Nothing."

Oates nodded. "Well, I guess that answered my question."

"Eddie, it was the only answer to your question."

Chapter 37

Oates and Rivette rode north into the teeth of the keening winter wind. A few flakes of snow cartwheeled around them and the leaden sky promised more to come.

They smelled the chimneys of Heartbreak before they crossed a rise, then rode across the bridge onto Main Street.

Despite the snow flurries, there were people on the street. There was no sign of Darlene McWilliams.

Rivette looked around him at the glittering lamps in his saloon, lit against the darkness of the afternoon. "A day like this makes a man feel glad to be home, huh, Eddie?" he said, smiling.

"My home is where Nantan is," Oates said. "I'm sure of that."

"Well, Nantan is here, so that makes Heartbreak your home, right?"

"Nantan and me are passing through, Warren. Just passing through."

Rivette waited until they were in the livery and had stripped the rigging off their mounts before he brought up the subject again.

"You didn't mean that, about just passing through?"

"There's nothing for me here," Oates answered, scooping oats to the horses. "Come spring, I think Nantan and me will head west a ways. I always believed that if I fell on hard times, I might prosper in the lava rock business."

Rivette took off his hat and ran his fingers through his thick black hair before he once again settled the Stetson on his head. "Eddie, you and Nantan can't leave this town. You were here from the beginning and you're as much a part of it as any of us. Hell, Stella is already driving me crazy, planning on all the clothes she's going to buy your little girl."

"It could be a boy," Oates said, smiling.

"Nah, Stella and Lorraine say by the way Nantan is carrying, it will be a girl. Nellie says it's a boy, but I think that's only to cross Lorraine." Rivette grinned. "Nellie has become real uppity since she started walking out with Luke McCloud"—he made a face—"my esteemed competitor in the saloon business."

"She could do worse. McCloud looks like he's thriving."

Rivette shrugged. "I guess a man who struts around with a diamond stickpin and carries an extra ace in his sock is thriving. I don't like him much."

The gambler looked into Oates' eyes. "Eddie, don't even think about leaving Heartbreak. Me, Stella, everybody else in town need you here. You get a long Yankee face on you sometimes, but you're a rock, and this town needs a rock to prop up its shaky foundations."

Rivette smiled. "Tell me you'll think this thing through before you do anything rash."

"I'll think about it, Warren, but I can't make promises, not right now."

"Well, that's good enough for me. Now get home to the increasingly generous bosom of your family."

"You look so cold, Eddie, frozen stiff," Nantan said. She helped him off with his coat and hat and sat him by the fire. "I have good hot soup ready. That will warm you."

As he ate the soup, Oates told Nantan about the dead puncher and what he had said about Darlene McWilliams.

"She's got nothing against you, Nantan, but be on your guard just the same," he said. "Don't go out anywhere unless I'm with you." He looked at his wife. "Promise me."

"Of course, Eddie, I promise."

Oates ate in silence for a while, then looked around at what Nantan, who had learned it from the nuns, called the parlor. The shabby room had little furniture and what there was had been bought secondhand or scavenged from abandoned houses and showed more than its share of scratches, dents and wear. But the wood floor was scrubbed to a honey color and chairs, settee and table gleamed from constant polishing.

It was a warm, homey and welcoming place and Oates found it easy to understand why Stella and

Rivette spent so much time here, away from the plush, red velvet and brass splendor of the Golden Garter.

The hot soup and warm fire had relaxed him, and as he wiggled his toes to the flames, he realized just how lucky he was to have Nantan. She was already showing, but not hugely, and the cheap, gingham dress she wore accented the curves of her slim figure. Her hair was drawn back in a loose bun that complemented her broad, high cheekbones and gave full play to her vivid black eyes.

Oates allowed to himself that his wife looked what she was, a Lipan Apache girl disguised as a respectable Victorian matron. But he wouldn't have her any other way or, no matter how she might change in the future, love her more.

Night fell and the snow fell heavier. The north wind prowled around the house and set the doors to rattling on their hinges. Red and orange flames guttered in the fireplace, sizzling now and then as melted snow dropped down the chimney.

Someone knocked on the front door, waited a few moments, then knocked again.

"Who would be out on a night like this?" Oates asked, surprised, as he rose to his feet.

"Probably Stella." Nantan smiled. "She thinks she has to bring food to the pregnant woman at all hours of the day and night."

Oates padded to the door on his sock feet, then opened it a crack.

The door slammed into him with tremendous force, slamming Oates against the wall to his right. Mash

Halleck, looking tall and terrifying in a bearskin coat and hat, went after Oates as he tried to rise. Halleck brought down the butt of his rifle on Oates' head and before he passed out, he heard a woman's voice yell, "Don't kill him, you idiot! We need him."

It was Darlene McWilliams' voice.

A cold wind rushing through the door helped Oates come to his senses. He rose groggily to his feet and staggered into the parlor. He had not been unconscious for long, because the fire still burned as before and the lamps were as bright.

The only difference was that Nantan was gone.

Oates called his wife's name several times, but there was no answer. Then he saw the knife that pinned a note to the table. He worked the knife free, took the note closer to a lamp and read.

If you want to see your wife again, do as you are told. We will be in touch. If you try to trick us, Clem Halleck will cut the baby from the squaw's belly. YOU KNOW DAMNED WELL HE WILL.

There was no signature, but Oates knew what had happened. Darlene McWilliams had Nantan.

Oates pulled on his boots, then buckled his gun belt. He quickly shrugged into his blanket coat and knotted the ties of the fur hat under his chin. He grabbed his rifle, and, with one last look at the parlor where the woman he loved had been only a few minutes before, he rushed out of the house and ran through the snow to the livery stable.

Oates rode across the bridge, following tracks that were being rapidly obliterated by the snow. He had not considered for one moment asking Rivette for help.

Nantan was his wife. The responsibility was his and his alone.

Chapter 38

Oates was not a tracker, but as near as he could judge, Darlene and her party had crossed the bridge, then headed north. But they would stay close, and probably swing west for the cover of the Gila.

After an hour of fruitless search, the snow stopped, the clouds cleared and the moon dappled the silent, shadowed land with a hard glitter.

Any tracks Darlene had left were buried under the snow. Maybe an Apache or an experienced army scout could have found the way, but Oates did not possess those skills.

His breath smoking in the cold air, he rode as far north as Cuchillo Negro Creek, then turned and headed south again, his eyes constantly searching the mountain foothills.

He neither saw nor heard anything.

After another half hour, Oates gave up. The bladed moonlight cast too many shadows among the arroyos and high ridges of the Gila where an army could hide and never be seen.

He rode into a shallow gulch thick with juniper and sage and swung out of the saddle. He loosened the cinch on the paint's saddle and let the little horse graze, then found himself a hiding place among the trees.

Oates sat on something hard, reached under himself and threw it aside. It was a round, white rock. He looked closer and saw dark eye sockets and under those, long, yellow teeth grinned at him. A skull!

He sprang to his feet, spooked. All around him, scattered by coyotes, lay the bleached bones of a man. Two steps away was another, the bones of this one more intact. Scraps of cloth and leather still clung to the skeleton and in the stark moonlight Oates could make out the rusted remains of a revolver still clutched in the man's bony hand.

It was too dark to see more. A man who had inherited his fair share of the Westerner's dread of folks long dead and their ha'ants, Oates grabbed the mustang's reins and backed out of the arroyo.

Oates spent a sleepless night among some boulders on the lee side of a wedge of rock that protected him from the worst of the north wind. Curiosity driving him, at first light he took his Winchester and walked back to the dead men.

Were they victims of Darlene McWilliams? Maybe Circle-T punchers?

But when Oates saw the skeletons again, he realized these men had been dead for many years.

He found a second revolver close to the first skull he'd discovered, and something else—two round bullet holes in the man's breastbone. He saw an obvious wound in the more intact skeleton, several of its ribs shattered by a heavy caliber ball.

No flesh remained on the dead men, but their story was writ plain enough in guns and bone. These two, whoever they were, had gotten into a gunfight in the arroyo and killed each other.

Both revolvers were old cap-and-ball models and the degree of rust suggested that they'd lain out in the elements for at least a decade.

Oates scouted around and after a few minutes discovered the reason why these men had died. Several burlap sacks, so rotted that coins had spilled out onto the ground, lay at the base of a juniper, half hidden under drifting sand and dirt.

He kneeled beside the tree, dragged the sack toward him, and counted the coins, then scrabbled under the juniper for the rest. When he finished he had a pile of one thousand and two double eagles, more than sixty pounds of gold.

Oates whistled between his teeth. That amounted to twenty thousand dollars, a fortune, enough to keep him and Nantan in style for years.

The gold fever fled Oates as quickly as it had come and despair took its place. Where was his wife and could he find her in this wilderness?

He would gladly part with the money to get her back. . . .

Sudden inspiration came to Oates and he nodded to

himself. Lying at his feet was his bargaining chip. He no longer need depend on Stella. He'd give Darlene the five thousand, and, if need be, each and every one of the double eagles for the return of his wife. The avaricious woman would jump at that offer.

Oates returned with his horse and filled his saddlebags with the gold. When he stepped into the saddle, the paint resented the extra load and bucked his resentment. But when he was pointed in the direction of town, the mustang began to have visions of hay and a warm barn and settled down to a steady canter.

The morning offered little promise of warmer weather and the black sky was in complete agreement. Snow tumbled in the air and the air was chill and hard to breathe, like gulping down draughts of ice water.

Heartbreak lay under a pall of wood smoke as Oates trotted over the bridge and rode to the barn. At this hour there were few people about, the bitter cold and the tang of frying bacon keeping them indoors.

He stripped the paint's rigging, rubbed him down with a sack, then forked him hay and a generous supply of oats.

That done, he shouldered the heavy saddlebags and walked to his home. He stashed the gold in the parlor, now cold and echoing emptiness, and was glad to seek the warmth and bustle of Hermann Schmidt's restaurant.

A dozen miners sat at tables and most nodded when Oates entered. He took a seat and one of Hermann's plump daughters wrote down his order, then poured him coffee.

Oates had just started to eat when Warren Rivette stepped into the restaurant. He took a seat opposite and said, "I tried your house, but you and Nantan weren't there, so I figured you two had gone out for breakfast." He looked around him. "Where is your lady wife?"

"She's gone, Warren. Darlene McWilliams has her."

He answered the question that formed on the gambler's face by recounting what had transpired the previous evening. "They left this," he said, and passed Rivette the note.

After the man read, Oates chewed on a piece of steak, swallowed, then said, "I went out last night, looking for Nantan."

"You didn't see anything?"

"Only snow."

"Why didn't you tell me, Eddie? I would have come with you."

"She's my wife, Warren, my responsibility. I had it to do."

"She's a citizen of Heartbreak. That also makes her my responsibility." Rivette waited for an answer, got none, and asked, his voice edged, "Has Darlene found a way to get in touch with you?"

"Not yet."

"I wish you had asked for my help, Eddie."

"I will . . . next time."

The waitress poured coffee for Rivette and the gambler lit his morning cigar.

"This may come as a surprise to you, Eddie, but I like you and Nantan and I guess everybody in town does. Your welfare is our concern."

Oates dipped a piece of bread into his egg yolk and popped it in his mouth. "I already owe you, Warren. I haven't forgotten what you did for me back in Alma."

Rivette smiled. "Eddie, I did that to prove to myself that I wasn't completely worthless. That I could show even that small modicum of compassion for another human being came as a complete surprise to me."

"When I look back on it, you made me feel less worthless. Not much, but a little."

"Well, it's water under the bridge. Our immediate problem is getting Nantan back home safe and sound."

"I have an idea about that," Oates said. "You're going to find what I'm about to tell you hard to believe, but the proof is back at my house."

"Ah, Eddie, you're always such a man of mystery. Now, tell away."

And Oates did.

When he was finished talking, Rivette looked around him, making sure no one was eavesdropping, whistled through his teeth and said, "Twenty thousand is a heap of money, and it's a lot to pay for a woman, any woman."

"I'll offer Darlene the five thousand and all of it if I have to. I don't care about the money, but I do care about Nantan." He sat back and let the other Miss Schmidt pour them coffee. When the girl was gone, Oates said, "Of course, maybe you think I should find the gold's true owner."

Rivette laughed. "Yeah, you go to a bank and ask, 'Say, did you lose twenty thousand dollars in gold about, oh, ten, fifteen years ago?' What's the answer going to be? 'Damned right we did, and thanks for returning it. Here's a dollar. Go buy yourself a cup of coffee.'

"The railroad? Same thing.

"Hell, Eddie, even the Army would jump at the chance of free money. 'Yeah, that's one of our stolen payrolls. Now just leave the gold right there and light a shuck afore we throw you in the guardhouse.'"

The gambler shook his head. "Finders keepers, Eddie. That's one of Rivette's laws, never to be broken."

Despite the worry riding him, Oates had to smile. "You've got larceny in your soul, Warren, just like me."

"Damned right."

"I guess all we can do now is wait until Darlene makes her next move, huh?"

"My guess is it will be soon. That dying puncher wasn't lying to us, no. If the Circle-T is still after her like he said, she'll want to get out of the territory as soon as possible."

Rivette rose to his feet. "My advice is to head home. After Darlene contacts you, we'll go from there." A slightly puzzled expression crossed the gambler's face. "I never knew you loved Nantan this much."

"Neither did I, until yesterday."

"You could buy the whole Lipan tribe for twenty thousand dollars."

Oates smiled. "I only want one of them."

Rivette nodded, smiling. "Keep in touch, Eddie."

Chapter 39

Oates, feeling cold and empty inside, returned to a bleak, empty house.

He lit a fire in the parlor and sat in his chair. As the room warmed he grew drowsy. Soon his chin dropped to his chest and, utterly exhausted from his cold night in the Gila, he slept.

Outside, morning faded into early afternoon with no change in the light, though the day grew colder and frost laced windows all over town.

People came and went in the street, and at twelve noon there was a commotion in Hermann the German's place when a miner suddenly took a header into his beef and onion soup. The man was dead by the time other diners got to him, and it was later agreed by all present that the whiskey had finally done for him.

At one in the afternoon a tight V of geese flew across the sky above town, though no one noticed, and at two a woman named Martha, the wife of a miner from

Cornwall, England, badly burned the palm of her left hand on a hot iron.

Then, at three, or very shortly thereafter, a man knocked on Eddie Oates' door.

Oates was awake instantly. He rose, slipped his gun into a pocket and stepped into the hallway. "Who's there?" he asked.

"You Eddie Oates?"

"That's me."

"I have a letter for you. It's cold out here, open up."

Oates opened the door a crack, his hand on the butt of the Colt. A miner, as big and shaggy as a grizzly, had a scrap of paper in his extended hand. He looked like a man whose patience was rapidly wearing thin.

"Feller asked me to give you this. He paid me two dollars to deliver it safe. He said you'd know who it's from."

The miner shoved the paper into Oates' hand and waved before turning away. "Cold day, huh?"

Oates took the paper inside and read it at the window.

Wait until nightfall. Then head north toward
Cuchillo station.
Watch for our fire and bring the money.
No funny business or fancy moves.
CLEM HAS SHARPENED HIS SQUAW STICKER.

The note was written in the same female hand as the previous one, scribbled in some haste by Darlene Mc-

Williams. The woman was evil and she would not hesitate to carry out her threat against Nantan.

It was still a couple of hours until dark, but it was a ten-mile ride to the stage station. Impatient to be going, Oates dressed, then shouldered the saddlebags, staggering a little under their weight as he headed for the door.

He had not begged Rivette for help before, but he would now. His wife was in terrible danger and his pride had no more value than a rooster crowing on a dung heap.

Oates walked through the icy day to the Riverboat. When he stepped inside it felt like he was coming home.

The saloon was warmed by a cherry red, potbellied stove and the thick air was made fragrant with the smells of bourbon, spilled beer, sawdust and cigars. Oil lamps cast a golden glow on the brass rails of the mahogany bar, burned with radiant fire inside every amber bottle, their soft halos of smoky light beckoning to him, welcoming him home like a prodigal son.

For a few moments, Oates stood transfixed, like a mortal in the presence of a deity. He touched the tip of his tongue to his top lip and his eyes glazed, his throat working.

A man who enters a room and stands deathly still, staring at something only he can see, will attract attention. Conversation among the miners died away to a few whispers, and all eyes turned to Oates and the heavy burden he carried on his right shoulder.

Rivette sat at a table with three other men, a stack of chips in front of him. Like the others, he looked at Oates. Then he turned and called out to the bartender, "Adam, come play this hand, then cash me out."

He laid his cards on the table, stood and moved aside as the bartender took his seat. "I'm sorry, gentlemen," he said to the other players. "We'll continue our game later."

Rivette put on his hat and sheepskin and walked to Oates' side. Taller and bigger than the other man, he removed the saddlebags from Oates and shouldered the load himself.

"They've been in touch?"

Oates' eyes searched Rivette's face. Then, a man slowly emerging from a dry drunk, he slurred, "Huh?"

Reading the signs, the gambler took Oates by the arm and gently but firmly led him outside.

The cold hit Oates like a hard slap. He shook his head, trying to clear his foggy brain, and looked at Rivette. "Sorry . . . for a while there I was home again."

Rivette nodded. "It's a battle you'll have to fight every day for the rest of your life, Eddie."

"Suppose one day I lose?"

"Don't worry about that now. Take each day as it comes and never fight tomorrow's battle today."

Oates nodded. "I'll try to play it that way."

"Don't try, Eddie. Do it."

Oates was silent for a few moments. Then he handed Rivette the note. He waited until the gambler read it and said, "I need your help, Warren."

"I wouldn't have it any other way." He looked into

the gray day and at the gunmetal sky. "Well," he said, "shall we get it done, you and me?"

As daylight faded and the temperature plummeted, the air took on a crystalline quality, as though traced through and through with spiderwebs of frost. The trunks of the aspen on the high ridges shone like burnished silver and the canopies of the juniper were covered with snow and looked like lines of old men in white nightcaps marching off to bed.

Oates huddled into his blanket coat, his breath smoking into the freezing wind.

"Best we slow up some, Warren," he said. "We're only a couple of miles from the station and it's not dark enough to see a fire from the distance."

"I could smoke a cigar," Rivette said. He nodded to a stand of pines at the base of a ridge. "We'll hole up over there for a spell."

The trees sheltered Oates and Rivette from the worst of the wind and gave the illusion of warmth. Fine snow was drifting down from the branches as Rivette cupped his hands around his cigar and fired the tip.

"Care for one, Eddie?"

Oates shook his head. "They say smoking stunts your growth and I can't afford to be any more stunted than I already am."

Rivette grinned. "Height isn't the measure of the man. It's what's inside that counts, and you've got sand, Eddie."

"You think so? Then how come right now I'm scared stiff?"

"So am I, but we're out here anyway. I guess that means something."

Slowly the day shaded into night, and the two riders left the trees and headed north again. Coyotes were calling out in the hills and the mountains were lost in darkness.

After ten minutes Oates saw the fire twinkling in the distance like a fallen star. To his surprise, the fire was to the northwest among the Gila foothills, not in the direction of the stage station.

He and Rivette rode directly for the blaze, letting the horses pick their way along the unseen trail. When they were close enough to smell smoke, a huge, shadowy figure emerged from the gloom.

The man got within hailing distance and drew rein. "Identify yourselves!" he yelled.

"Eddie Oates and Warren Rivette," Oates called out.

The rider rode closer and solidified into the shape of Clem Halleck. In the firelight, the man looked enormous in a bear fur coat, a muffler wrapped around the bottom half of his face.

"Rivette," he said, "what the hell are you doing here?"

"Oates is my friend, Clem. I came along for the ride."

"Then don't try nothing slick with that gun o' your'n, Rivette. Any fancy moves an' I'll cut the squaw's belly to ribbons."

"You're such a fine man, Clem," Rivette said with a smile. "It's an honor to know you."

"Yeah, well, I ain't forgetting what you already

done, Rivette. You played hob helping them Alma whores."

"It passed the time, Clem."

Halleck ignored the gambler and his eyes sought Oates in the darkness. "You bring the money?"

"Uh-huh, all of it."

"Then follow me, an' be on your best behavior, just like you're visiting kinfolk."

Halleck had a bucket of water handy and he immediately extinguished the fire. He, better than any of the others, knew the risk they were taking if the Circle-T posse was still on the prowl.

The big gunman led Oates and Rivette into an arroyo that began narrow enough to permit the passage of only a couple of horses, then widened out into an open space about twenty acres in extent. A small fire burned close to a sheer wall of rock and a gigantic, maverick cottonwood.

Darlene McWilliams and her brother, Charles, stood in front of the fire, and a little ways off Mash Halleck had his left arm around Nantan's neck, a wicked-looking bowie knife clenched in his right fist.

Clem led Oates and Rivette closer to the fire, then pointed at them. "Light and set you two. An' that ain't an invite—it's an order."

Oates did as he was told and Rivette followed. Clem slapped his horse away, then walked beside Darlene, carrying his rifle. Despite the cold, Charles McWilliams had removed his coat, and the ivory handles of his Remingtons caught the firelight. The man was grinning, confident, and he looked ready and eager to kill.

At that moment it dawned on Oates that Darlene McWilliams had no intention of letting him and Rivette—and Nantan—leave this place alive.

He'd have to bargain with the whole twenty thousand.

Chapter 40

"You, the drunk," Darlene said, "did you bring the money?"

Oates nodded. He glanced at Nantan. His wife's eyes were wide in the shifting scarlet light and she looked scared.

"I've got twenty thousand in gold in my saddlebags," he said, "and it's all yours, Darlene. All you have to do is let my wife go free." He hesitated a moment. "Put her on her horse and send her home. Now!"

Charles looked at his sister and the grin on his handsome face grew insolent. "You going to let a tramp like that call you by your name?"

"Shut up, Charles. Go see if he's telling the truth."

The man retrieved the saddlebags and returned to Darlene.

"Well?" she asked.

"Double eagles, hundreds of them."

"It seems that you weren't lying to me, Oates," Darlene said.

"Then let my wife go."

The woman shook her head. "I'm sorry, but that's impossible. I have enough problems at the moment, and I don't want to add to them by leaving any of you alive to dog my back trail."

"We'll let you be, Darlene," Oates said. "I swear on a stack of Bibles."

Darlene made no answer. She turned to Clem. "Load up the money. We've got to get out of here fast."

"What about her?" Halleck said, nodding to Nantan.

"After the rest of us leave, you can have her."

Halleck smiled. "I'll be busy for an hour or two. Then I'll catch up." He looked at Charles. "The tall one's name is Warren Rivette, Charlie. He's the gun."

"I can take him." Charles McWilliams grinned.

Grim old Mash Halleck threw Nantan away from him and she landed heavily on the frozen ground. "Leave the little one for me, Charlie," he said. "He killed my boy." His eyes measured the ground between him and Oates. "Remember him?"

Nantan was rising slowly from the ground and anger fired Oates. "He was just like you, Halleck, low-life scum."

Then he moved. It was unexpected and it caught Darlene and her men flat-footed.

Ignoring Mash Halleck, Oates drew and fired at Charles, the fastest of them. He hoped that Rivette would follow his lead and take on Mash. For the moment Clem was out of it, somewhere in the shadows loading the saddlebags on his horse.

Oates had opened the ball, but he'd drawn too quickly and nerves and anxiety over Nantan spoiled his aim. A clean miss.

Charles had drawn both Remingtons and was shooting them both, a grandstand play.

He missed with his left hand, scored with the right. Oates staggered as the bullet hit him low in the left side of his waist. Despite the tunnel vision a man gets in a gunfight, he was aware of Rivette shooting and Mash Halleck down on one knee, spitting blood.

Oates fired again.

He'd aimed for Charles' belly, but the gunman's fisted right revolver was directly in front of him. Oates' bullet hit the Remington on the trigger guard, ranged downward and neatly severed all three of the fingers Charles had wrapped around the ivory handle.

The man screamed, dropped both his guns and turned to his sister. "Darlene, he's maimed me!"

Her face furious, the woman shrieked, "Weakling! Pick up your gun and get to fighting!"

Suddenly Oates was aware of Mash Halleck lurching toward him, his bloody face twisted and made terrible by rage. "Die, and be damned to you!" the man roared.

He and Oates fired at the same time.

Halleck missed; Oates didn't. His bullet crashed into the man's chest and Halleck staggered a couple of steps and fell on his back.

Rivette was still shooting.

Clem Halleck staggered out of the gloom, firing his

gun into the air. He opened his mouth to speak, but his words died with him and he collapsed onto his knees, then stretched out facedown on the ground.

Out of the corner of his eyes Oates saw Darlene dive for Charles' gun. He fired a shot in front of her. The woman jerked to a halt as if she'd been burned, raised her hands and smiled.

"You wouldn't shoot a woman?" she said.

"He might not, but we would."

Oates turned, his head spinning from blood loss and the pain of his wound.

A few yards away a dozen riders sat their horses, their shadowed faces grim as death. One of them carried ropes, the hangman's knots dangling at his stirrup.

Nantan threw herself into Oates' arms and he hugged her close. "Eddie, you're hurt," she whispered.

Oates made no answer, his eyes on the one of the riders who had moved out from the others, a big, bearded man riding a shaggy cow pony.

"You made it easy for us, Darlene," he said, drawing rein. "At night a man can see a fire for as far as his eyes are good. Maybe you figured we'd let up and gone back. You were wrong."

"What do you want, Blackie?"

"What do I want? Not a damned thing, Darlene, except to see you hang, you and Charlie there and them other two, if'n they're still alive."

Holding his arm, his wounded hand dripping blood, Charles McWilliams reeled toward the man. "Don't hang me, Blackie. I was always good to you, huh? Always gave you respect in front of the men."

"Charlie, you murdered my boss and I ride for the brand. Me and the boys talked it over, and we decided on what was justice and what wasn't. A hanging is justice—we agreed on that."

Blackie had said he was loyal to the brand and there was no arguing that. Its roots went too deep, back a thousand years to medieval Europe when mounted and belted men pledged undying allegiance to their lord and proudly wore his badge. It was a bond that was seldom broken, not then and not now.

Desperately, Charles tried another tack. "Look at my hand!" he shrieked. "Damn you, haven't I been punished enough?"

"Shut your mouth, Charles!" Darlene snapped. Her eyes lifted to Blackie. In the crimson firelight the granite-faced man looked like the specter of death.

"Blackie, I remember the way you used to look at me, stripping me naked with your eyes, riding me hard in your mind," Darlene said, standing with her legs spread, her hips thrust forward. "I have twenty thousand dollars, Blackie. We can go away, Mexico, anyplace, just you and me, like you always dreamed."

The big man nodded. "You're a fine-looking woman, Darlene, and no mistake. But it's way too late for all that." He smiled in his beard. "You know what's funny, Darlene, a real snapper? Tom Carson was dying. He found out about a week after you moved into the ranch house. The doc in Alma said Tom had a cancer, deep in his belly, and it was killing him. He didn't want to tell you, but I was his foreman and he confided in me."

Blackie shook his head. "All you had to do was wait.

A couple of months, no more than that, and the Circle-T would have been yours."

Darlene swung on her brother. "You fool! You talked me into killing him. I should never have listened to you."

Rivette moved beside Oates and Nantan. He looked at the man called Blackie.

"Mister," he said, "I've heard some mighty loose talk about hanging. I've seen men hanged—didn't like it much. I figure I'd like it even less if it were a woman."

The Circle-T foreman took no offense. He nodded as if he'd carefully considered what Rivette had told him, then said, "Warren Rivette, I've played poker with you many times back in Alma, lost my shirt each time, but I got no kick coming about that—you deal honest cards. A friendly warning, don't take sides in this. Those two are as guilty as sin. You heard it out of Darlene's own mouth. There will be a hanging whether you approve or not."

Oates left Nantan's side and walked in front of the riders. Even in the dark he recognized the hangdog face of the taciturn puncher he'd met on the trail when he went to visit the Circle-T.

Their eyes met and Oates said, "Can you do something?"

The man shook his head. "What's done is done and there's no changing that. Now we'll do what still remains to be done."

Blackie said, "Rivette, my advice is to saddle up and get out of here. And in her delicate condition, there's no need for the little lady there to see what's coming."

Oates stepped back to Rivette. "Warren, we can't fight all of them." He managed a wan smile. "And I'm not sure I can stay on my feet for too much longer."

"You're wounded," Rivette said, seeing the blood on Oates' coat for the first time.

"Yeah, I'm shot through and through."

The gambler's eyes again lifted to Blackie. "Is there anything I can say? A way to change things?"

The big foremen shook his head. "No, Rivette, not a damned thing."

A few minutes later, Oates and the others passed the Circle-T riders on their way out of the arroyo.

"Hey, Warren," Blackie said, "was Darlene on the level about the twenty thousand?"

"It was a lie, Blackie," Rivette said evenly.

"Figured that."

As they left the clearing, Oates heard Blackie say, "All right, boys, do your duty."

He looked back. Charles was on his knees, begging loudly and vainly for his life. Beside him Darlene stood silent, her head lifted, proud and defiant as she watched angry, merciless men come for her.

Oates was impressed despite himself.

She was the worst of them, and the best of them.

Chapter 41

Despite his protests, Nantan insisted that Eddie Oates spend the next two weeks in bed while the wound in his side healed.

By the third week he was up and around, and even in that short time Heartbreak had grown. The permanent population was now almost a hundred, swollen to several times that number by wintering miners and roistering punchers.

The stage now stopped on a regular basis, and Bill Daley was moved to lodge a formal protest with Wells Fargo, complaining that he was losing the passenger food trade.

During his confinement, Rivette and Stella visited often, but, busy with their own businesses, did not linger long.

Unable to find odd jobs, Oates grew restless. He had twenty thousand dollars, enough for him and Nantan to live in some style, but he needed something useful to do, a task that would make him feel he was truly part of the community.

The parasite label the city fathers in Alma had stuck on him still rankled. He never wanted to be branded with that mark of shame again.

Sitting by the fire one night as a gnawing wind prowled around the house like a hungry wolf, Oates brought up the matter to Nantan.

"I thought we could move on," he said, "to a place nobody knows me, Arizona maybe, or Texas. We can get a fresh start, the three of us." Nantan was sitting at his feet and he stroked her hair. "I reckon I could prosper in the hardware business."

Nantan turned her head and looked at him. "I will go where you go, Eddie."

"You don't mind leaving here?"

She did not answer that question. "It is a wife's duty," she said. She turned away and watched the flames dance in the fire.

"I'll make you happy, Nantan."

"I'm already happy."

"Happier."

"I don't know how that could be, like trying to add more water to a full jug." She smiled at him. "It can't be done."

"I'll try, trust me."

In the silence that followed, the logs in the fireplace cracked and crimson sparks rose into the chimney.

"I hear that there are no hard times in the Arizona Territory," Oates said finally. "Silver is being mined in the Dragoon Mountains and a nearby town called Tombstone is booming." He nodded to himself, but said aloud, "Yes, indeed, no hard times coming down in Tombstone."

Oates turned his head as someone pounded on the door. Then it opened and a voice called out, "Is the Oates family to home?"

"Come in, Warren," Oates yelled.

Rivette stepped inside, a few flakes of snow on the shoulders of his sheepskin. After the usual pleasantries, he said, "We need both of you down to Hermann the German's place. Town meeting and you should be there." He smiled. "There's coffee and Lorraine baked a cake, if you can believe that."

Oates shook his head. "Warren, Nantan and me have been talking. We plan on moving on as soon as the weather breaks. Maybe the Arizona Territory."

The gambler seemed to take it in stride. "Well, at least come down for the cake. You two have been cooped up in this house for weeks. How is the side, by the way?"

"Healed up mostly. Warren, I—"

"I like cake, Eddie," Nantan said. "Can't we go?"

Unwilling to refuse his wife anything, Oates made a gesture of surrender. "All right, we'll go. But I've got nothing to contribute to a town meeting."

"You'd be surprised, Eddie," Rivette said slyly.

The restaurant was crowded with people when Oates and Nantan walked inside with Rivette. Judging by the grins on most of the male faces, they'd earlier decided to fortify themselves with something stronger than the proffered coffee and cake.

Stella was there with Sam Tatum and Lorraine. Nellie, dressed in jewels and fine silk, was clinging to the finely tailored arm of Luke McCloud. He and Rivette exchanged cool nods, no love lost between them.

Willing volunteers found a seat for Nantan, brought her cake, and generally fussed over her, much to the dazzling Nellie's obvious chagrin.

After Nantan was settled, Rivette called for order. "We all know why we are here tonight," he said, "to honor a man who has done more to bring about the revival of Heartbreak than any of us."

As hearty shouts of "Hear, hear!" rang out, Oates looked around, trying to figure who was being honored. Hermann the German, fat and jolly, was beaming, nodding to everyone. Well, he deserved it. His restaurant had been a much-needed addition to Heartbreak.

"I should also add . . ." Rivette waited until all the whispers had died way. "I should also add that the man we have invited here is the bravest and coolest hand in a shooting scrape I have ever known."

A man yelled, "Huzzah!" and Oates realized, to his surprise, that many of them were looking in his direction.

"Mr. Eddie Oates, will you please rise," Rivette said.

To loud applause Oates rose to his feet, his cheeks burning.

The gambler stood in front of him. "Before you arrived here, Eddie, by unanimous vote, all present agreed to appoint you as town marshal, at a salary of"—Rivette waited until the noise faded—"eighty dollars a month!"

Amid more cheering, he leaned forward, winked, then whispered in Oates' ear, "You'll be the richest town marshal in the history of the West."

Rivette turned away and faced the crowd again. "Now all that remains is to present Marshal Oates with this silver badge of office"—he produced a five-pointed star from his pocket and held it up for all to see—"made, at great expense, I might add, by an Italian craftsman in Silver City."

There was more cheering and Rivette held out the star to Oates. "Look, see right here? It says 'Marshal.'" He looked into Oates' eyes. "Will you accept the appointment, Eddie? This town is your home. We, all of us, respect you and we need your cool head." He grinned. "Especially when I become mayor."

To Oates, it seemed that Alma was already a distant memory and the move to Tombstone forgotten. He pinned the badge on his coat. "Everybody . . . I . . . well, thank you, and of course I accept."

"Three cheers for our new marshal!" Hermann Schmidt yelled.

Nantan rose to her feet and smiled at her husband. "Is this our home now, Marshal Oates?"

"Of course it is." Oates grinned. "Where else would we go?"

After the huzzahs were done and the handshaking was over, the restaurant began to clear out until only a few people were left.

Sam Tatum approached Oates shyly, a framed picture in his hand. "Marshal, I made one of these for Mr. Rivette and one for you." He smiled. "I sure hope you like it."

Oates took the drawing and grinned. It showed him and Rivette. To minimize the height difference, the gambler sat in a chair, Oates standing beside him. Tatum had caught them perfectly, two Western men sporting big, dragoon mustaches, looking grim and determined against a winter backdrop.

"It's great, Sammy," Oates said, warmly taking the boy's hand. "I plan to hang this on my wall."

"In the marshal's office, huh?" Tatum said.

"Sure thing, in the marshal's office." He smiled. "On the wall opposite the door where everybody is bound to see it."

Nellie and McCloud were next to give their congratulations, followed by Stella and Lorraine.

"Now, you two," Lorraine said sternly, "what this town needs, in addition to a doctor and a bank, is children. After this one is born, you get busy making more babies."

Nellie, conscious of her elevated status as a kept woman, sniffed. "Get busy making more babies. How very crude. You're such a whore, Darlene."

"Takes one to know one, Nellie," Lorraine said.

Eddie Oates looked around him as people left, the smile on his lips fading. He touched his tongue to his dry top lip.

God, he needed a drink.

Historical Note

During its brief, violent life, the town of Alma saw more murder, mayhem and bloodshed than any other settlement in New Mexico, culminating in the Apache siege of May 1880.

The Apaches, led by Victorio and aided by the even more terrible Nana and Geronimo, killed thirty-one whites in and around the town before the siege was finally lifted by a mixed force of soldiers, miners and local ranchers on May 15, 1880.

But other Apache raids followed and in 1882 two troops of the Eighth Cavalry camped near the village, remaining in the area for sixteen months.

During its boom years, Alma was a hangout for Butch Cassidy's Wild Bunch, and William Antrim, Billy the Kid's stepfather, was a permanent resident. Billy stayed with him from time to time.

Alma is now a ghost town, and one adobe building and a tiny cemetery filled with victims of Apache raids and murder are all that remain of one of the West's most turbulent settlements.

"A writer in the tradition of Louis L'Amour
and Zane Grey!"
—*Huntsville Times*

National Bestselling Author
RALPH COMPTON

NOWHERE, TEXAS
AUTUMN OF THE GUN
THE KILLING SEASON
THE DAWN OF FURY
BULLET CREEK
FOR THE BRAND
GUNS OF THE CANYONLANDS
RIO LARGO
DEADWOOD GULCH
A WOLF IN THE FOLD
TRAIL TO COTTONWOOD FALLS
BLUFF CITY
THE BLOODY TRAIL
WEST OF THE LAW
BLOOD DUEL
SHADOW OF THE GUN
DEATH OF A BAD MAN
RIDE THE HARD TRAIL
BLOOD ON THE GALLOWS
BULLET FOR A BAD MAN
THE CONVICT TRAIL
RAWHIDE FLAT
OUTLAW'S RECKONING
THE BORDER EMPIRE

**Available wherever books are sold or at
penguin.com**